Like many authors, Lesley started writing stories as a child. After a checquered beginning, including jobs as varied as actor, model, cabin crew and nightclub DJ, she fell into feature writing for publications including *Business Matters*, *Which? Computing* and *Farmers Weekly*.

She progressed to short stories for the vibrant women's magazine market and, following a Master's degree where she met her publisher, she turned to her first literary love of traditional British mysteries. The Libby Sarjeant series is still going strong, and has been joined by The Alexandrians, an Edwardian mystery series.

Praise for Lesley Cookman:

'Lesley Cookman is the Queen of Cosy Crime' Paul Magrs

'With fascinating characters and an intriguing plot, this is a real page turner' Katie Fforde

'Intrigue, romance and a touch of murder in a picturesque village setting' Liz Young

'A compelling series where each book leaves you satisfied but also eagerly waiting for the next one' Bernardine Kennedy

'Nicely staged drama and memorable and strangely likeable characters' Trisha Ashley

'A quaint, British cozy, complete with characters who are both likeable and quirky' Rosalee Richland

MURDER ON THE EDGE

LESLEY COOKMAN

ACCENT

First published in 2020 by Headline Accent
An imprint of HEADLINE PUBLISHING GROUP

1

Cataloguing in Publication Data is available from the British Library

ISBN 978 1 4722 7831 9

Typeset in 10.5/13pt Bembo Std by Jouve (UK), Milton Keynes

Printed and bound in Great Britain by Clays Ltd, Elcograf S.p.A.

HEADLINE PUBLISHING GROUP
An Hachette UK Company
Carmelite House
50 Victoria Embankment
London
EC4Y 0DZ

www.headline.co.uk
www.hachette.co.uk

Character List

Libby Sarjeant
Former actor and part-time artist, mother to Dominic, Belinda and Adam Sarjeant and owner of Sidney the cat. Resident of 17 Allhallow's Lane, Steeple Martin.

Fran Wolfe
Former actor and occasional psychic. Owner of Balzac the cat and resident of Coastguard Cottage, Nethergate.

Ben Wilde
Libby's significant other. Owner of The Manor Farm and the Oast House Theatre.

Guy Wolfe
Fran's husband and father to Sophie Wolfe. Artist and owner of a shop and gallery in Harbour Street, Nethergate.

Peter Parker
Freelance journalist, part owner of The Pink Geranium restaurant. Ben's cousin and Harry Price's partner.

Harry Price
Chef and co-owner of The Pink Geranium. Peter Parker's partner.

DCI Ian Connell
Local policeman and friend. Fran's former suitor.

DS Rachel Trent
DCI Connell's colleague.

Flo Carpenter
Hetty's oldest friend.

Hetty Wilde
Ben's mother. Lives at The Manor.

Lenny Fisher
Hetty's brother. Lives with Flo Carpenter.

Jane Baker
Chief reporter for the Nethergate Mercury.

Reverend Patti Pearson
Vicar at St Aldeberge.

Anne Douglas
Librarian and Reverend Patti's friend.

Edward Hall
Academic and historian.

Colin Hardcastle
Steeple Martin's newest resident.

Andrew Wylie
Retired history professor. Lives at Nethergate.

Mike Farthing
Owner of Farthing's Plants and partner of Libby's cousin Cassandra.

Joe and Nella
Owners of Cattlegreen Nursery.

Prologue

There was no one to hear the crash except the seagulls, who rose in a crowd of squawking protest, circling the cliff top before heading for the open sea, which continued its rhythmic, unrelenting assault on the rocks below. Someone looked over the cliff, paused, nodded and withdrew. The cliffs were left to the birds once more.

Chapter One

'So, I've decided,' said Colin Hardcastle, 'that I'm going to keep one of the flats for myself!' He beamed at his assembled friends, who all reacted with delight.

'Excellent!' said Libby Sarjeant. 'I always wondered why you hadn't done anything with the building yourself, being in property.'

'I know. I should have done.' Colin looked guilty.

'No need,' said Ben Wilde, Libby's significant other. 'You're doing it now. Let's have another drink to celebrate.'

He went to the bar, where Tim, owner of the Steeple Martin village pub, had been listening to the conversation.

'Different bloke now, isn't he?' he said as he pulled a new pint for Ben. 'Wouldn't recognise him from when he first came over in June.'

'Good job, too,' said Ben. 'And two halves of lager, please.'

'Weren't you going to take someone over to see that house near the Dunton Estate?' Patti Pearson, vicar of St Aldeberge, a village a little way from Steeple Martin, put in. 'It's just behind us, more or less.'

'Oh, yes!' Colin turned to her. 'This morning. But it was really odd. I told you last week, didn't I, that Gerald Hall was interested?'

'Who's Gerald Hall?' asked Libby, who had obviously missed the previous conversation.

'Bloke I met through the business. He said he wanted a base in England, and liked the idea of living on the coast.'

'How did you know about the Dunton Estate house?' asked Ben.

'That was someone else I met in Spain. I was talking about what had happened over here in June and he said he had a house near here that he wanted to sell. Apparently he and his wife had split up and he'd decided he was going to live permanently in Spain. And then I met Gerry and was telling *him* about what happened—'

'Does everyone in Spain know about what happened over here in June?' asked Libby, amused.

'Well, it was extraordinary,' said Colin defensively, 'you must admit. And I was explaining that I'd decided to make my base over here, you see . . .'

In June, Colin had been called back to England by the police after the discovery of a body in a semi-derelict property he owned. Far from giving him a dislike of the area, he had made friends and was becoming a part of the village community.

'So anyway, Gerry said he wanted to come back to England, too, and I mentioned Nick Nash.'

'He's the owner of this house?' said Patti, frowning. 'I think I know the name.'

'Yes, him and his wife Simone – although I'm not sure she actually part-owned it. It was his before they married. So I put them in touch and arranged to take Gerry over to see it. Nick was flying back specially. But he didn't turn up.'

'Nick Nash, Nick Nash,' Patti was muttering under her breath. 'Why do I know that name?'

'One of your congregation?' suggested Libby.

'No.' Patti shook her head. 'Something to do with the church, though, I'm sure.' She sighed. 'Oh well. It'll come back to me.'

'Do you think you got the wrong day?' asked Patti's partner, Anne. Patti came over to Steeple Martin every Wednesday to visit Anne and have a drink with Libby and Ben, her time being somewhat circumscribed as reverend of three parishes.

'No – I checked the message while we were over there. And tried to phone him. But it went straight to voicemail.'

'Do you think he's changed his mind?' said Ben.

'I suppose he might have done, but why not let me know?' Colin sat back in his chair with a sigh. 'I can't ask Simone because I don't know where she is. And I haven't got her mobile number – I never knew her very well. I didn't know Nick that well, either. He was just part of the ex-pat business community.'

'I don't suppose your friend Gerry's very happy, either,' said Libby. 'Where's he staying?'

'Hotel in Canterbury,' said Colin. 'He said he's going to look round the estate agents tomorrow – see if he can find something else.'

'Well, at least it isn't your responsibility any more,' said Ben.

'I brought Gerry over here, though,' said Colin miserably. 'What a waste of a journey.'

'Doesn't he want to buy one of your lovely new apartments?' asked Anne.

Colin shook his head. 'No, he wants a house. Preferably one with a bit of land and near the sea.' He turned to Patti. 'You must admit, the Dunton Estate's perfect.'

'Well, it's near the sea,' said Patti. 'Bit isolated, though. You remember, Libby? Where you thought it looked like Rupert Bear country, with tunnels leading down to caves?'

'Well, it did,' said Libby. 'That's where the illegal immigrants were landed.' She looked at Colin. 'There's a long history of smuggling in those parts. People and . . . stuff.'

'Stuff?' Colin looked alarmed.

'Drugs.' She nodded portentously. 'And tea and brandy in the past.'

'Tea?'

'Hugely valuable back in the eighteenth century,' said Anne, who worked in a Canterbury library. 'Even more than gin and brandy. You've heard the old rhyme, haven't you? "Brandy for the parson, baccy for the clerk"? Famous poem by Rudyard Kipling!'

'It rings a bell,' said Colin, looking nervous.

'Don't tease the poor man,' said Ben. 'Don't worry about it, Colin. They've found out about all these things over the years. They enjoy airing their knowledge.'

Patti, Anne, and Libby set up a chorus of protest.

5

'There must be some down near your mate Fran's place,' said Tim, who was leaning on the bar listening.

'I can't think of any with land, though,' said Libby. 'We could have a look, I suppose.'

'Who could?' said Ben. 'This isn't anything to do with you, Lib.'

'Just trying to be helpful.' Libby gave him a look. 'Aren't I, Colin?'

'Yes, Libby,' said Colin dutifully. He shot a quick glance at Ben, and said hastily, 'Would you like to come and see the flat tomorrow morning, by the way? It's shaping up quite nicely.'

Accepting the change of subject with good grace, Libby gave him a wry smile and agreed.

The following morning, after Ben had left for a meeting with the builders working on his restoration of the Hop Pocket pub, a project he had taken on during Colin's original visit, Libby followed him down Steeple Martin High Street, until she came to the scaffolding-wrapped former Garden Hotel. Not knowing quite where to go into the building, she made her way to the back, where the restored bat and trap pitch had been in use for several months now, to the delight of the villagers. An old game now being revived in Kent, it had proved surprisingly popular.

Colin appeared at the top of the external staircase that led from the top floor of the building. 'Come on up, Libby!' he called.

'Not going to be much fun climbing up here in the winter,' she puffed, as she reached the top.

Colin, slim, wiry, and at least fifteen years younger than Libby, grinned at her.

'We're building an internal staircase, too,' he said. 'We've had to re-position the old one because it cut two of the apartments in half. Anyway, come in. This will be a Juliet balcony when we've finished.'

Libby turned round and looked. 'Nice view,' she said.

The apartment was still an empty shell, still awaiting kitchen and bathroom fittings, but it was bright and airy, and bore little resemblance to the shabby, dilapidated building of a few months ago.

'No radiators?' said Libby.

'Underfloor heating throughout the building,' said Colin. 'Controlled from the basement.' He gave an involuntary shudder. 'No one wants to spend time down there.'

'No.' Libby took a deep breath. 'Well, you've certainly made it different. 'Are the other apartments as advanced as this one?'

'No – they haven't gone on the market yet. We're going to finish this one so people can come and view. Then they can choose their own finishes and fittings.'

Libby nodded. 'So when do you think you'll be moving in?'

'In time for Christmas.' He smiled. 'I have a fancy to spend a traditional English country Christmas for the first time in years.'

Libby beamed back at him. 'Excellent! And Nanny Mardle will be delighted.'

Mrs Mardle had helped bring the young Colin up, and lived next door to Libby and Ben in Allhallow's Lane.

'I'm going down to Nethergate to see Fran this afternoon,' Libby said as they descended the stairs. 'Do you want me to have a look in any estate agents while I'm there? I know you and your friend can do it online, but . . .'

'I thought Ben told you it wasn't your problem,' said Colin with a grin.

'I know.' Libby sighed. She thought for a moment. 'I still think it was odd, though, your friend not being there. The other friend, I mean.'

'I know what you mean.' Colin leant on the fence of the bat and trap pitch. 'We looked all round the house, in the windows and everything. And his car was on the drive.'

'You didn't tell us that!'

'No? Well, it was. He must have changed his mind.' Colin frowned. 'Shame, because Gerry really liked the look of that place.'

'Is it worth trying to get hold of him again?' Libby opened the gate to the lane that ran at the back of the building.

Colin shrugged. 'I can try. I might ask John Newman. He knows a lot of people from the Felling and Aldeberge area, doesn't he?'

'He seemed to,' said Libby. 'You could always ask. It depends how long ago this Nick Nash lived there, doesn't it?'

'Your Patti said she thought he had something to do with the church,' said Colin. 'He wasn't a vicar, was he?'

'How do I know?' laughed Libby. 'Patti just thought she'd come across the name somewhere.'

'I'll give Nick another try and then give up. I'll give John a ring later, too.'

John Newman had lived at the Hop Pocket, the pub Ben was having restored, when he was a child, while Colin had lived at the old Garden Hotel. He now lived with his wife in the tiny town of Felling, close to St Aldeberge and the Dunton Estate.

Libby put her head round the door of the Hop Pocket, where she found Ben, covered in plaster dust, up a ladder. He waved cheerfully.

'I'm going to see Fran,' she said.

'Don't start house hunting,' he warned.

But Libby didn't want to go house hunting. She wanted to know why the prospective vendor hadn't turned up.

Chapter Two

'Oh, Lib!' Fran Wolfe laughed as she poured boiling water into mugs half an hour later. A foot taller than Libby and considerably slimmer, her sleek dark hair was just beginning to show a little grey.

'What?' Libby looked indignant.

'You can't leave well alone, can you?'

'Well, it's odd.' Libby accepted a mug and retreated to the window seat in the front room. 'Colin told me this morning that this bloke Nick's car was actually on the drive. Why wasn't he there?'

'The lubberkin got him,' said Fran, following her.

'The what?'

'Lubberkin. It's a sort of Puck, or hobgoblin.' Fran sat down in the armchair by the fireplace. 'I was reading up about it. There's quite a lot of myth and legend about the whole area.'

Libby sipped her tea and looked out of the window at the grey sea, which grumbled and threw itself at the beach. 'Of course there is,' she said. 'Just remember Cunning Mary and the Willoughby Oak.'

'And it's coming up to All Hallow's Eve,' said Fran after a moment.

Several years ago, when Libby and Fran had first met Patti, over a rather unpleasant murder in her church, they had come across the legend of Cunning Mary, a local wise woman, who, in 1612, the same year as the Pendle Witch trials, had been forced out of her cottage, taken to the isolated Willoughby Oak, and hanged. Over the years, tales of unearthly goings-on about the tree had spread, particularly on All Hallow's Eve, or Samhain.

Libby sighed. 'Well, we don't want to get involved in anything like that again, do we?'

'We don't want to get involved with *anything*,' warned Fran. 'There's no mystery here, and it's nothing to do with us anyway. It's only marginally to do with Colin, after all.'

'Oh, all right.' Libby turned from the window and absentmindedly rested her mug on the head of Balzac the cat, who had slithered unobtrusively onto her lap. 'Amuse me, then. What other murky tales did you find out, apart from this Lubberkin?'

'Lots of stuff about the blackthorn tree.' Fran settled back in her chair. 'Did you know it's particularly associated with Samhain?'

'No. Is it a very witchy tree, then?'

'One of the witchiest. Its thorns are used in poppets, and—'

'Hang on. Poppets?'

'That's the little figures people make to cast spells on people.'

'The wax ones?'

'Yes, although apparently they can be made of all sorts of stuff. And not just in Voodoo religions, either. Very European – Germany and Norway.'

'Well, well!' Libby shook her head. 'Grimm's Fairy Tales, then.'

Fran nodded.

'So what started you on that?'

'Something popped up on one of the apps, you know.'

'What app?' Libby looked wary. 'You know I don't do apps.'

'Sorry. I forgot how internet-resistant you are!'

'Why were you looking? I thought you would have had enough of witches by now.'

Fran shrugged. 'Oh, you know. Hallowe'en. Brings out the weird and wonderful everywhere.'

'Well, unless this landlubber or whatever it is can make people vanish, I don't see what it's got to do with Colin's mate.'

'Neither do I,' said Fran. 'I was just looking into it for interest's sake. And because we occasionally get asked for Hallowe'en curios in the shop.'

Libby looked shocked. 'You don't do that sort of tat!'

'I know. It just made me wonder if there was a – I don't know – *classier* side to it all.'

'Good Lord, Fran!' Libby was disgusted. 'Whatever's got into you?'

'This from the person who's devoted to panto?

'Panto has a long and noble tradition,' said Libby loftily.

'Not half as long as Hallowe'en,' said Fran, amused.

'Ah, but not in its current form!' said Libby. 'Anyway, that's not what I came to talk about.'

'No.' Fran sighed. 'You came because you sense a mystery in the offing.'

'Come on, you must admit it's odd.'

'OK, I'll admit it's odd because someone anticipating a house sale – and presumably a lucrative one, at that – doesn't voluntarily just not turn up. That's what you're thinking, isn't it? That it isn't voluntary?'

Libby eyed her friend warily. 'Well – yes.'

'Even if it isn't, there isn't anything we can do about it, is there?'

'No . . .'

'So it's useless speculation.' Fran grinned. 'As it often is.' She stood up. 'More tea?'

'No thanks.' It was Libby's turn to sigh.

Fran sat down again. 'So tell me about this house, then. Is it big?'

'I don't know. It must be quite posh, I think. I can't think exactly where it is.'

'And you want to go and look at it, don't you?'

Libby felt the colour begin to seep up her neck. 'Erm . . .'

Fran laughed. 'You're so transparent!'

'Oh, all right! Yes, I do. But I suppose I can't. That really would look nosy, wouldn't it?'

'Yes, Lib. I really think you'll have to leave it be.'

'If Ian had been at the pub last night, we could have asked him,' said Libby. 'But he wasn't.'

Detective Chief Inspector Ian Connell frequently joined the

Wednesday party in the pub, but it was no surprise when, due to the exigencies of his job, he didn't turn up.

'I suppose someone will have to report him missing eventually, if he doesn't appear,' said Fran.

'Who, Ian?' Libby was startled.

'No, idiot! This Nick person.'

'Yes, I suppose so. Should I tell Colin to do that?'

'Isn't there someone else?'

'Colin said he couldn't get hold of the ex-wife. And I expect, as he seems to live in Spain a lot of the time, people would be used to him not being around.'

'It wouldn't hurt to mention it, I suppose. Informally.' Fran raised an eyebrow.

'The last time I tried to do anything informally with Ian, he got mad at me,' said Libby.

'Was that when you – er – *mentioned* something through Edward?'

'Yes. Well, Edward does live in the same building as Ian. It seemed like a good idea at the time.' Libby grinned reminiscently. 'Oooh, he was mad!'

'So were you, as I remember.'

'Yes, well. Anyway, I'll mention it to Colin, and if he wants to, he can tell Ian.'

'Let me know what happens,' said Fran. 'And now I'll have to turf you out. I've got to go back to the shop. Guy's got an appointment this afternoon.'

Back in the car, Libby wondered what to do next. There was a casserole in the slow cooker, so there was nothing to do for dinner, there were no rehearsals at the theatre that evening, and Ben wouldn't be home for ages. She decided it was a toss-up between Patti at St Aldeberge or a visit to Jane Baker up on Cliff Terrace. Jane was the grandly titled Online Editor of the Nethergate Mercury group of local newspapers, and worked mainly at home, as the group only maintained a very small office space.

On balance, she decided against Jane, as her daughter Imogen would be home from school. Patti, on the other hand, might be anywhere, but it was worth a try.

St Aldeberge was quiet. It usually was, although there was a healthy community spirit – and an even healthier support for the pub. Patti's own support in the village had been slow to pick up, but she had persevered, and after her involvement in the murders that Libby and Fran had helped to solve, it had strengthened. The only thing she didn't feel able to do was to bring Anne to live in the village. That might be a step too far, she felt.

Libby drove past the Community Shop, currently closed, down the side of the church, and onto the drive in front of the vicarage. Patti appeared at the front door, beaming.

'I've been looking things up!' she called, as Libby got out of the car. 'Is that why you've come?'

'I suppose so, sort of.' Libby locked the car and went up to the steps. 'I was just puzzled about that Nick person. His car was still on the drive, you know.'

'Was it?' Patti looked surprised. 'Colin didn't tell us that last night.'

'No, he told me today when he showed me round his new flat.'

'Oh.' Patti led the way into what she fondly referred to as her office. 'Look.' She pointed to a ledger lying open on her desk.

'What am I looking at?' Libby peered at it.

'Here.' Patti pointed at the handwritten heading

'Parish Officials,' read Libby. 'Nick Nash! Gosh! What was he? *Churchwarden?*'

'See? I knew I knew the name from somewhere. And he lives right behind the village. You remember the two cottages by the side of the inlet?'

'How could I forget?' said Libby with a shudder.

'Well, his house is right behind there, not far from Dunton House. You must have been able to see it when you and Fran went exploring.'

Libby nodded slowly. 'But no reason to take any notice of it then. How do you get to it?'

'You remember the little lane leading to the Willoughby Oak?

There's a lane leading the other way, straight up to it. That's the way Colin would have taken his friend.'

'Hmm.' Libby was thoughtful. 'Fran and I walked all over that land, almost down to the cliff. That was when I thought it looked like Rupert Bear smugglers' country.'

Patti nodded her head. 'I mentioned that last night. Rupert was a TV puppet, wasn't he?'

Libby was shocked. 'No! Well, they eventually made him into one, but he was originally a *Daily Express* strip cartoon character. Then they made him into annuals. Hugely popular. Still is.'

'Oh.' Patti looked doubtful.

'Anyway, what I was going to say,' Libby went on, 'was that we didn't think the land there was enclosed, or belonged to anyone.'

'I'm not sure it does,' said Patti.

'Doesn't belong to this Nick Nash, then?'

Patti shook her head. 'You're not going to look at it, are you?' she said, frowning worriedly at Libby. 'Because something always happens when you do.'

'When I do what? Look at something?'

'Yes – you know exactly what I mean, Lib. You've only got to remember this summer, when you started looking into Nasty Nigel.' Sir Nigel Preece had featured in last summer's adventures.

'Hmm.' Libby was thoughtful. 'Same area, wasn't it?'

'Libby!' Patti sounded exasperated.

'All right, all right!' Libby held up her hands in mock surrender. 'Anyway, it's interesting about Nash having been a churchwarden. You didn't find anything else?'

'Unlikely to be anything to find,' said Patti. 'We don't keep dossiers. 'I'll ask some of the older members of the congregation, see if they remember him.'

'When will you do that?'

'Don't be so impatient! Probably tomorrow. I'm doing a stint in the shop.'

St Aldeberge's Community Shop was just across the road from the church, and Patti often helped out there.

'Oh, I might come and do a bit of shopping, then,' said Libby, looking innocent.

'I'd really rather you didn't.'

'That's nice! There am I, offering to support your community enterprise . . .'

'And poke your nose in,' said Patti. 'Sheila Johnson and Dora Walters have never forgotten you.'

'I know.' Libby pulled down the corners of her mouth. 'All right, I won't come. Did the Nashes ever use the shop?'

'I don't know – they'd left before I arrived. As I said, I'll ask some of the ladies.'

With that Libby had to be content. She contemplated walking over to the cliff top as she and Fran had done in the past, but decided it was too cold and too muddy.

Her mobile rang just as she walked back through the door of Number Seventeen.

'Libby, it's me,' came Colin's voice. 'I've just spoken to John Newman.'

'Really? I've just come from over that way.'

'Oh, yes – you said you were going over to see Fran. That's not all that near to Felling, though.'

'No, I went to see Patti in St Aldeberge afterwards. And guess what? Your Nick Nash was a churchwarden! That's why Patti had seen his name.'

'Bloody hell!' said Colin. 'I can't imagine him having anything to do with the church!'

'She's going to ask some of the older members of her congregation about him. Anyway, what did John Newman have to say? Did he know him?'

'Well . . .' Colin paused. 'Yes, he did, but he was very cagey.'

'Cagey? How?'

'He said he didn't know Nick very well, just remembers him being around Felling when he first met Emma.'

'Yes, his wife. Could he have been part of Nasty Nigel's crowd?'

'I don't know. It would be a bit of a coincidence, wouldn't it?'

'You didn't press him?'

'I could hardly do that, could I?' Colin sighed. 'Anyway, I don't see that it's got anything to do with him not turning up the other day. Looks like he's not going to turn up at all.'

And, indeed, he wasn't.

Chapter Three

The weather turned even gloomier on Friday. Libby called Ben's mother Hetty and asked if she needed anything from the big supermarket in Canterbury.

'Not got enough to do?' asked Hetty shrewdly. 'No thanks, gal. I can get everything I need from the Eight 'til Late and Nella's farm shop.'

'You don't want a run out, then? said Libby. 'You and Jeff-dog?'

'We got enough good walking country hereabouts,' said Hetty. 'Go and see young Fran.'

'She's working,' said Libby. 'So should I be,' she added gloomily.

Hetty made a noise somewhere between a snort and a cough. Although many of her generation considered it right that a woman's place was in the home looking after her menfolk, Hetty had been brought up in a Cockney family where everyone worked, regardless of gender, and often of age.

'Plenty of opportunity,' she said now. 'Ever thought about runnin' a pub?'

'What?' shrieked Libby. 'No! Ben promised me I wouldn't have to have anything to do with it.'

'Hmph,' said Hetty.

Next, Libby called Fran, who sounded harassed and was obviously far too busy to chat. Finally, she switched off the phone, regretting the long gone days of the receiver and cradle. Much more satisfying to bang it down. She looked at her watch and wondered if she could get away with morning coffee in the Pink Geranium.

'What's up?' asked Harry, coming forward to greet her, as she trailed through the door. 'Lost a pound and found a ha'penny?'

She gave him a half smile.

'Well, it's either that or you've had another bust-up with someone.'

'If you must know,' she said, sinking into a chair at the big round table in the window, 'I'm feeling useless.'

'Uh-oh.' Harry put his head on one side. 'We've been here before.'

'Well, everyone works except me.' Libby was aware that her voice came out as a whine.

'I thought you painted pictures for a living?' Harry smirked at her.

'Don't mock. Fifty quid here and there is hardly a living, is it?'

'Hmm.' Harry frowned at her. 'Have you come in here for coffee?'

'Sorry!' Libby bridled. 'Aren't I allowed to come in for a chat, now?'

'Stop it, you silly old trout!' Harry snapped. Two ladies at an adjoining table looked up, startled. Harry gave them a shamefaced grin.

'Sorry,' muttered Libby.

'Come through to the back,' said Harry, holding her chair.

Libby followed him out through the kitchen and into the back yard, where he served her with an individual cafetiere and a battered ashtray. 'In case,' he said.

'I don't, any more,' said Libby. 'You know that.'

'I always like to be prepared,' said Harry. 'Now, what's brought this on?'

'Something Hetty said.'

'What, she told you to go to work?'

'No, but she suggested I might like to work in Ben's new pub.'

'What's wrong with that?'

'I don't know – nothing! Just that I felt she was criticising me for *not* working.'

'She's never done that before, has she? And she's always been pleased you've been there to help Ben – and her – with everything that goes on at the Manor.'

'It just doesn't feel like real work.'

'Look.' Harry leant forward with his elbows on the little wrought iron garden table. 'You're doing exactly what Fran does, when you come to think about it.'

'How do you make that out?'

'Fran goes and helps Guy in the shop. Takes over when he's painting, or away on a buying trip. Does she get paid?'

'I've never asked her!'

'I bet she doesn't. It's taken as her contribution to the family business. In the same way that yours is. You've put a lot into transforming the Hoppers' Huts, and running them and Steeple Farm as a business, and the bedrooms in the Manor, not to mention all you do for the theatre. Just because you don't want to work in the pub – tell me, is Ben going to work in there?'

Libby shook her head. 'No, he's going to put a manager in. Probably one who can live in. That's why he's doing up the flat at the same time.'

'So why do you think you should?' Harry sat back in his chair. 'And if you're worried about having to earn a living – why? You had enough to retire on when you moved into Bide-a-Wee, and Ben doesn't have to earn, either. Anything else is a bonus.'

Libby considered. 'When you look at it like that,' she said slowly, 'it looks a bit different.'

'Thought it might,' said Harry smugly.

'But Hetty said I hadn't got enough to do.'

'Perhaps at that time, you hadn't. It's not a permanent state, though, is it?'

'No.' Libby cheered up. 'I feel better now.'

'It's the old Protestant work ethic getting in the way,' said Harry. 'You feel you *ought* to be working.'

'Yes.' Libby nodded thoughtfully. 'I suppose that's it.'

'You're too sensitive by 'alf, you are,' said Harry, patting her hand. 'Even if you are a nosy old boot.'

'Thanks,' said Libby. 'Love you, too.'

However, she felt a lot more cheerful as she made her way back to Allhallow's Lane to pick up the car.

'Half the problem,' she told herself as she turned the car round, 'is not having the panto to do.'

Or, she realised, anything theatrical at all. In previous years, there had always been some kind of production on at the theatre, and she was almost always involved, either in the production itself, or the administration connected with it. Or even, as had happened last year, with a production elsewhere. And this year, *that* production was coming to the Oast House Theatre under the aegis of Dame Amanda Knight. Ben would be on hand to oversee the stage and technical aspects, and Dame Amanda had been casting lures to some of Libby's regular company to pad out her cast. But not, Libby told herself firmly, to her. However, Dame Amanda had very sensibly persuaded Tom, the Oast's regular pantomime dame, to reprise his role, as the regular audiences looked forward to seeing him every year. Libby had purloined him from the company both he and she had been with before her move to Steeple Martin, both of them being more or less retired professionals. Now, she knew, Dame Amanda – or Abby, as she liked to be known – had her eye on the equally popular double act consisting of Bob the butcher and Baz the undertaker. As this was a professional production, money was involved, but there would be more performances than usual, and it might be difficult, as both Bob's and Baz's professions tended to ramp up a gear in the winter.

What she could do, she mused, as the Silver Bullet sped along the Canterbury road, was run another Nativity play for Patti at her church, as she had done before.

'Or even,' said a voice in her head, 'one for Beth at your own Steeple Martin church?' Vicar Bethany Cole, a friend of Patti's and now of Libby, Fran, and all their other friends, quite cheerfully accepted Libby's avowed aversion to organised religion in the same way that she took most things in her stride.

By the time she reached the supermarket, she had regained her equilibrium and decided that perhaps in future she wouldn't be so hasty to cast off all things theatrical without making sure there was something to take their place.

As usual, the supermarket had sneakily moved things around, so the shopping took longer than she had anticipated. By the time she'd finally got home and unloaded, it was well past lunchtime.

'Soup,' she told Sidney. 'Lentil and vegetable.'

'Sounds fine,' said a voice from the kitchen doorway.

Libby turned so quickly she almost fell over.

'How did you get in?' she gasped.

'The door was open,' said Colin.

'Bother. I'm always doing that – coming in with bags of shopping and leaving it open behind me.'

'I've shut it now,' said Colin. He sat down at the table. 'Actually, I've got news.'

'Oh?' Libby raised an eyebrow.

'They've found Nick.'

'Uh-oh. That doesn't sound good.'

Colin shook his head. 'It seems he went out to mow the lawn—'

'I thought there wasn't a lawn?'

'Well, the grass up to the headland, I suppose, to make it tidier.' Colin heaved a sigh. 'And he went over the cliff.'

'*What*?'

'He was on one of those ride-on mowers.'

'Good grief!' Libby's hand flew to her mouth.

'I feel terrible, now.'

'Why? You didn't push him over!'

'No, but I was moaning about him not turning up.'

'Well. you weren't to know, were you?'

'No.'

'Who got in touch with you?'

'The police. They found a note of my name and address in his pocket, with the date and time and everything.'

Libby nodded. 'And who found him?'

'Some gardener woman. I don't know much about her. I think he'd hired her. He was obviously trying to tart the place up ready to sell.'

'Not much chance of that now,' said Libby.

'I don't suppose Gerry would want to buy it now, anyway,' said Colin gloomily. 'I expect that awful Simone will cop the lot.'

'Not keen, huh?'

'She's one of the most manipulative, grasping women I've ever met, and quite a bit younger than him. I wasn't surprised when they split up, nor when he said he was going to stay in Spain.'

'Well, at least you won't have to worry about it any more,' said Libby. 'Now, do you want soup? It'll take about half an hour.'

'No. Come on – I'll buy you lunch at the pub.' Colin stood up.

'All right,' said Libby, 'but you must come and have a meal with us this evening. You must be fed up with eating out all the time.'

'At least I haven't got to go and look at him,' said Colin, on the way to the pub. 'They just wanted me to confirm that I'd been going to meet him.'

'Someone must have identified him,' said Libby. 'After all, he could have been anybody.'

'He had all the right documents,' said Colin. 'You know, driving licence, credit cards . . .'

'What – with him while he was mowing the lawn?' Libby looked dubious.

'Some people carry their wallets with them everywhere, don't they?'

'Maybe.'

'I don't know, anyway. You're right, someone must have identified him. Do you suppose Patti knows anything about it?'

'Why should she?' Libby was surprised.

'You know – churches – centres of gossip.'

'Your John Newman's still more likely to know something. He and Emma have lived there a lot longer than Patti, and know a lot of the older residents better than she does.' Libby pushed open the door of the pub. 'Snug?'

Nevertheless, when Libby reached home after a substantial lunch in the pub, the first thing she did was to phone Patti.

'Yes, we've heard.' Patti sounded gloomy. 'The shop was alive with it.'

'Oh, yes, you were open today.'

'Yes, every Friday and Saturday up to Christmas, now. I was over there myself for an hour. The police actually came into the shop.' Patti sighed. 'And naturally, once they saw the dog collar . . .'

'You were appointed spokesperson.'

Patti sighed again.

'Well, what did they say?'

'Did I know him, did anyone know him, did we know what he was doing here – you know.'

'What did you tell them?'

'I said he was meeting Colin, and they said they'd got his address.'

'Yes, they were on to him straightaway. Did anyone else say they knew him?'

'Yes, a couple of them remembered him when he was a church-warden.' She hesitated. 'In fact, I got the impression that they weren't very – er, well – impressed.'

'Oh? Did they say why?'

'No. As I said, it was just an impression.' Libby heard her take a deep breath. 'Now listen, Libby. You're not to start turning this into another mystery. He fell. It was an accident. Nothing else.'

Chapter Four

Libby was quiet for a moment. Then, 'who would remember him as a churchwarden?'

Patti sighed gustily down the phone.

'I don't know! The couple in the shop – parishioners. Pensioners, too. You're *not* to go questioning them!'

'I wasn't going to. I just thought someone might remember . . .'

'But why? Why does it matter that he used to be a churchwarden here? The poor man's dead.'

'I don't know,' said Libby, privately resolving to get in touch with John Newman, as she had suggested to Colin. Why should it matter, though? Was she just trying to make a mystery out of an accidental death? And if so, why?

'I suppose I'm just used to mysteries,' she said out loud, with a sigh.

'You haven't got enough to do,' said Patti.

Libby gasped. 'You're the second person to say that to me today!'

'You're used to being busy. And at this time of year, you're usually involved with the theatre. You're missing it.'

'Yes, I'd come to that conclusion myself,' said Libby gloomily. 'I even thought about a Nativity play . . .'

'We've got ours organised. Ever since you did that first one for us, we've followed the same template every year. Why don't you ask Beth? Or does she already have one?'

'I thought of that, too.' Libby became brisk. 'No, I shall just have to make sure I've got enough to do on the Manor side of things—'

'What, the lettings? The huts and the rooms? But they don't do much business in the winter, do they?'

'Stop it! I shall just have to make work, then.'

'Or join in with Dame Amanda's panto!' said Patti mischievously.

Libby laughed. 'No chance! No I shall just go on making a nuisance of myself in the village until something turns up.'

She clicked off the phone and set about starting preparations for dinner, remembering belatedly she'd asked Colin to join them for the meal. It was after everything was underway, she'd lit the fire and sat down with a cup of tea, that the landline rang.

'It's me again,' said Patti's voice. 'Listen – something odd's happened.'

Libby's attention sharpened. 'Odd?'

Patti paused. 'Well, it's difficult.' She paused again. 'You know I said that one or two of the people in the shop remembered Nick Nash?'

'Yes?'

'One of them, Connie Barstow, turned up on my doorstep this afternoon, not long after you and I'd finished speaking.'

'Yes?' prompted Libby again, when Patti went quiet.

Patti sighed. 'I said it was difficult, didn't I? Connie told me what she and her friend, Elaine, remembered. Although,' she said hastily, 'she said they weren't all that sure of the details and it was only rumours anyway.'

'Well, what *are* the rumours?'

'It all sounded very vague to me,' said Patti, 'but Connie thought there were rumours about children.'

The both went quiet at this, then Libby groaned. 'Oh, no.'

'I know. Anyway, I said we couldn't really do anything about that now, and the man was dead, and she promptly reminded me of the scandals recently in the church about the abuse of children. Which rather silenced me, I must admit.'

'I bet,' said Libby.

'And then,' Patti went on in a rush, 'she said couldn't you look into it.'

'You? Golly! That would be—'

'Not me. *You!*'

Once again, Libby was silenced.

'Well, say something,' said Patti.

'I don't know what to say,' stammered Libby. 'Are you sure?'

'Yes. She quoted our famous murder at me, then the business with Sir Nigel, and the one about . . .'

'Yes, yes, OK. I get it.'

Libby heard Patti's deep intake of breath. 'I did try and discourage her. But she said it was the sort of thing you did. And you've been asked to help with things before, haven't you? I mean, it was Alice who asked you to help me, wasn't it?'

'I know, but . . .' admitted Libby grudgingly.

'And I remember Fran telling me you'd even suggested trying it professionally at one time—'

'I wasn't serious!' yelped Libby.

'Weren't you?' asked Patti innocently.

'No! You have to have licences and take exams and stuff. I can't do that. And I bet Ian would put his foot down.'

'You're a private citizen. Ian can't dictate what you do. All very well for him to stop you interfering in a police investigation, but—'

'No! Out of the question.'

'Then,' said Patti after a pause, 'why do you do it?'

'I'm nosy,' said Libby eventually.

'And you care about justice,' said Patti.

'Well, yes, but in this case, what justice is there to seek? I suppose you could blame the lawnmower . . .'

'Don't be facetious! Although it probably is the lawnmower's fault – or a fault within it, anyway.' She paused. 'What Connie seems to be worried about is twofold. First, whether there was any truth in the rumours she and Elaine remembered from years ago, and second, did it have anything to do with his death. And if so, did that make it murder.'

They both went quiet again.

26

'I suppose it does make sense,' said Libby slowly, 'even if it's a bit far-fetched, but not something I could look into. Can't she tell the police?'

'Would they take any notice? She's an elderly woman and what she's talking about is – I don't know – twenty years ago? And if nothing was done about it then, what's the likelihood of it being taken seriously now?'

Libby was frowning into space. 'But think of all those accusations of historic abuse that have been brought into the light over the last few years. Your Connie mentioned them. Saving your blushes, Patti, but it looks as if it was almost endemic within—'

'Don't say it!' Patti interrupted sharply. 'Look, I agree. It's why, in the end, I agreed to speak to you. What I thought was, could you perhaps talk to Connie and Elaine and see if they remember who the alleged victims were back then. And if any of them are still around.'

'Or their families,' put in Libby.

'I really don't want to get the Church involved,' said Patti, sounding distressed, 'but if it's something that's likely to come out during any subsequent investigation it's likely to get blown up by the media, isn't it?'

'But,' protested Libby, 'if I do find anything out, I'd have to tell the police and it would come out anyway.'

'But if you looked into it and found there was nothing in it, there would be nothing to come out.'

'Patti, you're not suggesting I look into it in order to cover it up, are you?'

'No!' Patti was obviously horrified. 'I just thought you'd be less – I don't know – official and heavy-handed.'

'I often tread on toes.' Libby was rueful.

Patti gave a small chuckle. 'You're not very heavy.'

Libby sighed. 'All right. When do I see this Connie?'

'I'll ask her. She might have second thoughts.'

'After all this? I hope not!'

'I'll ring you when I know.'

Libby clicked off the phone again and regarded her now cold cup of tea. Now what had she let herself in for?

She said nothing to Ben about Patti's request, but after Colin arrived and was sitting in front of the fire in the sitting room with a pre-prandial gin and tonic, she said casually, 'Do you remember any scandal about St Aldeberge when you still lived here, Colin?'

'Scandal?' Colin wrinkled his brow. 'Apart from my own? No, I don't think so. Are you thinking about Nick Nash?'

Ben groaned.

'Well,' said Libby, ignoring him, 'Patti's turned up a couple of people who remember him when he was a churchwarden.'

'*Churchwarden?*' echoed Ben.

'But he left. That was when he went to Spain, I suppose. I don't know when he got married. Do you?' She raised her eyebrows at Colin.

'No – I didn't really know her. The only reason Nick and I were vaguely drawn together was that we came from roughly the same area. And he returned regularly, whereas I didn't. He used to bring me news. I told you, I never really liked her, and I think that was why he wanted to offload the house in Kent and live in Spain permanently.'

'Hmm,' said Libby, frowning.

'Why?' said Ben suddenly.

'What?' Libby looked up, startled.

'Why this interest?'

Libby felt the familiar colour begin to rise up her neck.

'Come on,' said Ben. 'Or is it just plain old nosiness?'

Libby looked indignant. 'No! It's just . . .' she tailed off.

'Someone's asked you,' said Ben shrewdly. 'Who? Is it Patti?'

Libby nodded. 'Some of her older parishioners remember Nash, and asked her if they could speak to me.' She avoided Ben's eyes.

'Yes? And?'

'There was gossip.'

'About?' said Colin.

28

Libby cleared her throat. 'Children.'

She allowed a couple of minutes for the implications to sink in.

'You mean . . .?' Colin gasped.

'Only rumours,' said Libby. 'But Connie and Elaine thought someone ought to know.'

'Police,' said Ben firmly.

'As Patti said, they're elderly women and it's what? Twenty years ago?'

'Are you going to talk to them?' asked Colin. 'Can I come?'

'Yes, I am, but I don't think they'd want to talk to a stranger. They know me, you see.'

'From the last time she poked her nose into church business,' said Ben.

'Not the last time,' said Libby. 'There was the business of the monastery after that, and—'

'All right.' Ben stood up and patted her on the shoulder. 'I'll go and check on the dinner.'

Colin was frowning into the fire. 'Was it abuse?' he asked after a moment.

'I don't know.' Libby looked at him sideways. 'What do you think?'

He heaved a sigh. 'I was thinking of Nigel's happy band. Little Foxes, wasn't it called?'

'Were they into that sort of thing?'

'How should I know?' Colin looked grumpy.

'Would it be the right sort of time frame?'

'That's what made me think of it,' said Colin.

Ben reappeared. 'Almost ready. Come and sit down.'

They managed to stay off the subject of Nick Nash until Libby brought them all coffee in the sitting room.

'You mentioned the Little Foxes,' she said to Colin, sitting down on the sofa. 'Well, it couldn't be anything to do with them, could it? They'd all have been too young. You don't get to be a churchwarden in your twenties.'

'You might,' said Ben.

'I had the idea that anyone involved in – er – children would be the jaded businessman type,' said Libby.

'That's a bit biased,' Ben raised his eyebrows at her.

'Nick was in his fifties, I would say,' put in Colin. 'So twenty years ago he'd have been in his thirties.'

'Well, that's reasonable, I suppose.' Libby frowned at the fire. 'But he wouldn't have been anything to do with Sir Nigel Preece, would he?'

'I don't know.' Colin shook his head. 'Maybe Nick went to that school where his gang went.'

'Foxgrove – yes, but he would have been there before that club was started.'

'You don't know that,' said Ben. 'It sounded as though it was one of those secret societies that was originally started back in the twenties.'

'And it was used as the basis of their nasty shenanigans.' Libby nodded. 'Yes, that sounds likely. So maybe it was already pretty dodgy when Nick Nash went there.'

'Hey – steady on!' Ben laughed. 'We have no idea if he actually went to Foxgrove! He probably didn't even grow up near here.'

'Actually, I think he did. In Kent, anyway,' said Colin. 'I don't see what it has to do with him being crushed to death by a lawnmower, though.'

Ben and Libby looked at him in surprise.

'I was talking about him when he was a churchwarden,' said Libby.

'But why? Because you're trying to find a *reason* for his death. But it could have been an accident. In fact, it probably was.'

Chapter Five

Ben's gaze turned to Libby, whose own dropped to her lap.

'Come on, Lib, he's right.'

After a long moment, Libby sighed. 'I know.' She looked up at the two concerned faces peering at her. 'So what do I do now? About Patti's parishioners? Tell them I won't see them?'

'You can't do that,' said Ben reasonably. 'They aren't part of your "investigation", they went to Patti of their own accord. I'd see them, and if they have anything relevant to say, pass it on to the police and leave them to deal with it.'

'All right.' Libby stood up. 'Anyone for a drink?'

The following morning Libby heard nothing from Patti, which was hardly surprising, as it was Sunday, and Patti would have been to at least one of her other churches before Matins at St Aldeberge. By one o'clock she and Ben were on their way to The Manor for the ritual of Hetty's Sunday lunch. Any members of the extended family who were around would be there, along with Flo Carpenter, Hetty's best friend from childhood, with Lenny, Hetty's brother and Flo's partner. Today, Edward Hall, historian and university lecturer, and a particular favourite of Hetty's, was already seated at the big kitchen table with a glass in his hand.

'No Peter?' he asked after greetings had been exchanged.

'He helps Harry in the caff most Sundays in the run up to Christmas,' said Libby. 'You wouldn't believe how many people start having their works do this early.'

'Spoils it really, doesn't it?' Edward shook his head. 'Ian can't be here, either. He's got some new murder to deal with.' He laughed. 'They're trying to make him stay in the office and delegate again, but it doesn't seem to be working.'

'Where is it this time?' Libby asked nonchalantly, pouring herself a glass of Shiraz.

'Libby!' said Ben warningly.

Edward grinned. 'Not here! Although it is down near Patti again, a bit like—' He broke off as Ben groaned and Libby gasped. 'What have I said?'

Ben pulled himself together first. 'Do you know any more about it? How the person died, for instance?'

'Something about the cliffs,' said Edward looking puzzled. 'Why?'

Hetty came up to the table and helped herself to a glass of wine, shaking her head. 'You've done it now, young Edward. There they was, all tryin' to persuade our gal to stay out of it.'

'Out of *what*?' Edward almost shouted.

'It's a friend of Colin's,' Ben began.

'What?' Edward looked gobsmacked.

'Well,' said Libby, 'it might be a friend of Colin's. We don't actually *know* that.'

'Come on,' said Ben. 'Down near Patti? Cliffs? Who else could it be?'

'We'd better tell him the whole story,' said Libby, resignedly. 'You start.' She stood up and went to help Hetty put vegetables in dishes.

'You want to phone and ask that Colin up here for lunch?' asked Hetty in a low voice.

'Really?' Libby looked at her mother-in-law-elect doubtfully. 'He might have booked in at the pub. Or even Harry's.'

'Ask 'im.' Hetty turned away to poke the resting joint with a vicious skewer.

'Really?' said Colin, unconsciously echoing Libby. 'Are you sure she doesn't mind?'

'It was her idea. You'll see why when you get here. You hadn't booked in anywhere else?'

'No. Harry's full and I didn't fancy the pub again.'

'Come on, then. Quick smart.'

Libby turned off her phone.

'Colin's on his way,' she said, interrupting Ben's story. Edward and Ben turned shocked faces to her.

'My idea,' said Hetty abruptly. 'Seein' as you was talkin' about 'im. Poor bugger.'

'Another waif and stray?' said Edward with a grin.

'Hmph,' said Hetty, and turned back to her roast. At the foot of the Aga, Jeff-dog raised his head, looked at her enquiringly, and sighed.

'He got the measure of her pretty quickly, didn't he,' said Libby, reaching down to fondle his silky ears on the way back to her chair. Jeff-dog had been acquired during the course of an adventure with some turkeys some years previously.

'Of course,' said Edward. 'Another stray.' They all looked at Hetty's unresponsive back.

'Where had you got up to?' asked Libby.

'The two old ladies asking to see you,' said Ben.

'You should tell Ian about that,' said Edward. 'I don't think he knows much about the murdered man yet.'

'Well, that's as far as we've got,' said Libby. 'In fact, last night Colin and Ben were both persuading me I'd made mountains as usual and I was trying to make it into a murder.' She looked across at Ben triumphantly. 'Well, I wasn't, was I?'

They heard the big front door open, and Colin appeared, slightly red-faced, in the kitchen doorway.

'Sit down, boy,' said Hetty. 'Ben'll give you a drink.'

'Thanks, Hetty.' Colin sank into a chair.

'That was quick,' said Libby.

'I cut through the back way. Across the green,' explained Colin, accepting a glass from Ben. 'Hello, Edward.'

Between the back of the pub and the Manor and Oast Theatre was a green space, used variously as a car park, camping site, and, on one memorable occasion, a beer festival.

'So what's happened?' he asked, after a restorative gulp of wine.

Everyone began to speak at once, until Hetty banged a serving spoon on the table. When a surprised silence fall, she looked across at Colin.

'Your mate,' she said. 'Murdered.'

Colin's mouth fell open. 'Nick?'

'Yes.' Libby looked apologetic. 'Sorry, Colin. Ian's on the case, apparently.'

'Do you know – I mean, how?' Colin shook his head. 'Was it what you thought, Libby?'

'What did you think?' asked Edward, interested.

'The two ladies from Patti's church.' Libby turned to him. 'They thought they remembered him having something to do with . . .' she paused. 'Children.'

Edward looked horror-stricken. He shook his head and cleared his throat. 'In that case, you should *definitely* tell Ian. Now it's been proved to be murder.'

'Oh, blimey, he's going to hate me,' groaned Libby.

'Yes,' said everybody else.

'No,' said Colin, putting down his glass. 'I'll tell him. After all, I've already been questioned—'

'You didn't say that!' said Libby.

'Well, only about how I knew him and why he had my name and so on. But it wasn't Ian – it was a couple of uniformed constables.'

'But your name will appear in the files,' nodded Libby.

'So it would be better for you to speak to Ian,' agreed Ben.

'As long as it isn't me,' said Edward, giving a slight shudder. 'I remember what happened last time.'

'So does everybody, apparently,' said Libby.

After roast beef, Yorkshire puddings, carrots, Brussels sprouts, and roast potatoes with homemade horseradish sauce and gravy, followed by raspberry dumplings and custard, Hetty announced she was going into her own private sitting room for a nap. Ben and Libby offered to wash up, as usual, and, as usual, were told to load the dishwasher but leave the pots to her. Colin and Edward helped, and then, as per custom, they all trooped down the Manor drive to Peter's and Harry's cottage.

Peter let them in.

'Harry's still clearing up,' he said. 'Rushed off our feet, we were. Coffee, or alcohol?'

For once, everybody opted for coffee, which Peter was passing around when Harry arrived, still in his whites.

'Coffee?' He said, eyebrows raised in surprise. 'Well, not for me, thank you. I've had a hard day.' He flung himself down in a corner of the sofa. Ben and Edward shifted together.

'We've had an interesting one,' said Libby. 'We've got another murder.'

This raised a chorus of protest.

'It was the mate of Colin's, I suppose?' Harry looked up and accepted a glass from Peter, who perched on the arm of the sofa next to him.

'How do you know?' asked Colin.

'Because the old trout was trying to turn it into one. *Ergo* . . .'

Libby glared at him. Ben sighed.

'My fault,' said Edward. 'I merely reported that Ian couldn't come to lunch today—'

'Not unusual,' interrupted Harry.

'No. Because he had a new murder case, somewhere near Patti's village.' Edward shook his head. 'And that was it.'

'Do they know any more? Any ideas?' asked Peter.

'We don't know,' said Libby, 'but everyone thinks I should pass on my little bit of information. Colin's going to do it.'

'What information?' asked Peter and Harry together.

Between them they explained.

'Ian might know that already,' said Peter. 'They'll have gone into the victim's background by now, won't they? Do you know when they decided it was murder, Edward?'

'No idea. Ian knocked on my door to ask me to apologise for his absence at Hetty's. That's all I know.'

There was a short silence.

'Well,' said Harry, 'we don't know nuffink, so even our Lib can't speculate. We might as well talk about something else.'

A little later Ben and Libby strolled home along the dark and silent high street.

'Do you think Ian will want to talk to me?' asked Libby.

'What? Why?'

'Because of Patti's ladies.'

Ben turned to look at her. 'Probably. If only to ask who they are.'

'I don't know who they are.'

'Patti told you their names.'

'Yes. Um . . .'

They turned the corner into Allhallow's Lane.

'Connie – that was one.' Libby frowned.

Ben took out his key. 'Can't think of the other?'

'No.' Libby sighed in frustration. 'I suppose I'll have to wait until they get in touch.'

'Or Ian will track them down first,' said Ben.

The following morning, Libby was sitting at the kitchen table when the landline rang. Ben, on his way out, answered it and brought it over to her.

'Gird your loins,' he said.

'Is it Ian?' mouthed Libby. Ben shook his head and grinned.

'Hello?' said Libby tentatively.

'Libby, what do you mean by telling Ian about my parishioners?' said Patti. 'I didn't!' gasped Libby. Ben escaped through the front door.

'How did he know about Nick Nash being a churchwarden and

the rumours about him, then? He was on the phone not half an hour ago!'

Libby looked at the clock. Half past eight. 'I expect it was Colin.'

'And how did *he* know?'

Libby sighed. 'Look, Patti, let me explain.'

Patti made a sound suspiciously like 'Harrumph.'

Libby explained how Edward had unwittingly stirred up the whole situation the previous day.

'Colin had already been talked to by the police, so he thought he ought to let Ian know,' she concluded.

Patti sighed. 'Apparently he already knew who the body was—'

'Of course – all his documents were on him.'

'But he didn't know his history.'

'You mean about him being churchwarden?'

'Of course I do!' Patti burst out again. 'And he wouldn't have known about the rumours, either!'

Libby took a deep breath. 'Look Patti. It's murder. That's why it was decided – by all of us, not just me – that Ian needed to hear anything that had been said about Nash. And no one mentioned your ladies' names.'

'No, because he asked me who they were!'

Libby paused before answering. 'And did you tell him?'

'Yes.' Grudgingly.

'Well, they won't want to speak to me now, will they?'

'No.' Patti sighed. 'Sorry I made a fuss. I feel as if I betrayed them.'

'Of course you didn't. They wanted to talk about it, anyway.' Libby looked at the clock again. 'Shall I pop over this morning?'

'If you like.' Patti sounded tired. 'Ian wants to come and talk to me, too. I told him I never knew Nick Nash, but . . .'

'He'll want to look in the church records, I shouldn't wonder,' said Libby. 'Look, I'm going to call Fran – she doesn't know the latest, and she might want to meet the ladies.'

'They probably won't want to meet her,' said Patti darkly. 'All right. I'll expect you when I see you.'

Libby made a quick call to Fran, giving her a brief update on the situation and arranging to meet her at the St Aldeberge vicarage.

'And then,' said Libby to herself as she dashed upstairs to get ready, 'perhaps we'll begin to find out exactly what happened to Nick Nash.'

Chapter Six

Fran's Smart car was already parked in front of Patti's vicarage, and Libby was amused to find her still sitting inside.

'I didn't want to go in without you if Patti's ladies are already there,' she said, climbing out.

'What about Ian? Has he been here?'

'I don't know. He could have already come and gone.' Fran approached the front door. 'I hope he has.'

'So do I,' said Libby.

'He hasn't arrived yet,' said Patti, opening the door, 'but the ladies are here. I've just brought them tea, would you like some?'

'Not for me, thanks,' said Fran. 'What have they said about seeing me? Or both of us, come to that?'

Patti sighed. 'They seem to think Libby's more likely to help them than the police.'

Libby raised an eyebrow.

'They'll be happier confiding in her than in an intimidating policeman,' said Fran. 'I can understand that.'

'Come on, then.' Patti led the way into her sitting room, where two women sat, side by side on the sofa. 'This is Connie Barstow,' she indicated the woman with close cropped grey hair, 'and this is Elaine Roberts.' Elaine, short and stout, with improbably brown hair, smiled nervously.

'Hello.' Libby held out a hand to each of the ladies, which was rather tremulously shaken. 'I'm Libby Sarjeant, and this is my friend, Fran Wolfe.'

'You're the medium, aren't you?' Connie peered at Fran.

'Not quite.' Fran smiled in return.

'I thought you . . .'

'Fran occasionally thinks of things we don't necessarily see,' Patti cut in hastily. 'The police trust her.'

'Oh.' Connie still looked vaguely suspicious.

'What did you want to see us about?' asked Libby, sitting on one of assorted chairs Patti had assembled to cater for her frequent meetings.

'Well,' Connie and Elaine looked at each other. 'See, we thought if we told you what we remembered, we wouldn't have to tell the police.'

'But I'm afraid, as I've told the ladies,' said Patti to Libby, 'the police will want to know.'

'Don't worry, though,' said Fran. 'They're very fair, and they won't want to put you on the spot.'

'So what do you remember about Nick Nash?' asked Libby. 'He was a churchwarden, wasn't he?'

'Yes,' said Connie.

'It was when Reverend Turner was here,' said Elaine. 'He wasn't very popular, I'm afraid. And Mr Nash always was.'

They fell silent.

'But Patti said he wasn't,' said Libby.

'Well . . . no. Not after . . .'

'After what?' asked Fran.

'It was the girls, see,' said Elaine. 'In the choir and the youth club.'

'What happened?' asked Libby, when they seemed to dry up again.

'A couple of the girls in the choir left, and then the girls in the youth club stopped going. And Mr Nash, he'd been very active in keeping the choir going, and the youth club. And people started to talk.' Connie gave a decisive nod and folded her arms over her handbag.

'What were they saying?' asked Patti.

'That it was his fault,' said Elaine.

'Who were these people?' asked Patti again.

'Everyone. Gossip, you see. People wondered.' Connie compressed her lips.

'Did you know any of the girls personally?' asked Libby.

'No.' Connie tightened her lips again.

'Yes, we did, dear,' said Elaine. 'You remember young Pamela? And that Kerry? And Amy's niece . . .'

'Well, all right,' snapped Connie. 'But not to say personally, did we?' Elaine subsided.

Libby, Fran, and Patti looked at each other.

'And what did you want Libby to do, exactly?' Patti leant towards the women. 'What are you worried about?'

The colour came up in Connie's face and drained from Elaine's. Eventually, it was Elaine who spoke.

'Well, see, we thought that Mrs – er – Libby could find out if it was someone who, like, held a grudge about Mr Nash. If it really was him that made the girls leave . . .'

'Did they just leave the church?' asked Fran. 'Didn't they tell anyone?'

'Went away,' said Connie. 'Two of 'em never seen again.'

'What about the police?' said Patti. 'Weren't they reported as missing persons?'

'Folk didn't want a fuss,' said Elaine. 'They seemed . . . well . . .'

'Embarrassed?' suggested Libby.

Elaine nodded gratefully.

'And are any of those people still around now?' asked Fran.

Elaine looked at Connie. 'There's still Amy's family, isn't there? Don't know any of the others. Pam and Kerry's families moved away.'

Libby was frowning. 'It's not really very clear,' she said slowly. 'I mean, you have no concrete evidence that there was anything going on – or have you?'

'He was a wrong'un,' said Connie firmly. 'Everyone knew it. And them girls – well, why wasn't they around any more?'

She stood up and Elaine followed suit.

'You find out, Libby. We want to know if we got some kind of madman killing people.'

With that, they left.

'Hardly a madman,' said Fran as Patti came back after seeing the ladies off. 'Only one man dead.'

'They're scared,' said Patti.

'Yes, but what of?' said Libby. 'They've got no real evidence that anything was going on, no one seems to be around to talk to about it . . . It just sounds like village gossip to me. You know – of the girls-who-are-no-better-than-they-should-be type.'

'Nudge nudge, say no more,' said Patti.

'Exactly. I thought that sort of thing had died out by now.'

'Are we going to stay and talk to Ian?' asked Fran.

'I don't see much point, frankly,' said Libby. 'We don't know anything, and Patti can tell him what the ladies said – which is nothing.'

'I agree,' said Patti, 'although I would have liked the moral support.'

'We'll stay if you want,' said Libby.

'No, you go. He might get irritated with you. He won't with me.'

Libby opened her mouth indignantly, but Fran laughed.

'Absolutely right. But before we go, those ladies we met before – Sheila, wasn't it? And who was the lady in the shop?'

'Doris?' suggested Libby.

'Dora Walters,' said Patti. 'I can ask them if they remember anything – see how widespread this gossip was.'

'Good idea,' said Libby. 'And now, we'd better get a move on if we don't want to bump into Ian. And I don't.'

'Where now?' she asked Fran, as they prepared to get into their cars. 'Do we need to have a confab?'

'What you mean is – *you* want to have a confab,' said Fran.

'Well, yes.'

'OK. Come to mine. We might have to go into the shop, but it won't be busy.'

Libby followed Fran to Nethergate, where she was able to park almost opposite Coastguard Cottage.

'I'll just pop along to the shop and see if Guy needs me,' said Fran. 'You all right here for a moment?'

'I'll just look at the sea,' grinned Libby. 'Very soothing.'

The sea was fretting a little at the beach, grey and irritable-looking. A couple of dog walkers strolled along, but otherwise it was very quiet. Fran appeared at her shoulder.

'No, he doesn't need me. Come on, I'll make tea.'

'Well,' said Libby, when they were settled with tea, 'that was a bit inconclusive, wasn't it?'

'Yes and no,' said Fran. 'They're obviously scared of something, but I can't understand exactly what. If girls did go missing and there was gossip about Nick Nash, I can understand there being a lot of unsettled feelings at the time, but it was twenty years ago! Why would they be scared now?'

'Because they're scared it might all be stirred up again?' Libby shook her head. 'No, that doesn't work. Unless there's someone still around from that time who they thought was connected with it all?'

'That makes sense,' said Fran.

'Do you suppose it got as far as the local papers?' suggested Libby. 'We could ask Jane to do a bit of digging for us.'

'No – but I'll tell you who might help,' said Fran. 'What about Fred Barrett?'

Barrett was a retired reporter they had met while investigating the twenty-year-old murder of a young singer from Felling.

'Gosh – yes! I bet he remembers. Sort of case he'd be interested in, isn't it? Have you still got his number?'

'In my phone. Let's think about it first, though.'

'What's to think about? We want to find out – he's bound to have some kind of evidence.'

'Not evidence,' said Fran. 'From the sound of it, it'll just be hear-say. The ladies didn't seem to think the police had been involved.'

'I find that very odd,' said Libby. 'Do you think they've got it wrong? The girls didn't actually disappear?'

Fran frowned. 'I wish we could talk to someone who was around at that time.'

'Well, Connie and Elaine were.'

'Someone else. That girl's family, for instance.'

'Amy something? They wouldn't talk to us,' said Libby. 'No, the best bet is Fred Barrett. And he'd know we weren't just being nosy for the sake of it.'

'All right.' Fran sighed and stood up. 'Where's my phone?'

However, Barrett's phone went straight to voicemail, so Fran had to leave a message.

'Suppose he died?' said Libby. 'After all, he was quite old, wasn't he?'

'Not that much older than we are!' said Fran. 'I don't think we need worry about that. And the phone's still connected. So while we're waiting for him to ring back, let's write down what we've got so far, with names.' She retrieved a pad and pencil from the table beside her.

'The police will be doing all this,' said Libby. 'In fact, now Patti's told Ian what the ladies had to say, I expect he's all over it.'

'I expect so, but I would think their priority is finding the wife, wouldn't you?'

'Yes, but they can run several lines of enquiry, can't they?' Libby glanced at the carriage clock on the little table. 'Look at the time! And we haven't had any lunch!'

'Can't you survive until dinner time?' asked Fran, amused.

'No! And I don't even know what we're going to have for dinner, either. Because we go to Hetty's every Sunday, there aren't any convenient leftovers for Monday.'

'Air pie and doorknobs,' said Fran with a grin.

'Haven't heard that for years,' said Libby. 'And it'll be up in Annie's room behind the wallpaper.'

'I wonder how many people remember those old phrases?' said Fran. 'Apart from us.'

'No idea. But – er – back to our muttons – shall I pop down to Mavis and see if I can get a couple of sandwiches?'

Mavis owned The Blue Anchor cafe at the end of Harbour Street, next to The Sloop Inn.

'Go on then. I'll wait here in case Barrett phones.'

Libby hurried along Harbour Street and waved madly as she saw Mavis just about to pull down the blinds on the cafe.

'Just caught you!' she said breathlessly. 'Got any sandwiches left?'

Mavis sighed. 'Come in, then,' she said grudgingly. 'You been off snooping again?'

Libby grinned, as Mavis ferreted about behind the counter for sandwich ingredients. 'You could say that. Trying to find out what happened twenty years ago in St Aldeberge.'

'Thought you did that already.'

'That was Felling, if you mean that business with Sir Nigel.'

'So what's this then? More of the same?'

'Don't know, really. Some girls who went missing, as far as we can tell.'

Mavis paused and looked up, startled. 'You don't mean Kerry Palmer?'

Libby's mouth dropped open.

Mavis put down the knife she'd been holding. 'What do you want to know for?'

Libby found her voice. 'Someone said she and some other girls from the choir had moved away, and there was talk—'

She got no further. 'I'll say there was talk! So what's brought it up again now?'

'Someone was killed,' said Libby, choosing her words carefully, 'and the police want to find out as much as they can about him.'

'Well,' said Mavis, picking up her knife again, 'he deserved it, if it was that Mr Nash.'

Libby sank onto one of the stools at the counter. 'OK, Mavis. What do you know about Nick Nash?'

Chapter Seven

Mavis went back to constructing sandwiches. 'Rumours.'

Libby blew out her cheeks. 'That's all we've got. And it *was* him that was murdered.'

Mavis looked up briefly. 'Don't know as it's my story to tell,' she said.

'What about this Kerry Palmer? We heard her name earlier.'

'Who from?' Mavis asked sharply.

'Two ladies who live in St Aldeberge. Do you know her?'

'Did. Know the family. They live here, now.'

Libby surveyed her thoughtfully for a moment.

'I don't suppose they'd talk to me?'

'No.' Mavis tightened her lips. 'No use bringing it all up.'

'All *what*?' Libby wanted to ask. Aloud, she said 'The police will find out. They'll probably want to talk to them.'

Mavis looked up and pointed the knife at her. 'You don't say nothing to them, d'you hear?'

Startled, Libby shook her head.

Mavis grunted. 'I know what you're like.'

Not for the first time, Libby cursed her reputation.

A few minutes later, Mavis wrapped the sandwiches in grease-proof paper and handed them over.

'No,' she said grudgingly, when Libby proffered money. 'Sorry if I was rude.'

Even more startled, Libby thanked her and left the café.

'Guess what?' she said, bursting through the door of Coastguard Cottage. 'Mavis knew one of those girls!'

Fran appeared from the kitchen. 'She *what?*'

Libby handed over the packet. 'This is what she said.'

As she related the conversation with Mavis, Fran put the sandwiches on plates and handed one over.

'So the Palmer family live here, now?'

'Yes, although we're forbidden to talk to them or tell the police about them.'

'The police will find out anyway,' said Fran, sitting down in her usual chair.

'I told her that.' Libby stared out of the window at the sea. 'Whatever it was must have been bad, mustn't it? I wonder why we've never heard of it before?'

'No reason we should, I suppose.'

'Yes, but it was the same time as all the Sir Nigel stuff, wasn't it? And not so far away, either. I'm surprised we didn't hear about it then.'

'That's why we're asking Fred Barrett, isn't it?' Fran looked at her watch. 'And he hasn't returned the call.'

'I expect he's busy,' said Libby. 'And I suppose I ought to be going home. Ben will think I'm poking my nose in, as usual.'

'Well, you are, aren't you?' Fran was amused.

Libby shrugged irritably and finished the last of her sandwich. 'I'd better go.'

She drove home slowly, mulling over what she'd been told that morning. In fact, it didn't seem as though previous events had anything to do with Nick Nash's involuntary dive off the cliff top, but, in true Libby fashion, it was far too intriguing to let it go altogether. After all, there were those girls to find justice for . . .

Before going back to Allhallow's Lane, she detoured to the Hop Pocket, where she found Ben sitting in what would eventually be the bar with a mug of tea.

'Find any houses?' he asked with a grin.

'Didn't look for any.' Libby perched on a window sill next to him. 'Saw the two old ladies, though.'

'And? What did they have to say?'

Libby related the story she'd been told, and followed it up with Mavis's surprising revelations.

'So there is something for Sarjeant and Wolfe to look into!' Ben gave her a knowing wink.

'Well, there's certainly something for Ian to look into.' Libby stretched her legs out in front of her. 'Fran's left a message for Fred Barrett.'

'Who?'

'The ex-journalist from the *Mercury,* who helped us with the Sir Nigel stuff – you remember.'

'Do you think it's got something to do with all that? Young girls might be significant.'

'It is the same time frame, but . . .' Libby sighed and shook her head. 'I don't know. Best wait and see. Anyway, you didn't want me getting involved.'

'That's never stopped you before.'

'No . . . but oh, I don't know. I feel a sort of sense of responsibility.'

Ben looked at her in surprise. 'For what?'

'Those girls. No one seems to have looked into their disappearance. Which I find very odd. If they really did go missing, why didn't it make the news? At least regional, if not national. That's what usually happens. And this was the twenty-first century not back in the seventies or eighties. Anyway, Connie Barstow and Elaine Roberts trusted me.'

Ben tried to hide a grin and failed. Libby punched him on the arm.

'I'm going home. Any ideas for dinner?'

Libby had just lit the fire and boiled the kettle for tea when the landline rang.

'Have you plans for dinner?' asked Edward.

'No!' Libby was taken aback. 'I was just wondering what to have, as a matter of fact.'

'Well . . .' Edward was hesitant. 'Ian wondered if you'd like to have dinner with us at the pub?'

'He – what?' Libby was even further taken aback. '*Ian* did?'

'Yes. Apparently, he thought you might say something rude if he asked himself.'

Libby laughed. 'I can imagine! But I can't see why that would worry him. We've known one another for a long time, now. What does he want?'

'"Matters arising" he said.'

'From the Nick Nash murder, I suppose. Doesn't he want Colin?'

'Just you. And Ben, of course.'

'In that case, lovely. Thank you for inviting us.'

'Don't thank me – thank Ian. His treat. Eight at the pub, all right?'

Libby called Ben to tell him the surprising news and sat down in front of the fire to enjoy her tea.

It was an hour later when her mobile rang.

'Me,' said Fran. 'Fred Barrett just rang back.'

'Great! And?'

'He did remember. And it wasn't anything to do with Sir Nige, apparently. A different thing altogether. Are you sitting comfortably?'

'Yes, yes. Get on with it.'

'Apparently, it really was just rumour. He picked up on it, but no one reported any of the girls missing to the police.'

'What? But what about Kerry? And Pam, wasn't it?'

'The parents thought they had just – well – gone off. Like girls do, they said.'

'But what about the church involvement?'

'That was gossip among the parents, too. They and several of the girls had belonged to the choir and the church youth club – not much else to do in those days – and they had all stopped going. They parents thought it must be something to do with the vicar, or Nick

49

Nash, because he ran the youth club. In fact, one or two of them tackled him.'

'It must have been slightly more than that, if people are still talking about it today,' said Libby.

'That's what Fred thought. So he did a bit of digging. Talked to some of the girls who were still in the village, but they were – strangely, he thought – reluctant to talk. He said they seemed scared of something.'

'Didn't he do anything about it?'

'Yes. He talked to the police. Of course, there wasn't a local bobby, but there was a small police station in Felling. A sergeant there knew St Aldeberge, and he dismissed the whole thing. More or less said girls would be girls. You know the sort of thing.'

'And what about the vicar and our Mr Nash?'

'Above reproach, according to this policeman.'

'Hmm. So will I tell Ian?' She repeated Ian's surprising invitation.

'Well, Patti will have told him what Connie and Elaine said this morning. I expect he wants to talk about that, so yes, I'd tell him, if I were you.'

'Even if he thinks we've been going above and beyond the call of duty?'

'You usually do!'

'Oi! So do you!'

Fran laughed. 'All right, all right. But yes. Tell him. And don't forget to report to me.'

Before they left for the pub that evening, Libby discussed everything with Ben. 'And you can't say I'm poking my nose in, now. Not if Ian wants to talk to me.

'No,' said Ben thoughtfully, pulling on a shoe. 'And I must say, I'm quite interested myself. Come on, let's go and partake of DCI Connell's largesse.'

Ian, tall and faintly saturnine, and Edward were already ensconced at a table with menus when they arrived. Ian stood up.

'Ah – Ben and Libby. What will you have to drink?'

'I'll get them,' said Ben.

'No – my treat,' said Ian. 'Libby – I've ordered a bottle of Tim's finest red, or would you prefer something else to start with?'

Libby settled for red wine, while Ben opted for bitter, and they settle down to wait for the inquisition.

'Now,' said Ian. 'Connie Barstow and Elaine Roberts.'

'Yes?' said Libby nervously. 'They asked to see me.'

'I know they did, so none of this is your fault.' Ian smiled at her. 'Don't worry. I'm simply wondering if your well-known detective instincts have unearthed anything else.'

'Well,' Libby glanced at Ben, 'actually, Fran and I wondered about that ex-journalist, Fred Barrett. So we rang him.'

'Ah.' Ian leant back in his chair, a look of satisfaction on his face. 'And?'

'He rang Fran back late this afternoon.' Libby reported what Barrett had told Fran.

Ian frowned. 'Yes . . . in fact I got someone to dig out the files from back then, and he's right. Peacock, the sergeant he mentioned, had logged the report, concluding that there was nothing in it. Surprisingly, though, there were reports of a couple of attacks on both the vicar – Reverend Turner, I think – and Nicholas Nash.'

'Attacks?' Edward looked shocked.

'On their property, not on their persons,' clarified Ian. 'So there was definitely ill feeling in the village.' He frowned again. 'I just wonder why more wasn't made of it at the time.'

'That's what I couldn't understand,' said Libby. 'Missing children – or teenagers – are front page news, aren't they?'

They fell silent.

'Do you think this has anything to do with Nash's death?' asked Libby.

Ian looked up. 'Who knows? But we have to look into these things. The fall off the cliff wasn't accidental. Someone had been performing surgery on the insides of that lawnmower.'

'What about the wife?' asked Ben. 'Colin said she wasn't er – very likeable.'

'We're trying to trace her,' said Ian. 'She isn't at the address we found for her, so obviously she's a person of interest. On the other hand, she does not inherit the property, nor the one in Spain. Although no doubt she will claim against the will. They were officially still married.'

'So it's a question of looking for motives in the rest of his life?' said Edward.

'Sorry to interrupt,' said Tim, coming up behind them. 'But would you like to order?'

'Do you think he'll manage to turn this into a gastropub when you open the Hop Pocket?' asked Ian, as they watched Tim disappear into the kitchen.

'He'll have a good go,' said Ben. 'The food's quite good already, and he's already on the search for a new chef.'

'So back to motives,' said Libby. The other three laughed.

'In answer to Edward's question, yes we're looking for other motives,' said Ian. 'But I'm not sure a vague rumour of girls going missing twenty years ago is enough.'

'But those women said the vicar and Nick Nash both left the parish at about that time,' said Libby. 'That's suspicious, surely?'

'We'll look into it,' promised Ian. 'Now, has Colin said anything else to you?'

'No,' said Ben. 'Simply that he didn't know Nash very well, or Simone, come to that. He knew nothing about his background except that he came from round here and used to come back more frequently than Colin himself did.'

'He asked his friend John Newman from Felling if he knew Nick Nash,' said Libby. 'John said he remembered him, but was a bit cagey, Colin thought.'

'Oh?' Ian looked interested. 'Might that link up with Sir Nigel Preece?'

'We've all wondered that,' said Libby.

'Well, you have,' said Ben.

'Worth looking into,' said Ian. 'You never know what might turn up. There are a lot of unanswered questions about that man and his unholy gang. Now, I'm going to relax and forget all about work.'

Chapter Eight

'I think,' said Libby, on the phone to Fran the next morning, 'we ought to speak to John Newman and Emma.'

'I thought Colin had already spoken to him?'

'He did, and he said John was a bit cagey.'

'That doesn't surprise me. Look how disturbed they were when we asked them about Sir Nigel.'

'But that's what I mean,' said Libby. 'That sounds as though Nash could have been part of Nasty Nigel's gang.'

'Hmm,' said Fran. 'He might clam up. After all, we're being a bit intrusive.'

'Well, I'm going to ask, anyway. I think Ian will, as well.'

Luckily for her, Libby had kept Newman's number in her phone from their last encounter. To her surprise, Emma answered.

'We just wondered if you'd remembered any more about this Nick Nash Colin asked about the other day,' said Libby.

'I didn't know he had,' said Emma. 'Why?'

'Well, he was found dead. Didn't you know?'

'Yes. Some accident, wasn't it?'

'Not exactly,' said Libby. 'The police think it was murder.'

'Oh, no!' Emma gasped. 'Not again!'

'Not exactly,' said Libby. 'He wasn't anything to do with Felling, he was a St Aldeberge man, but we thought, Fran and I – you remember Fran? – that he might have been mixed up with Sir Nigel.'

There was a moment's silence. Then, 'I don't think so. At least, I don't remember his name. But then, I didn't know many names, did I? Do you think he could have been at . . .' she paused, 'that party?'

'I don't know.' Libby sighed. 'But if you don't remember his name I don't suppose you met him.'

'Why did you think he might have been one of those awful people?'

'He had a bit of a reputation at about that time. In St Aldeberge.'

'I wouldn't know about that, would I?' Emma sounded petulant, and Libby imagined her shaking her blonde curls in annoyance.

'No, I suppose not. It was only a bit of a mystery about some girls going missing from a youth club . . .'

'Oh, *that*!' Emma gave a phony laugh. 'What a fuss about nothing.'

'Really? You knew about that, then?'

'Yes. People thought it was daft. After all, girls do go off, don't they?'

'So you didn't know him? Colin rather thought John did.'

'Really? I'll ask him, if you like.'

'Would you?' said Libby, surprised.

'Yes.' There was an implicit shrug in Emma's voice. 'Why are you interested this time?'

This brought Libby up with a start. What did she say?

'Well,' she began slowly, 'Colin knew him in Spain, and—'

Colin again. He's more trouble than he's worth.' Emma puffed out a sigh. 'Anyway, I'll ask John. Has he got your number?'

'As I had this one, I expect so,' said Libby. 'And thank you again for your help.'

'Definitely a flake,' she told Fran when she rang back to report. 'We thought so last time, didn't we?'

'Interesting what she said about the Felling attitude to missing girls, though,' said Fran.

'Sounds similar to the attitude of certain people to pandemics and climate change,' said Libby. 'They think it's all a load of hogwash.'

'They can't all be stupid, though.'

'Oh, I don't know,' said Libby darkly.

'It might explain why it wasn't taken seriously.'

'I told you about the policeman, didn't I? He came from Felling.'

'That fits, then, doesn't it? So is it – well, hogwash?'

'I honestly don't think so,' said Libby. 'Or am I just wanting it to be a proper mystery?'

'Partly, I expect. But we have got Connie and Elaine's testimony, if you want to call it that.'

'I wish they could tell us more,' sighed Libby. 'Or at least where we could find one of the girls who are left.'

'They've probably married and moved away,' said Fran. 'It was twenty years ago.'

Patti rang later that afternoon.

'I don't know how much use this will be,' she said, 'but a couple of things have come to light.'

'Really? What sort of things?'

'Just listen and I'll tell you. First of all, I dredged up everything I could find about the Reverend Turner. And there wasn't much. I found an old parish magazine with an editorial, but it was very short and didn't say a lot. There was also a short piece about the choir, which apparently needed new members, and another about the youth club, which was about to close.'

'That's interesting,' said Libby. 'Falling numbers in both cases, do we assume?'

'Looks like it,' said Patti. 'And there was a sort of official thank you notice concerning the donation of a thousand pounds to the repair fund.'

'A thousand? Gosh! Who was it?'

'Doesn't say. You know, "thanks to our anonymous donor".'

'Well! And was there something else?'

'Yes. Rather odd, really. Elaine turned up on the doorstep.'

'Elaine! Without Connie?'

'Exactly. And seemed very nervous.'

'She wasn't that full of confidence yesterday, was she?'

'No.' Patti obviously thought for a moment. 'She asked if it would be all right to speak to you again.'

'I hope you said yes?'

'Of course! I said I would ask you down here again, but she said no, she would rather ring you. She gave the strong impression that she didn't want Connie to know.'

'Now, that *is* interesting! Did you give her my number?'

'I did, but she said she'd prefer it if you rang her. I think she might chicken out if we leave it to her.'

'Fine. Give me her number, then. Did she say what would be a good time?'

'Before dinner, she said. Which she probably has early.'

'And watches the news,' agreed Libby. 'Right.' She checked the time. 'It's half four now, so five o'clock, do you reckon?'

On the dot of five o'clock, with a fresh cup of tea, Libby rang the number Patti had given her.

'Hello?' said a quavery voice.

'Elaine?' asked Libby. 'Libby Sarjeant here. You asked me to ring you.'

'Ah – um – yes.' Elaine cleared her throat. 'The thing is . . . you see, Connie didn't want . . . well, she didn't really know. I mean – do you still want to know about Nicholas Nash?'

'Anything you can tell me,' said Libby, wondering what she could say to reassure the woman. 'Our friend Colin, well, he brought Mr Nash over here this time, so he feels responsible, and,' Libby crossed her fingers, 'the police are obviously looking at him rather closely, too.'

'Oh, dear! And he had nothing to do with it?'

'No! He hardly knew anything about Mr Nash, except that they lived in the same area of Spain.'

'Spain! Oh. Is that where Mr Nash went when he – when he left here?'

'We don't know. Colin's only known him for a little while, and because he knew someone who wanted to buy a house near the sea and Mr Nash was selling his . . .'

'I see.' Elaine went silent. 'He was a businessman, wasn't he?'

'Mr Nash? Yes. I don't know what field he was in. Do you?'

'No . . .'

Libby let the silence go on for a moment.

'So what did you want to tell me, Elaine?'

'Well . . .' Elaine became confidential. 'He had these friends, you see. They used to meet at the church. After the youth club.'

'They did? At the *church*?'

'Yes. Amy's niece told me. She didn't like it.'

Libby felt a little lurch in her solar plexus. 'Did she say why?'

'No, not exactly. But I think Mr Nash used to ask some of the girls to serve them tea and biscuits when they had their meetings.'

Libby repressed an exclamation. 'And was that why she left the youth club?'

'I don't know. I just didn't see her any more. Amy's still here. But I don't like to ask Amy.'

'No, of course not,' said Libby, her mind racing. 'So why did they all keep going?'

'The Reverend, wasn't it? I expect he'd be cross if they stopped.'

'The Reverend? He was one of these – er – men?'

'Oh, yes. I couldn't understand why.'

'Perhaps,' said Libby, 'it was a sort of fund-raising thing? We heard about a thousand-pound donation to the repair fund.'

'Maybe.' Elaine sounded doubtful. 'But we'd have known.'

'Not if they wanted to be anonymous,' said Libby. 'That thousand-pound donor did.' She paused. 'Who told you about this, Elaine?'

'It was general knowledge. I mean, there were never any announcements in church or anything like that, but we all knew about it. We'd see them go off into the vestry after evensong sometimes. Those of us who went to church, that is.' She sniffed.

'Do you know who they were? Were they regular members of the congregation?'

'A couple were, but I don't remember their names. The others I never knew at all.'

58

Libby thought about it.

'Elaine, do you mind if I pass this on to the police? I think they ought to know.'

'Yes, dear! Do!' Elaine sounded relieved. 'I hoped you would. Connie would . . . I mean, Connie will . . .'

'Be cross with you? But why? She wanted to talk to me in the first place.'

'I think she thought you could just find out who killed Mr Nash and be done with it,' said Elaine. 'Bit silly, really, wasn't it?'

'Very,' said Libby dryly, having encountered this attitude before. 'Well, I'll tell Chief Inspector Connell and we'll see what happens after that, shall we? Do any of the other ladies in the village remember all this?'

'Oh, yes. Dora Walters does.'

'Yes, I remember Dora. She implied to me that all sorts of things go on in a village. *And* she mentioned the young people.'

'That was when you was looking into those other murders, was it?'

'That's right,' said Libby. 'Quite helpful, she was.'

'Terrible gossip, though,' said Elaine, with unconscious irony.

'Well, that's been very helpful, Elaine,' said Libby. 'Now, I must let you get on.'

'Thank you, dear. Yes, it's time for my tea.'

Libby sat for a long time after the phone call, ignoring her now cold cup of tea. Finally, she called Fran.

'Well,' said Fran, when she had finished relating what Elaine had told her, 'it's certainly worth telling Ian, even if it is based mainly on gossip.'

'Should I tell Patti, too? After all, it could reflect on her church.'

'I suppose so.' Fran sighed. 'It does seem unfair, doesn't it? She hasn't had much luck with that church.'

'I think I'll have to go down there again, you know,' said Libby.

'What for? You can't talk to anybody, can you?'

'I expect I can . . . A lot of them remember me for the Nativity play, if not for the murders.'

'Well, be careful. And tell Ian and Patti first.'

'I will,' promised Libby, and mentally girded her loins to report to Ian.

However, Ian was unavailable, so Libby left a message on his private mobile number and went to prepare dinner.

It was getting on for ten o'clock when Libby's mobile rang.

'Ian,' she mouthed at Ben, who turned off the television.

'So what have you got for me?' asked Ian, sounding tired and faintly irritable.

Libby launched into Elaine's story, leaving no gaps to allow him to comment along the way. When she finished, she waited.

There was a fairly long silence. Then, 'Do you believe this?'

Surprised, Libby nodded, then realised he couldn't see her. 'Yes. I believe she believes it, anyway. And it was worrying her enough to come to me with it.'

'She's not just trying to make herself important?'

'She's too timid for that. And a bit scared of her friend Connie.'

Another silence. 'I think I remember that other woman – Doris?'

'Dora.'

'Yes. A gossip.'

'Yes, but gave me some information that turned out to be important.'

'Do you think she'd confirm this?'

'If you turned up asking her, I think she might balk.'

'What you mean is, you ought to soften her up first.'

'I didn't say that!'

Ian laughed. 'All right, go and talk to her. And you can tell me all about it tomorrow night. But tell Patti first.'

'Yessir!' said Libby smartly.

'What you could do,' said Ben when she told him, 'is let me take you over and drop you there and you could come back with Patti. She'll be coming here tomorrow, won't she?'

'I'll ring her in the morning,' said Libby. 'Now let's watch the end of the news.'

Chapter Nine

Although dubious about Libby's proposed chat with Dora Walters, Patti was perfectly amenable to Ben's plan, and suggested lunch.

'Pensioners' lunch?' asked Libby, grinning at Ben. 'I thought that was Thursdays.'

'No, vicar's lunch,' said Patti. 'In my kitchen.'

Ben dropped Libby off and drove off to see an independent supplier he was interested in for the Hop Pocket.

'Do you want coffee before you embark on your interrogation of Dora?' Patti asked.

'Yes, please. I'm slightly putting it off,' said Libby. 'Where is she likely to be at this time of day, do you know?'

'At home, I should think. The shop opens at twelve, but I don't know if she's on duty today.'

'I'll risk it,' said Libby. 'I hope she won't mind.'

'I told you, she remembers you all right,' said Patti with a grin. 'And it'll give her a chance to gossip, won't it?'

Coffee finished, Libby set off for Dora Walters' cottage, a mid-terrace like Libby's own, but there, as Libby remembered, the similarity ended. Dora opened the door, looking surprised and still as though she was living in the nineteen fifties, as Libby also remembered.

'Mrs – Libby!' she said.

'Hello, Dora.' Libby smiled. 'I wondered if I could talk to you about something.'

Dora nodded wisely and opened the door wide. 'Better come in, then.'

The living room was even more crowded than Libby remembered, knick-knacks and presents from Brighton jostling for space on every surface.

'Sit down, and I'll put the kettle on,' said Dora, making for the kitchen.

'No, no,' said Libby hastily, 'the vicar's just given me coffee.'

'Oh.' Dora looked disappointed, but came and perched on an aggressively carved upright chair. 'What is it you wanted, then? About that Nash, is it?'

Unsurprised, Libby nodded. 'I just wondered what you remembered about him? When he was churchwarden?'

Dora nodded. 'Connie Barstow been talking, has she?'

'And Elaine Roberts.'

Dora raised her eyebrows. 'And what do she know about it?'

'She said something about a – a gentlemen's club in the church.'

Dora laughed scornfully. 'Gents' club, eh? Den of iniquity, more like! And in the church, too! Sacrilege.'

'I thought you were Chapel?' said Libby, amused.

'Still sacrilege,' said Dora stubbornly.

'So you remember it, too?'

'Gambling,' uttered Dora portentously.

'Gambling? Really?'

Dora shrugged. 'What I reckoned, anyway.'

'I see. But why? Gambling wasn't illegal.'

'Wouldn't be drinking, would it? Not in a church.'

Libby ignored the confused logic of this statement.

'So they weren't – I don't know – Friends of St Aldeberge, or something? Fundraisers?'

'Dunno. Don't think so. Never heard of them doing nothing like that. Just the vicar, old Turner, that Nash, the policeman, and some others. Shop owner from over Felling. Don't know the others.'

'*Policeman?*' Libby's eyes opened wide.

'He was from Felling, too.'

'Sergeant Peacock?'

Dora shrugged again. 'Might have been.'

'And what about the girls? Who left the youth club?'

'There's always talk about the young ones,' said Dora. 'When there isn't nothing to tell, folk make things up. Kids get up to all sorts. Leave home, don't they?'

'I thought some of them were too young to leave home?'

'Dunno. I told you, don't go to church regular, being Chapel. Don't go there neither, these days. So I wouldn't know.'

'You didn't know any of them, then?' asked Libby, disappointed.

Dora shook her head. 'Thought that Connie knew them.'

'Well, she and Elaine mentioned a couple. Pam and Kerry. And a niece of someone called Amy.'

'Amy's still here. Palmers moved away.'

'So I believe,' said Libby, making a note to try and get Mavis to open up about the Palmers.

'Anyway, there was talk. And that Nash, he stopped his meetings in the church, far as I know, and next thing, he's upped and gone. And vicar not long after. Didn't have one for more'n a year after that.'

'An interregnum,' said Libby.

'A what?'

'A gap in ministry,' said Libby. 'Well, that's very interesting, Dora. Thank you very much.'

'You looking into it, then? With the police, like last time?'

'Yes,' said Libby. After all, Ian had given his sanction to this visit. 'Now, I'd better get on. Having lunch with the vicar.'

'Ah.' Dora looked knowing. 'And I'm at the shop.' She stood up. 'You in the panto this year, then?'

'Not this year.'

'Wasn't last year, neither. Went to that one in Nethergate where that bloke got murdered. You had something to do with that, too, didn't you?'

'Er —yes.' Libby stood and picked up her basket. 'Maybe next year.'

'Well?' said Patti, opening the vicarage door. 'How did it go.'

'All right.' Libby followed her into the kitchen. 'She didn't actually know anything. Thought these meetings in the church were for gambling!'

'Gambling?' Patti burst out laughing. 'For goodness' sake! We're not still in the fifties.'

'I know. But then, she's Chapel. I expect she disapproves on principle.'

'And the girls?'

'Claims to know nothing. Said as she's not a member of the church she didn't know any of the girls.'

'I suppose that could be right,' said Patti, assembling lunch ingredients on the kitchen counter, 'but church member or not, most of the old girls in the village know everything. Or perhaps they don't, these days, with so much television and . . . and . . .'

'There wasn't quite so much "and" back then,' said Libby, pulling out a stool, 'but yes, I'd have thought so, too. She did know Amy was still here and that Kerry Palmer's family moved away. What's Amy's other name, do you know?'

Patti's forehead wrinkled. 'Wright, I think. I'm not sure.' She brightened. 'I know! You could ask your friend Alice! She'd know.'

'Oh, Lord,' groaned Libby. 'Not Alice.'

Alice had known Libby years before and been instrumental in introducing her to Patti and the village.

'No, all right, not Alice. Sheila Johnston?'

'I don't suppose she'd want much to do with me.'

'Look, no one holds anything against you, you know.' Patti looked her earnestly in the eyes. 'And it's all over now.'

'Until this.' Libby sighed. 'Bloody Nick Nash.'

'There,' said Patti, with a decisive nod, 'I thoroughly agree with you. He's brought the church into disrepute – again.'

'Well, we don't know that there was anything actually illegal going on,' said Libby.

'He's been murdered.' Patti tightened her lips. 'And it looks as though, whatever it was, the vicar was involved.'

'Have you looked him up? Do you know where he went?'

Patti sighed. 'No, he just disappears from the records. Ian can look him up if he wants to.'

'I think we ought to try and speak to Amy,' said Libby.

'Not me,' said Patti nervously. 'I've got to carry on living and working here.'

'OK.' Libby sighed and picked up a hunk of bread. 'This looks good.'

They finished their lunch, and cleared away the dishes, just as the doorbell rang. Patti frowned.

'They all know Wednesday's my day off.'

Nevertheless, she went to the door, and a moment later reappeared in the kitchen, a look of surprise on her face.

'Libby – this is Amy.'

She stepped aside and revealed a lady about as unlike Connie, Elaine, and Dora as she could possibly be.

'Amy – Wright, is it?' Libby went forward hand outstretched.

'Lister, actually, Wright was my maiden name.' Amy Lister came forward and shook Libby's hand. 'Good to meet you, Mrs Sarjeant.'

'Libby, please.' Libby resumed her seat on her stool, and Patti ushered Amy to one of the kitchen chairs.

'Shall I leave you?' she asked.

'No, please, vicar.' Amy smiled at them both. 'I came on the off-chance because I saw a strange car, and Dora in the shop said you'd been to see her this morning. Very secretive, she was.'

'She would be!' said Libby. 'Loves to think of herself as the recipient of all secrets.'

'Doesn't she!' Amy sighed. 'Anyway, it struck me that this would be to do with that man Nicholas Nash, and it was quite likely that my niece's name would have come up.'

Not quite sure what to say, Libby looked at Patti for guidance.

'It did,' said Patti. 'Connie Barstow and Elaine Roberts mentioned her.'

'Three of the worst gossips in the village.'

'Oh, I'm sorry! But—'

'Don't apologise,' said Amy quickly. 'I expect you're information gathering on behalf of the police again, aren't you?'

Libby felt her cheeks heating up.

Amy crossed her legs, and Libby admired her rather nice trousers. Squashing an urge to ask where she got them, she said 'Yes, actually. The police are aware that I – er – helped in the previous investigation, so they kindly allowed me to ask some questions. Although,' she added hastily, 'they don't know how an unproven historic case could possibly be of relevance.'

Amy smiled. 'I'm with them there. Which is why I thought I ought to speak to you.'

Libby and Patti both sharpened their attention.

'Twenty years ago – or thereabouts – my sister Angela decided to allow her daughter Sarah to come to the youth club here. One or two of her schoolfriends attended, and as their house was – is – rather isolated, they arranged a rota of lifts. And Sarah used to come to me for a meal beforehand, straight from school. The problems, if problems there were, began when some of the girls were asked to help out with tea and biscuits at meetings held after youth club had finished.'

'Yes, we heard about that,' said Libby.

'I bet you did,' said Amy, her lips twitching. 'Well, it wasn't convenient for everyone. Some of the older girls went, but a lot of the younger ones didn't want to. Including Sarah. I think she went once, but didn't like it, and as she relied on a lift from the mother of one of the younger girls, it was easy to make excuses.'

'Do you mean to say that there was nothing suspicious about all this after all?' Patti said, her face a mask of astonishment.

'Not quite,' said Amy, and shifted uncomfortably in her chair. 'In fact, I was rather pleased when Sarah said she didn't want to go. I didn't like the fact that the meetings were all men, even if they were run by the vicar. And several of the girls left – the younger ones because the numbers were falling, and the older ones . . . well, I'm not sure. But, as the numbers were falling off in the choir, too, the rumours began to circulate.' She looked at Libby. 'I'm sure you know how that happens.'

'Indeed I do.'

'Anyway, it struck me that all you – or the police – were likely to get were these inflated rumours and perhaps it would be better to speak to someone who was actually there. And Sarah's staying with her mother right now.'

Libby and Patti stared at her with their mouths open.

Amy laughed. 'It's all right, she's agreed to talk to you. I called Angela before I came over.'

Libby found her voice. 'I don't know what to say! You've taken the wind out of my sails.'

Patti got to her feet. 'Tea is called for,' she said. 'Can you stay, Amy?'

'Of course. I expect Libby probably wants to ask me some questions.'

'I think I probably do,' said Libby.

67

Chapter Ten

'You were involved in that unpleasant business with Sir Nigel Preece, weren't you?' asked Amy, while Patti boiled the kettle for tea.

'I was,' said Libby, wrinkling her nose.

'And I can see that our so-called missing girls would have seemed to fit in with that story?'

'The police did wonder,' admitted Libby.

Amy sighed. 'Look, as far as I could see at the time – and I was working full time, so I didn't have my finger on the pulse of the village – there was very little suggestion that there was an underground paedophile ring connected with the church, which is what the old biddies seem to be saying.'

'Why would they do that?' Libby frowned. 'Connie Barstow was positively vitriolic about Nick Nash.'

'Yes, there was definitely bad feeling. But, as I say, I didn't know much.'

'Where were you working?' asked Libby, as Patti placed mugs on the table and frowned at her. 'Oh, sorry, I'm being nosy!'

Amy laughed. 'That's all right. I was – am, I suppose – a research chemist.'

Libby and Patti gaped.

'Not at . . .'

'Yes, that one,' said Amy, amused, assuming correctly that Libby referred to a very famous establishment a little way down the coast.

So definitely not one of the village old biddies, thought Libby.

'Do you suppose Sarah will be able to tell me any more?' she asked.

'Well, she's very willing to talk to you, according to Angela, so it's worth a try. Certainly before bothering the police with it.'

'I think that's why our Inspector's allowing me to do this while he gets on with the proper work,' said Libby.

'Otherwise she'd be getting a telling off,' added Patti.

'So how did you get involved in all this?' asked Amy, waving a descriptive hand.

'Murders?' said Libby. 'I'm nosy.'

'Well, I wasn't going to say it,' said Patti.

Libby gave a brief outline of her and Fran's careers as investigators.

'So you aren't professionals?'

'Fran was, at one time,' said Patti.

Libby gave an even briefer outline of Fran's career as a so-called psychic investigator for a high-end estate agent.

Amy looked interested. 'And you're OK with that?' she asked Patti, who shrugged.

'It works. I've seen it. And she has actually saved lives.'

Seeing that Amy was about to ask more questions, Libby stood up quickly.

'About time I got off to see Sarah,' she said. 'Patti and I have to get to Steeple Martin this afternoon.'

'Oh, dear, I hope I haven't held you up,' said Amy, also getting to her feet.

'Not at all,' said Patti. 'Actually, if I run you over there, Libby – wherever it is – we can go on from there.'

Amy supplied them with details of Angela's address and left, with mutual expressions of regard.

'Nice woman,' said Libby, as Patti loaded her holdall into her car. 'Seems an unlikely resident of St Aldeberge, somehow.'

'We're not all bumpkins, you know,' said Patti.

'I've been thinking,' said Libby, as she settled in the passenger seat. 'If Nash popped back every now and then, as Colin said he did, why did none of the residents seem to know about it?'

'Perhaps they did. And gossiped about it among themselves.'

'You'd think they'd have said something now, wouldn't you?'

'Yes, but they haven't been officially questioned yet, have they?'

Angela Elliot's house was, as Amy had said, rather isolated on the way to the Nethergate road. Four-square and Victorian, it seemed to inspire confidence. Patti drew up on the drive.

'I'll stay here,' she said. 'Don't want to overwhelm them.'

Libby pressed the old-fashioned bell and almost immediately, the big front door swung open.

A very pretty young woman stood there, cradling a sleeping baby in her arms. She beamed at Libby.

'Hello – are you Sarah? Mrs . . .?'

'That's me – and it's still Elliot. My partner and I aren't married.' She peered over Libby's shoulder. 'Is that the vicar? If she wouldn't disapprove of me, why doesn't she come in?'

'She doesn't disapprove of anything much. Hello, Sarah – I'm Libby.' She turned and beckoned Patti, who climbed hesitantly out of the car.

A woman bearing a striking resemblance to Amy appeared in the hall behind Sarah and held out her hand, smiling broadly. 'And I'm Angela.'

Introductions performed, Libby and Patti were ushered into a comfortable sitting room at the front of the house.

'Can I offer you anything?' asked Angela. 'Tea? Coffee?'

'We've just had tea with your sister,' said Patti. 'I must say, it's awfully good of you to see us. Well, Libby.'

'I'm sure Amy explained why,' said Sarah. 'Nobody wants gossip spread around, do they?'

'No,' said Libby curiously. 'Can I ask how you got to hear about – well, all this?'

Sarah looked at her mother and smiled wryly. 'Mum's cleaner. She was full of Mr Nash's death and chattered on about what they were saying in the village. Mum tried to shut her up, but she would go on.'

'So I called Sarah and told her,' said Angela, 'and we decided that, as she was still at home with Thomas—' she indicated the baby, 'she'd come over for a few days and we'd see if we could do anything to stop it.'

'Or put things right, anyway,' said Sarah. 'You see, I was in the thick of it, and I guessed no one else would talk to you.'

'Why did you think that?' asked Patti.

'Tell me what's been said to you – or the police.'

So between them, Libby and Patti related all that Connie, Elaine, and Dora had told them.

'And,' said Libby slowly, 'someone else I know, in Nethergate, also told me that Kerry Palmer's family had moved there, and wouldn't talk to me. I'm afraid that's partly because my reputation goes before me.'

'That sounds ominous,' said Angela, with a lift of one eyebrow.

'It's because she gets involved in things,' said Patti. 'And she certainly helped me a few years ago. But some people are caught in the fallout.'

'I remember. The murder of those flower ladies,' said Angela.

'Yes,' said Libby, 'so if you want to stop now, that's fine.'

Sarah laughed. 'No, you sound just what I want. Someone to put a stop to some of this gossip that seems to be going round. Goodness knows what the police will make of it.'

'So what is it you wanted to tell me?'

Sarah stared into space for a moment. 'I expect you've heard that girls started going missing. Well, that wasn't quite true.'

'Dora said you told her about it,' said Libby.

'As far as I remember,' said Sarah, with a smile, 'Dora asked me what was going on with "all those men" in the church. I said I wasn't interested, so I'd stopped going. Which I had.'

'And Pam and Kerry?'

'They were the only two from the youth club who stayed on as waitresses. To tell you the truth, I wasn't altogether happy about the situation. Nothing had actually been said, but it was the atmosphere, you know?' Sarah adjusted the position of baby Thomas and frowned over his head. 'So I didn't know what happened with Pam and

71

Kerry. They weren't actually friends of mine, so when I left the youth club I didn't see them any more. They were a bit older than I was, I think. Fifteen? Sixteen?'

'And the choir?' asked Patti. 'The ladies mentioned that, as well.'

'The youth club was actually started from members of the choir, so as far as I know, the same people drifted away. But it was nowhere near the scandal that was being whispered about at the time – or now, it seems.'

'And to my recollection,' said Angela, 'most of the gossip arose after Nicholas Nash left.'

'So the gossip put the cart before the horse?' suggested Libby.

Angela and Sarah looked at each other. 'Looks like it,' said Sarah.

'Just goes to show how reputations can be ruined,' said Patti, sighing.'

'I'm really grateful you've told me this,' said Libby. 'I'm sure it will help.'

'Are you sure you won't have tea?' asked Angela.

'No, thanks,' said Libby. 'Patti and I have to get back to Steeple Martin this afternoon.'

'Day off, Vicar?' asked Sarah.

'Well, afternoon and evening. A group of us meet in Steeple Martin for dinner and drinks every Wednesday.'

'Lovely restaurant in Steeple Martin,' said Sarah. 'The Pink Geranium – you must know it.'

'Yes, it's run by my friend Harry,' said Libby. 'That's where we have dinner.'

She and Patti departed with many expressions of thanks.

'But whether we save Nash's reputation or not,' said Libby, as Patti drove off, 'he was still murdered by somebody.'

'But maybe it was one of his business associates. Or his wife.'

'She's the obvious suspect, isn't she,' said Libby. 'But Ian said they haven't been able to locate her yet. Still, I suppose that's the end of our involvement.'

'Your involvement,' said Patti.

'You've been involved, too,' said Libby. 'Don't try and get out of it.'

Back in Steeple Martin, Patti dropped Libby at home, where she called Harry to ask if he had room for two extra for dinner, then called Fran to update her on today's revelations.

'So nothing there, then,' said Fran.

'No. I'll tell Ian tonight and he can discount it if he wants. I'd still like to know about Kerry Palmer, though.'

'Why? It doesn't matter any more, surely?'

'No – but it's a puzzle. It sounds as if there was something there, according to Mavis.'

'Probably something quite different,' said Fran. 'She got caught shoplifting or got pregnant. Something the family felt brought shame on them.'

'But Mavis was quite definite about Nick Nash being involved. I'd like to know why.'

Fran sighed. 'Please don't upset Mavis. Or Ian, come to that.'

'I won't. But I must ask Mavis.'

When Ben arrived, Libby told him they would be eating at the Pink Geranium, before asking him if he thought she ought to warn Colin about what she'd learnt before seeing him that evening.

'Might be wise,' said Ben. 'After all, it's his friend, isn't it?'

'Not that much of a friend,' said Libby. 'I get the impression that Colin didn't like him much.'

However, she called Colin's mobile and gave him a brief outline of her findings.

'And I didn't go looking, Colin,' she said. 'The old ladies of the village came to me.'

'So you said. So the rumours about children weren't true, then?'

'Doesn't look like it,' said Libby. 'Although there's still something there, I'm sure of it.'

Colin sighed. 'Don't go digging around, Libby, please. It's bad enough as it is.'

'I know, but in this case it was Ian asking me to investigate. I did it with his authority.'

'Which has now ended. Leave it alone, please.'

'There. Good job you did tell him,' said Ben. 'Now it won't come as a surprise.'

'Hmm,' said Libby, slightly grumpy. 'Even when I'm allowed to ask questions you don't like it.'

'I didn't say I didn't like it. Colin might not.'

'Yes. Patti did tell the Elliot women that people get caught in the fallout. That's true, isn't it? Even if it isn't my fault. All those lives that are ruined, or at least changed, after a murder investigation. It's so sad.'

'Right.' Ben got up from his perch on the edge of the table. 'As I shall be seen by the general public this evening, I'd better go and get rid of the plaster dust.'

Libby grinned at him. 'I don't know. It's quite attractive in a rough diamond sort of way.'

'You watch yourself, woman.' Ben grinned back and made for the stairs.

Libby was faintly surprised, when they turned up at the Pink Geranium later, to find not only Anne and Patti at the big table in the window, but Colin, Edward, and Fran and Guy.

'Bit of a squash, as usual,' said Harry, distributing menus. 'Just hope Ian doesn't turn up on the off-chance.'

'He said he'd come straight here as soon as he was able,' said Edward. 'Mind you, that was when he left this morning, so anything could have happened.'

'He's expecting a report from me,' said Libby, 'so I'm sure he'll come if he possibly can.'

Ian, in fact, made quite an entrance at the end of the meal by being dropped off by a police car.

'Thought we could share a cab home,' he said to Edward, accepting a glass of wine from Ben. 'So, Libby. What have you got to tell me?'

Chapter Eleven

'I'm sorry to have to repeat all this to everyone else,' said Libby. 'Perhaps they'd all like to go to the pub while we catch up?'

There was a chorus of denial.

'No,' said Edward. 'We want to hear what Ian has to say.'

So Libby embarked once more on her recital of the day's events.

'Patti was there for most of it,' she finished up. 'Is there anything you'd like to add, Patti?'

Patti shook her head, and Anne reached across and squeezed her hand.

Ian looked at Patti. 'You know these people . . .' he began.

'No,' said Patti. 'I'd never met Amy, or Angela and Sarah. All of this happened years before I arrived. I barely know the old ladies, either.'

'So how accurate do you think these stories are?'

'I know the gossip that goes on. St Aldeberge is a small community, so it's inevitable. I do appreciate that Sarah wanted to put her side of the story, so I suppose it's a matter of – what? Reading between the lines?'

'Wheat from the chaff,' said Guy.

Ian nodded.

'Do you think it's helped?' asked Anne.

Ian turned to Colin. 'You haven't said anything, Colin. What do you think?'

'I don't know.' Colin looked miserable. 'I just feel guilty that this is all my fault.'

There was another chorus of denial.

'How do you make that out?' said Ben.

'If I hadn't told Gerry that Nick was selling his house, Nick would never have come over and this would never have happened.' Colin stared at his empty glass.

'He probably would have come over at some point anyway as he was selling the house,' said Ian. 'Nothing to do with you.'

Colin didn't look reassured.

'Why don't we adjourn,' said Ian. 'Then Harry and Peter can close up and join us.'

Bills settled, they all trooped out to the pub, where they settled at their usual table and Ben, Guy, and Ian went to the bar.

'I do know what you mean, Colin,' said Patti. 'I'd feel the same. And after all that other business . . .'

Colin smiled at her gratefully.

When they all had drinks, with a glance at Patti, Libby turned to Ian.

'One thing I was surprised by was when Dora told me who some of the other men who met in the church were. She said "that policeman". Would it be the sergeant from Felling? Peacock?'

'I don't know. I know as little about it all as Patti.' Ian looked round the table.

'But you could look up the files,' said Fran.

Ian smiled. 'Don't you think we've already done so? It's all part of looking into Nicholas Nash's background.'

'And you've found nothing?' asked Libby.

'I didn't say that,' said Ian, 'but you really can't expect me to tell you that sort of information.' He laughed at Libby's expression. 'And don't say you've told me yours!'

'Well, I don't see that it gets you much further,' said Edward. 'Anyone ready for another drink yet?'

The conversation became more general, and Ian got up and came to stand by Libby's chair.

'A word?' he said quietly.

Surprised, Libby stood up and followed him to the window.

'What else was there you didn't mention?'

Libby looked down.

'Come on – there was something else.'

She looked up. 'Well, there was Kerry Palmer.'

'You mentioned her, or rather, Connie Barstow did.'

'It turns out Mavis knew her. You remember Mavis? Owner of the Blue Anchor?'

'Yes?'

Libby told him what Mavis had said.

'And you want to look into it?' Ian shook his head. 'Don't go badgering people, Libby.'

'Don't you think it could be important?'

'Maybe.' Ian frowned.

'No one's said much about her. We know about Sarah now, but nothing about Pam or Kerry. They really did seem to be girls who disappeared. Sarah made light of the whole thing, but it does seem rather odd.'

'I'll get someone to check the records for them. Do we know Pam's surname?'

'No. But it doesn't seem as though they were reported to the police at the time. Which is also odd.'

'All right, I'll do my best. But be careful. I've trusted you far more than I should, you know that, and I don't want either you or me getting into trouble over this.'

They returned to the table, where both Ben and Fran treated Libby to curious looks.

Harry and Peter arrived soon after this.

'No, I don't want to know all the gory details,' said Harry, flinging himself down in a chair. 'I'm sure The Grand Inquisitor will come and tell me all over a free lunch sometime this week.'

Everyone laughed and Libby tried to look affronted.

After eleven o'clock, people started drifting away. Edward and Ian's taxi arrived, Fran and Guy departed for Nethergate, and Anne and Patti left for Anne's little house, until just Colin, Peter, and Harry were left with Libby and Ben.

'What did Ian want?' Colin asked.

'It was something about one of the girls who are supposed to have disappeared,' said Libby.

'And are you going to look into it?'

'I don't know,' said Libby. 'He is.'

'And do you think Nick is actually something to do with it?'

'Honestly, Colin, I don't know.' Libby looked at him, troubled. 'Don't forget, I didn't go barging in, people asked for me. And Ian authorised me to talk to them.'

'No.' Colin sighed. 'I just feel guilty.'

Harry smiled and leant across to squeeze his arm. 'Look, mate, you've got nothing to feel guilty about. And the old trout only ever means to help, whatever we think about it. So you just carry on getting your luxury des res in order and leave the rest to them what knows.'

'Because,' said Peter, 'we're all expecting to be invited to a spectacular house warming in time for Christmas.'

Colin grinned at last. 'Or maybe next Christmas.'

Neither Thursday nor Friday did Libby hear anything from Ian or anyone else about the murder case, until on Saturday morning Fran called.

'Odd thing just happened,' she said. 'I'm in the shop. We're just getting busy in time for Christmas, so I'm helping out.'

'That doesn't strike me as odd,' said Libby.

'Libby! No, what I was going to say was, Mavis came in.'

'Really? She doesn't seem the type to frequent an art gallery.'

'Exactly, she looked very uncomfortable.' Fran paused. 'Then she asked if you were – or we were – still looking into "that business with the girls", as she put it.'

'Blimey!'

'Exactly. So I said not as far as I knew.'

'No. After Wednesday I decided it was more or less hands off. Although Ian did mention Kerry Palmer.'

'That's just it. Apparently, Mavis spoke to Kerry's family and her mother asked if she could speak to you – us. The dad wasn't so keen.'

'What did you say?'

'I said I'd ask you. I'd really like to know why, though, wouldn't you?'

'I certainly would.' Libby thought for a moment. 'Tell you what, why don't you ask Mavis when would be convenient, then we'll decide. And a phone number if possible.'

'All right. I'll pop down at lunchtime – I think she's still opening at lunchtimes. Ring you this afternoon.'

Too wound up to settle, Libby took herself for a tramp across the fields at the end of Allhallow's Lane, past the restored Hoppers' Huts and as far as the Manor, where she tapped tentatively on the big front door. Receiving no answer, she pushed it open and discovered Hetty dozing in a chair by the Aga in the kitchen, Jeff-dog asleep at her feet.

"Lo, gal.' Hetty opened remarkably alert eyes, while Jeff-dog stood up, eagerly wagging his tail.

'Sorry to disturb you,' said Libby. 'I wondered if Jeff-dog would like a walk?'

Hetty raised her eyebrows. 'Want a walk yourself, do yer?'

Libby grinned. 'I'm going anyway,' she said.

'Go on, then. Lead's on the door.'

Jeff-dog obediently sat and panted at her while she fastened the lead, and decided which way to go. The woods at the top of Allhallow's Lane seemed a good idea, so she retraced her steps.

The morning was grey, dank, and cold, very typical of an English winter day. There was little colour in the landscape and no wind. When she reached the woods, she was surprised at how eerie they felt.

'Mind you,' she told Jeff-dog, who was nosing happily in a carpet of fallen leaves, 'I normally don't come in here much. It's probably lovely in the spring.' She peered round. 'Good place to hide, though.'

Woods. She stopped dead. A vivid picture of the woods behind the Dunton Estate had just come into her mind.

Turning round, she dragged an unwilling Jeff-dog out of the wood and up on to the top path back towards the Manor. Now why, she wondered, as she let the dog off his lead, had that picture of the woods come so vividly to mind?

She remembered one of the last times she had been there. The night something awful had happened at the Willoughby Oak. The woodland was much more dense than their own, guarded by the rusty gates that led to Dunton Manor, and away towards the sea, was open heathland, which was, presumably, what surrounded Nick Nash's house.

'Rupert Bear country,' Libby murmured to herself. Jeff-dog came rushing back at the sound of her voice. She smiled down at him. 'Come on, boy, I need to get back.'

Jeff-dog delivered safely back to the Manor, Libby went home to forage for lunch. Ben was having sandwiches at the Hop Pocket, where he seemed to be thoroughly enjoying himself. Taking her sandwiches into the sitting room, she sat at the table in the window with her laptop and a map of Felling and its surroundings. She had just spread it out in front of her when Fran called.

'We've got another secretive woman,' she said.

'Oh?'

'Doesn't want us to go and see her at home, but said could we go and see her at the Blue Anchor.'

'And what does Mavis think about that?'

'She was a bit grumpy, but seemed OK. She suggested tomorrow, but I said you were busy. So she said this afternoon. Can you make it?'

Libby checked the time. 'I suppose so. What time?'

'About three?'

'That's fine. Hey, listen. I just had a thought. I don't know where it came from, but I was walking through our woods, and I suddenly thought of the woods on the Dunton Estate.'

'Yes? What about them?'

'Very isolated, weren't they?'

'Yes? Get to the point!'

'Good place to hide someone – something.'

'Libby!' Fran made an exasperated sound. 'Don't start going in for flights of fancy!'

'But I saw it so clearly!'

'Look – you don't have "moments". I do. Occasionally. Your sub-conscious is running riot just trying to create a mystery.'

'Hmm,' said Libby. 'Well, I'll be over just before three. See you then.'

Nevertheless, she didn't put the map of the Dunton Estate away, nor did she stop reading her notes from eight years ago.

At twenty minutes to three, Libby parked behind the Blue Anchor and walked down to Coastguard Cottage.

'How do we play this?' asked Libby, as Fran opened the door. 'Do we tell this Mrs Palmer what the other old ladies said?'

'I think we'll have to play it by ear,' said Fran. 'Again, she's vol-unteered, so it's up to her, isn't it?'

They looked at each other wordlessly for a moment.' Come on, then,' said Libby. 'Let's get it over with.'

Chapter Twelve

Mavis, unsmiling as ever, let them in through the side door which led directly to the flat upstairs.

'Not here yet,' she said. 'Not sure about this.'

'She asked, didn't she?' said Fran.

Mavis shrugged. 'Never given up hope.'

Libby's heart sank.

They followed Mavis upstairs and into her sitting room, which looked as if she didn't actually do much sitting in it.

'Make yourselves comfortable,' she said, and disappeared.

'I'll try,' said Libby, perching on a wooden chair not far removed from those outside the cafe.

'I don't think she spends much time up here,' said Fran, looking around.

'I certainly wouldn't,' said Libby. 'Let's hope Mrs Palmer doesn't feel too uncomfortable.' She paused. 'Listen – I think that's her.'

The door opened and Mavis came in, followed by a small, brown-haired woman in a heavy coat and leggings.

'This is Liz Palmer,' she said. 'Kerry's mum.'

Libby stood up and held out her hand. 'Hello, Mrs Palmer. I'm Libby Sarjeant.'

'And I'm Fran Wolfe,' said Fran, following suit.

Liz Palmer shook both their hands. 'Liz, please,' she said in a shaky voice. 'Thank you for seeing me.'

'Want me to stay?' asked Mavis gruffly.

'If you like.' Liz Palmer nodded.

Mavis pulled up two more chairs.

'What did you want to tell us?' asked Libby.

'Or ask us?' added Fran.

Liz Palmer looked from one to the other. 'About Kerry.'

They nodded encouragingly.

'Oh, it's so difficult.' Liz sighed. 'You know they say those girls disappeared?'

Libby nodded again.

'Well, they did and they didn't.'

This *is* going to be difficult, thought Libby.

Fran smiled. 'Well, we rather thought that a lot of it was just gossip. As far as we can make out, the only two who really left St Aldeberge were someone called Pam and your Kerry.'

'That's it.' Liz nodded. 'Pam White. Do you know about the vicar's meetings in the church?'

'Yes,' they both said.

'Well, Pam and Kerry were the eldest girls, you see, so the vicar wanted them to help with serving, like, tea and biscuits, sort of thing.'

'Did the other girls not join in?' asked Libby. 'We were told they didn't like it.'

Liz shrugged. 'They just talked about it together, you know. And decided it was a bit – well – dodgy. But my Kerry wouldn't have gone if it was.'

'So it really was exaggerated,' said Fran.

'I think so.' Liz sounded doubtful. 'And the Scouts was all above board.'

'Scouts?' echoed three voices.

'Yes – they had Scouts there, didn't you know?'

'Not a word,' said Libby. 'Who ran the scouts?'

'That policeman. He was – what d'you call it – scoutmaster.'

'Let me get this straight,' said Libby, frowning. 'There was a scout troop there – held when? On the same evening as the vicar's meetings?'

83

'Yes – before them. There was youth club, mainly for the girls, and Scouts. I don't think they did much of the sort of thing Scouts normally do, you know, like camping and that.'

'All on the same evening,' said Fran.

Liz nodded.

'So what actually happened to Pam and Kerry?' asked Libby.

Liz stared out of the window. 'She – changed.'

Fran and Libby looked at each other, then at Mavis, who shrugged.

'Changed how?' asked Fran gently.

'Well, got grumpy. Like teenagers do. But she hadn't been like that before. And then . . . one day, she didn't come home.'

'From the church?' said Libby.

'No.' Liz shook her head. 'Gone to meet friends after school. Told me she was going that morning. But she never came home.'

Observing the imminent arrival of tears, Libby changed the subject.

'What about Pam? What do you know about her?'

'She just ran away. Her mum and me talked about it. She came to see me – see if I thought they'd gone together. But she'd been to school the day after . , . after . . .'

'So they weren't together,' said Fran. 'What about the police?'

'That Sergeant Peacock, he didn't take it seriously. First of all, he said, girls ran off. They'd turn up. And when they didn't . . .'

'And were the police looking into any of the other girls?' asked Libby.

'That was all just people making stuff up. That made it worse. Just looked as though we all were.' Liz looked down at her lap. 'And then when Pam's mum heard from her, well, that kind of put the lid on it.'

'So Pam turned up?' said Libby.

'Yes.' Liz nodded. 'About six months later, it was. Wrote from Dover.'

'Did she say why she'd gone?' asked Fran.

Liz shook her head. 'Not as her mum told me.'

'Do you know if she's still there?' asked Libby after a pause, and without much hope.

'No. Haven't spoken to her mum since we came here. They moved, too.'

'What do you want us to do?' asked Fran.

'Well,' said Liz slowly, 'I just thought if you're trying to find out about that Mr Nash, you might find out about Kerry, too.'

'It's the police who are investigating Mr Nash's death,' said Libby. 'We tell them everything we know, of course, but I don't know that they're connected.'

'Everyone thought he was.' Liz sat up straight. 'And it was him who really ran the youth club, more than the vicar.'

'But it was probably just gossip,' said Fran. 'The same as the gossip about the girls. What we really need to find is some of the girls who were there at the time. We've spoken to Sarah Elliot.'

'She was there.' Liz was much sharper now.

'Yes,' said Libby, 'but she and her mother have both explained what happened to her.'

'Yes? And what did she say?' Liz was glowering.

'She left before Pam and Kerry because she didn't like the atmosphere. There was no more to it than that. She also said that most of the gossip about missing girls started after Mr Nash had left.'

Liz deflated. 'Yes.'

They fell silent, while Mavis glared stonily out of the window.

'Look,' said Fran, exchanging a fleeting glance with Libby, 'I think the best we can do is to tell the inspector in charge of the case everything you've told us, and if he wants us to look into it any more, we will.'

'And one of the first things we'll do is try to trace any of the other girls, especially Pam White,' said Libby. 'She might be able to tell us a bit more, don't you think?'

'How will you do that?' asked Mavis suddenly.

'Ask people.' Fran smiled at her. 'You know what we do, Mavis.'

'And maybe find out about the scouts,' said Libby thoughtfully.

'Ask that vicar friend of yours,' said Mavis.

'She's already been very helpful,' said Fran. She leant forward and smiled at Liz. 'We'll do anything we can, Liz, I promise you. Have you got a photograph of Kerry?'

Liz fumbled in a pocket. 'I brought this one. Her dad isn't too pleased with dragging it all up again. He'd rather forget it – and her. So I keep the pictures out of his way.'

She handed over a small snapshot. Libby and Fran peered at it together.

'Pretty girl,' said Libby, aware of unexpected tears threatening to appear.

'Where was this taken?' asked Fran.

'In the back garden. She'd just come home from school. She'd got the results of some test or other . . .' Liz's voice trailed off.

'Good results by the look of it,' said Fran.

'Yes. She was clever.' Liz took a breath. 'You can keep that.'

A few minutes later, she left, and after a decent interval, Libby and Fran came downstairs and Mavis saw them out.

'Thanks for this, Mavis,' said Fran. 'You've been very helpful.'

Mavis scowled. 'Poor cow.'

'Yes,' said Libby. 'Couldn't agree more.'

They walked back in silence to Coastguard Cottage, where Libby turned aside and leant on the wall overlooking the deserted beach.

'What do we think?'

'I think she's dead,' said Fran.

'So do I.' Libby sighed heavily. 'I can't think why she's not been heard of otherwise.'

'There are cases . . .' said Fran.

'Not many. Remains usually turn up. Or some sort of forensic evidence.'

'Only if the case is still open. This looks as though it didn't even become a case.'

'I just can't understand why the police didn't look into it,' said Libby, thumping the wall.

'Sergeant Peacock again.' Fran frowned at the grey sea. 'He does keep popping up.'

'And what about these scouts? Should we see if any of them are still around?'

'We're going to carry on, then?' Fran looked at her sideways.

'Yes!' Libby was surprised. 'Ian didn't say we couldn't. After all, it's not directly connected to his investigation.'

'How do we go about it?'

Libby thought. 'Scouts, and try and track down Pam White.'

'How do we do that? We don't know her parents' names, nor where they moved to.'

'And it didn't sound as if Liz Palmer knew, either.' Libby turned away from the sea. 'I'll think of something. And ask Patti if she knows anything about the scouts.'

'Not today, though. She's usually busy at the weekends. What are you doing tonight?'

'We've got a one-nighter and I'm on the bar.'

The Oast Theatre hosted various events during the year, apart from their own productions, touring plays and musical events including Shakespeare and ballet companies and single-evening events with comedians, big bands, and tribute acts. Ben, Peter, and Libby, as directors of the theatre, usually pitched in and helped where necessary, and tried to provide support in areas where the visitors were lacking, principally backstage and in the sound and lighting departments. And, of course, the bar.

'And Hetty's tomorrow?' said Fran.

'Yes. I'm so predictable.' Libby sighed.

Libby drove home and spent the rest of day pottering in the house, preparing an early dinner and finally putting on her bartender's hat and going to the theatre. As tonight's event was a mildly popular comedian, the theatre was full. A few people Libby knew were in the audience, but there was little chance for socialising. At the end of the evening, when the audience and the performer and his crew had gone, Libby, Peter, and Ben sat down

87

in the bar for a well-deserved drink. They were joined by Harry, big with news.

'Guess who was in tonight?" He flung himself onto one of the little wrought iron chairs while Peter fetched him a glass of wine.

'Go on, who?' Libby smiled at him indulgently.

'Colin and Ian!'

'Together?' Ben looked shocked.

'Yes, together. And very chummy they looked. You don't think Ian's been turned at last, do you?' He leered significantly at Libby.

'Don't be ridiculous. Just because Colin's gay . . .'

'Not that he's shown much evidence of that since he's been here,' said Peter.

'I think he's a bit off relationships just now,' said Libby. 'And who's he likely to meet stuck down here?'

'So what were they doing together?' asked Ben. 'To do with the case, I suppose.'

'Off the record interrogation?' said Libby. 'Ian's allowed him access to all the information we've had, so he can't be a suspect.'

'Trying to find out about Nick's background in Spain, I expect,' said Libby. 'I think that's going to be the line the investigation's going to take. Not all this stuff about the missing girls, which seems to be vague at best, and mostly gossip.'

'What else have you found out, then?' asked Peter. 'Hal and I aren't up to speed, so you might as well fill us in.'

Libby gave them a brief outline of that week's findings.

'So the only real person worth looking into is this Kerry?' said Harry.

'Looks like it,' said Libby, 'although I would like to know about the Scouts.'

'Why?' Peter raised an eyebrow.

'They were there at the same time as the girls, and – well, you know – scouts and scout leaders . . .'

'And the scout leader?' asked Ben.

'The ubiquitous Sergeant Peacock,' said Libby. 'As Fran said, he does keep popping up. And he appears to have shut down any official investigation into whatever was going on.'

'But it really doesn't sound as though much *was* going on,' said Harry.

'I could still bear to find out a bit more about Sergeant Peacock, though,' said Libby. 'He's the key, I'm sure.'

Chapter Thirteen

At Hetty's on Sunday, they caught up with Edward.

'Yes, Ian took Colin out to dinner last night. I only know because he came to apologise for not including me – we don't live in each other's pockets, but we do socialise, as you know. But he said this wasn't social, it was work. Which is where I assume he is today. The car was gone when I got up.'

'I bet it's what I said.' Libby nodded. 'Looking into Nick Nash's more recent background.'

'I have to admit that seems to make more sense,' said Ben.

'They talkin' murder again?' said Flo, from the other end of the table, where she sat with Lenny.

Hetty, busy with vegetables, grunted.

'Someone to do with that Colin, I heard?' Flo squinted at Libby.

'Yes, Flo.' Libby gave her a grin. 'No one you'd know.'

'Never know,' said Flo, gnomically.

'Know lots of people in Spain, do you, Flo?' said Ben.

'Pfft. Spain.'

'I did.' Lenny had a reminiscent look in his eye.

'Your London gangster friends?' asked Libby.

'Some.' Lenny winked.

'Old reprobate,' said Ben.

'No way to talk to your uncle,' muttered Hetty.

Edward, amused by the conversation, turned to Hetty. 'You have a very interesting family, Hetty.'

'Not what I call it,' replied Hetty.

'Raises a question, though,' said Libby. 'A lot of rather questionable types did set up home in Spain, didn't they?'

'And you think Nick Nash might have been mixed up with them?' said Ben.

'It's a possibility, surely?' said Edward. 'I bet Ian's thought of that.'

'Colin wouldn't have been, though,' said Libby.

'Maybe not, but he might have suspected something,' said Ben.

'I doubt if he'd have been friendly with Nash in that case,' said Libby loyally.

'Lamb,' announced Hetty, bearing a noble leg to the table.

When Edward, Libby and Ben arrived at Peter and Harry's later that afternoon, Harry, as usual, was still in his chef's whites, sprawled elegantly on the sofa.

'Colin popped in,' said Peter, distributing mugs of coffee. 'He wanted to know if anyone fancied joining him for a drink this evening.'

'Where?' said Libby.

'In the pub – where do you think?'

'Well, he might have wanted to christen his new apartment.'

'No furniture,' said Ben. 'Although I think I saw the kitchen fitters on Thursday.'

'Did he say why?' pursued Libby.

'No!' Harry was impatient. 'You don't have to give a reason to want to go for a drink with someone.'

'Just . . . under the circumstances . . .'

'Oh, Lib!' said four voices.

'Well, he might—' began Libby grumpily.

'He might just want company,' said Ben gently.

'Anyway,' said Peter, 'I said we'd pop in sometime after eight. You coming?'

'I won't,' said Edward. 'I've got work tomorrow, and anyway, I might be intruding.'

Despite protests, Edward stayed firm, and in the end, just after eight o'clock, Libby and Ben arrived in the bar, where Colin sat in solitary, and rather mournful, state at the table.

'Thanks for coming,' he said, as they joined him at the table.

'What's up?' said Libby, without preamble.

'How do you know anything's up?' He gave her a slight smile.

'Because something is. Is it to do with your meeting with Ian last night?'

'Yes.' Colin sighed. 'Peter and Harry told you?'

'They said you looked very chummy.'

'He wanted information.'

'We gathered. About Nick Nash's life in Spain?'

'Yes. They can't seem to get anything out of the Spanish authorities.'

'Is there anything to find out, though?' asked Ben.

'Ian suspects there might be.' Colin looked round as Peter and Harry came in. 'Can I get anyone a drink?'

'I think it's what we thought,' said Libby, sotto voce, as Colin went to the bar.

'What, Spanish gangsters?' said Harry, grinning evilly.

Libby shook her head at him.

Peter sat a little way back from the table looking remote.

'And what's up with you, coz?' said Ben.

'Don't want him to feel crowded,' said Peter.

Colin came back to the table with a tray.

'So Ian's looking into Nash's background?' said Harry.

'And not the goings on in St Aldeberge?' said Libby.

'He seems to think it's far more likely to be a more recent connection. The murder, I mean.'

'So do I,' said Peter. 'The St Aldeberge connection seems a little tenuous to say the least.'

'And from what Lib's learnt, mainly dreamt up by the old ladies of the village,' said Ben.

'Have you found anything at all that makes you suspicious while you've been looking into it?' Colin asked Libby.

'Not really. There's one girl who really did disappear at the time, and we've talked to her mother, but to be honest, we couldn't see any connection. Beats me why they didn't make more fuss about that.'

'Yeah, that's odd. Why didn't they make more fuss about all of it?' said Harry. 'You know what villages are like.'

'You'd think it would be different these days, with all the other distractions on offer. Television, internet . . .'

'How many old ladies play with the internet?' asked Harry. 'Does Hetty? Or Flo?'

'No,' said Ben, 'but they do love their daytime telly.'

'And think of all the daytime crime dramas,' said Peter, 'lots of village mysteries.'

'Which give them ideas,' said Libby.

Colin laughed. 'Well, I'm not sure I wouldn't prefer what Ian's hinting at rather than child abuse stuff.'

'And what's that?' asked Libby.

They all looked at him expectantly.

'Ian thinks he may have been mixing with the wrong types in Spain.' Colin looked down at his drink.

They were silent until Libby said, 'The Costa del Crime squad, I suppose.'

'More or less.' Colin looked at her sharply. 'You'd already guessed that, hadn't you?'

'I wondered.'

'We slapped her down,' said Ben.

'Well, she's right. And the worst of it is, I'm pretty sure he thinks I would have known about it.'

'Surely not!' said Peter.

'I doubt he'd have taken you to dinner if he had you down as a Spanish gangster,' said Libby.

'He just kept prodding!' There was the suggestion of a whine in Colin's voice.

'Well, of course he did,' said Peter. 'We've all suffered from it at one time or another. If any of us know one of his cast members—'

'Cast?' Colin looked bewildered.

'People of interest in an investigation,' said Ben.

'If we do,' Peter went on, 'then Ian – or his team – will ask all sorts of questions trying to find a crack. The police figure that those who know subjects personally will have better access than the heavy mob.'

'Even if they're not heavy,' said Libby.

'You ought to know by now,' said Harry. 'This is the second police investigation you've been involved in within a year!'

'Don't remind me!' groaned Colin. 'And there was I, leading a perfectly blameless life in the sun . . .'

'How about,' said Libby, 'you tell *us* all about it? What did Ian ask you? We might unlock something, you never know.'

'And I expect you clammed up a bit the more Ian asked,' said Peter, 'even if you didn't realise it at the time.'

'You're right.' Colin looked surprised. 'I was so worried I'd say something stupid.'

'I think that often happens,' said Libby. 'That's when TV cops have to say "This is a murder investigation, you know!" because people so often don't want to say the wrong thing. So they keep back evidence without meaning to.'

'I've never thought of that,' said Colin. 'Yes – I think I'd like to talk it through with you.'

'So what did he want to know?' asked Harry. 'Tell all.'

'Actually, it was boring stuff. He wanted to know if I'd met any of Nick's business associates, of course, and who they were. The trouble was – I didn't know. I used to bump into him in bars and restaurants, and sometimes he was with people, sometimes I was, but we didn't seem to have any friends in common.'

'Didn't anyone you knew know who he was?' asked Ben.

'Yes, plenty of people knew his name. But neither of us belonged to the same clubs – you know, like Rotary. Not that I belonged to the local Rotary. I got to know some of the faces I saw him with regularly, enough to nod to, but I don't think I was ever introduced to any of them. Whereas,' Colin looked thoughtful, 'he seemed to know a lot of people I knew, even if they didn't know him. He would address them by name.'

'Did you tell Ian that?' asked Libby.

'Sort of.'

'Only that's slightly suspicious in itself, don't you think?'

'Mmm . . .'

'His circle seems to be a bit exclusive,' said Harry.

'How did you meet him?' asked Peter.

Colin frowned. 'I'm not exactly sure. It was some time ago . . . at a party, I think. He said he'd heard I came from Kent and which part. So we got chatting. And when he'd been home, he always made a point of speaking to me when he came back. I told you that.'

'And your friend who was interested in buying his house? Was he part of your community?'

'Gerry? Oh, yes. And last time Nick had been back here, he mentioned that he was going to sell up – I told you – and then when I was talking to Gerry he said he wanted to come back home, so it seemed obvious to put them together.'

'They didn't already know one another, then?' said Libby.

'No. Different circles entirely.'

'Well, it does look to me as if Nash's circle could be a bit dodgy,' said Ben. 'Anybody else?'

Peter, Harry, and Libby all agreed.

'I can see that now,' said Colin, 'but there was nothing to suggest it at the time.'

'But you never knew what any of his friends actually did?' said Peter.

'No – but then you don't, do you? In a group of acquaintances? Especially if they're just people you've met at a party or in a bar.'

'That's true,' said Libby. 'I might, because I'm nosy and I ask, but other people don't.'

'Well, if you gave Ian any of that information,' said Harry, 'he'll have picked up on it, the same as we have. Could you give him any names?'

'A couple, but most were just Christian names, or even nicknames.'

'Is he going to talk to Gerry?' asked Peter.

Colin looked startled. 'No – why should he?'

'He might want to know why Gerry wanted that particular house.'

'Just because I told him about it!'

'It does seem a tad coincidental,' said Libby. 'I daresay there's nothing in it, but I bet he looks into it, if he hasn't already.'

'I do hope not!' said Colin. 'I don't want to . . .'

'To what?' asked Harry.

'Drop him in it,' mumbled Colin.

More silence.

'Anyone want another drink?' asked Libby brightly, standing up. 'My round.'

Ben went with her to the bar.

'What are you up to?'

Libby looked innocent. 'Nothing.'

Ben looked doubtful.

When they were all seated again, Libby turned again to Colin.

'You said completely different circles,' she said.

'Yes.' Colin looked nervous.

'Look, don't get all defensive.'

'I wasn't.'

'You said you'd be happy to talk it over with us. I just wondered if there was something you weren't telling us?'

'Er – nothing important.' Colin shifted in his seat, attracting a sharp look from Harry and a more kindly one from Peter.

'Just remember who you're sitting with,' said Libby, and took a deep breath. 'I don't suppose Gerry was gay, was he?'

Colin went bright red.

'Why didn't you say?' Harry was impatient. 'Was he coming here because of you?' He grinned at Libby. 'Well spotted, old trout.'

Colin seemed to sag in his chair. He took a healthy swig of his drink and sighed. 'I didn't want to say anything. Especially to Ian. We were just going to see how it went . . .'

Libby patted his arm. 'And now you think it's spoiled? Don't be daft, of course it isn't. And that's why he didn't want one of your apartments, isn't it? In case it didn't work?'

Colin nodded with a shamefaced grin.

'I think we'd like to meet Gerry,' said Peter.

'Just to see if he's good enough!' said Harry.

Chapter Fourteen

'I've had an idea!' said Libby.

'Oh, no!' chorused assorted male voices.

'No, listen! Gerry's marooned over in Canterbury, isn't he, Colin? Wouldn't you both prefer him to be here?'

'There's only the pub,' said Colin, 'and we agreed we wouldn't be comfortable both staying here. We're taking it slowly.'

'Both moving back to the same area of Kent?' said Harry. 'That's not exactly slowly.'

'Well, we didn't want to move in together,' said Colin. 'Not yet, anyway.'

'Two suggestions, then,' said Libby. 'One of the rooms up at the Manor, or, even better, Steeple Farm.'

'I couldn't stay with Hetty!' protested Colin, going even redder than before.

'Steeple Farm's a good idea,' said Peter.

'What is it? Where is it?'

'It's the house my mother used to live in,' Peter explained. 'Just up the road here.' He gestured vaguely. 'Ben had it restored –'

'For him and Libby to live in,' added Harry, grinning.

'Yes, well; that didn't work out, so it's been let out as a holiday rental ever since.' He smiled at Colin. 'Quite a few refugees have stayed in it over the years.'

Colin was looking bewildered. 'Have you lot always got an answer for everything?'

'By no means!' said Peter, amid general laughter. 'But occasionally we can help. We'll even deliver the odd take-out!'

'Can I ask Gerry?' Colin took out his phone.

'Of course, but hadn't you better have a look at the place first?' said Ben.

'But not tonight,' said Libby firmly. 'You can have a look on Ben's phone. I haven't got the right equipment.

'Last of the technology dinosaurs, our Libby,' said Ben, scrolling through his own phone. 'There you are. That's the ad that goes in the glossies when we want to let it. We don't that often, these days.'

Colin began to look through the details.

'One of your better ideas, Lib,' said Ben.

'I don't know why we didn't think of it for Colin before now,' she said.

'We didn't know him well enough?' suggested Peter.

'We did by the end of that last business,' said Libby.

Colin looked up from the phone. 'What are these other places?'

'Oh – the Hoppers' Huts. We restored those, too, and let them out during the summer. Not that suitable during the winter – a bit muddy up there.'

'The Hoppers!' Colin smiled. 'I remember all about them.'

'One of the reasons I've restored the Hop Garden,' said Ben.

'And the Hop Pocket! I get it now!' Colin beamed. 'You're certainly into restoration in a big way!'

'I suppose so.' Ben looked surprised. 'It just seemed to grow up around me.'

'Well, it looks perfect,' said Colin. 'I'm going to call Gerry now.' He got up from the table and moved to the window.

'I hope Gerry won't mind that he's been discussing him with us,' said Libby.

'I should imagine that Gerry's heard all about us,' said Harry.

'He didn't seem to mind you saying we ought to meet Gerry,' Libby said to Peter.

'He's an honorary Loony,' said Harry. 'If we hadn't thought he'd be OK with that sort of thing, I'd never have admitted him.'

Harry had nicknamed their group of friends Libby's Loonies some years ago, and appointed himself membership secretary.

Colin came back to the table. 'Gerry says he'd like to come over and have a look, too, if that's all right?'

'Perfect!' beamed Libby. 'When?'

'Tomorrow morning?'

'About eleven? Gives me time to pop up and make sure everything's shipshape,' said Libby.

'Now,' said Peter, 'that calls for another drink.'

As they were leaving some time later, Colin took Libby aside.

'Will you tell Ian what we talked about?'

'If you'd like me to,' said Libby. 'I'll call him in the morning.'

'I expect, though,' Libby said to Ben as they walked home, 'he's already picked up on the possibly dodgy connections, don't you?'

'I expect he's also looking into Gerry, too,' said Ben. 'You'd better tell him that Gerry's possibly coming to Steeple Martin. Might make it difficult for off the record chats.'

Before setting off on her housekeeping mission the following morning, Libby sent Ian a text. To her surprise, he called back immediately.

'If you were going to tell me of Gerry Hall's prospective move to the nerve centre,' he said, 'I already knew.'

'Oh.' Libby was taken aback. 'Who told you?'

'He did, of course. He very sensibly called to tell me of his possible change of address, as we'd asked him to keep us informed if he moved around.'

'Did he tell you why?'

'He said Colin Hardcastle suggested it.' There was a faint question in Ian's voice.

'Well, they are friends,' said Libby. 'I'm sure Colin will tell you if you ask. And the other thing was, we were talking to Colin last night and we rather got the impression that some of Nick Nash's friends in Spain could be – well . . . perhaps not quite . . .'

'You mean criminals.' Libby could hear the smile. 'Yes, we'd worked that out. And you no doubt know that was what I was trying to find out from Colin on Saturday night.'

'Yes.' Libby was relieved. 'I said you'd picked up on it.'

'Well, now you know the investigation's in safe hands. And don't go letting anything out to Mr Hall, either.'

'We'd worked that one out, too,' said Libby. 'See you Wednesday?'

'If not before,' said Ian, and rang off.

Libby walked up the hill, past the dewpond, to Steeple Farm. The windows in the thatched roof still looked like secretive eyes peering out at her, no matter how well she now knew the house.

Inside, she checked that all was well, flicked the more obvious dust away from some surfaces, and sprayed a little air freshener around. At eleven o'clock on the dot the doorbell rang.

'Hi!' said Colin nervously. 'This is Gerry.'

He stood aside and a sturdily built man of about his own age stepped forward with a friendly grin and outstretched hand.

'Hello, I'm Gerry Hall. And you're Libby?'

Libby smiled at them both. 'Welcome to Steeple Farm. Come in.'

'This is a lovely house,' said Gerry, looking around the hall. 'Thank you so much for suggesting it.'

'I can't believe Colin didn't know about it,' said Libby.

'You haven't told me everything about your life yet,' said Colin with a relieved grin.

'I bet you've told Gerry all about us, though.' Libby gave him an answering grin.

'He has.' Gerry turned back from inspecting one of Libby's paintings. 'I know all about your adventures.'

'Oh, dear,' said Libby. 'Well, how about I leave you to wander around on your own? I'll wait in the sitting room.' She gestured to an open door. 'Take your time.'

In fact, it was twenty minutes before Gerry and Colin reappeared, by which time Libby had relocated to the kitchen from where she was surveying the paddock behind the house, where, had she and Ben moved there, she would have achieved her childhood dream of owning a pony.

'Does that belong to the house, too?' Gerry came up alongside her at the sink.

'Yes. I'd have had a pony in there if we moved here.'

'So would I if it was my house.' Gerry was almost misty-eyed as he gazed out at the paddock.

'You're only going to rent it,' said Colin, bringing them back to earth.

Gerry and Libby exchanged a complicit smile.

'Yes, please.' Gerry held out his hand. 'What do we do next?'

'I email Ben with your details and he sends you whatever it is you've got to sign.' Libby shook his hand.

'When can I move in?'

'Whenever you like.'

'Now?'

'Now?' echoed Libby.

Gerry gave a shamefaced grin. 'I checked out of the hotel this morning. I've got all my stuff in the car. There isn't much.'

Libby laughed.

'I should have known when Ian told me you'd given him your change of address.'

'So we're all above board?' Colin gave Libby a meaningful look.

'Yes.' Libby patted his arm. 'Ian's fully up to date.'

Colin smiled. 'We'll go and get Gerry's stuff, then, shall we?'

'Yes. You can park the car at the side. Just let me get his details.'

Libby gave them the keys and left them to it. As she walked home, she called Fran and brought her up to date.

'So what now?' said Fran. 'Do you still want to chase up Pam White?'

'Or her mum, at least. Although I don't see how.'

102

'Shall I try Fred Barrett again?'

'Could do. He talked to some of the girls, didn't he?'

'He did, but he seemed to think the same as everyone else – there wasn't much to it,' said Fran.

'But he did say they seemed scared of something,' said Libby.

'That was then, though. They were young.'

'And giggly and wanting to be scared.' Libby remembered being that age herself. 'I think I'll phone Patti, just to keep her up to date.'

A quick visit to the Hop Pocket, which was now actually looking a bit like a pub, and Ben updated with Gerry's installation, Libby went across to the Pink Geranium, feeling unreasonably disappointed when she remembered it was closed on Mondays. However, Harry was behind the counter frowning over the computer and saw her.

'Coming for a sneaky soup, are we?' He opened the door. 'Come on then. What happened with Colin?'

Libby followed him inside and told him about Gerry's enthusiastic response to Steeple Farm.

'He'll be wanting to buy it next, you'll see,' said Harry, departing kitchenwards to heat soup.

'No – Colin said he wanted to be near the sea.'

'Hmm,' said Harry. 'Sit down. Want a drink?'

'No, I'd better not.' Libby sat at a table near the counter. 'So, tell me what you really think about all this business.'

'What does that mean? Do I think you should be poking your nose in?'

'Well, do you?'

Harry shrugged. 'You've got Ian's blessing this time, haven't you? And it doesn't look as if you're on the main investigation trail. You're just looking into a load of old gossip.'

'That's true.' Libby sighed. 'I would like to know about all that old gossip, though. The policeman in particular.'

'What policeman?' Harry held up a hand. 'No don't remind me – I'm sure you told us. If not, I'll find out.'

They ate their soup in companionable silence.

'Do you think Colin will move in to Steeple Farm now?' asked Harry, pushing his bowl away.

'They're supposed to be taking it slowly,' said Libby. 'And he wanted to be in his flat by Christmas, didn't he?'

'Steeple Farm's a much nicer place to spend Christmas,' said Harry.

'Well, let's hope nothing else happens to spoil it, then,' said Libby.

Apart from updating Patti on the story so far, and Fran reporting that Fred Barrett was going to have a look at his notes from the time, nothing disturbed the normal round of life in Steeple Martin. On Wednesday, Colin brought Gerry to the pub, where he was accepted cheerfully into the little group. Ian appeared late, and no one dared to ask anything about the case.

'Sorry about this,' Colin said to Gerry while Ian was at the bar, 'but I did tell you he was a friend.'

'It's all right,' said Gerry with a grin. 'He hasn't marched me off in handcuffs yet.'

By Thursday, Libby was feeling restless.

'It's panto-itch again,' said Ben. 'You really will have to go back to it next year.'

'I know,' said Libby. 'It's not just that, though. I feel as though I'm waiting for something to happen.'

'Don't you start going all psychic on me,' Ben warned. 'Come down to the Pocket and help me paint the bar.'

In fact, Libby found slapping paint on to the newly plastered walls of the Hop Pocket's lounge bar quite therapeutic. Until she was interrupted by a phone call.

Chapter Fifteen

'Libby.' Patti's voice sounded shaky.

'What? What's the matter?' Libby turned away from the wall.

'I came home this morning . . .'

'And?'

'The police have found a body.'

'*What*?'

'They came and told me.'

'Who did? Who came?'

There was a gulping sound. 'Two officers – constables.'

'Why? Why did they come and tell you?'

Ben came over and stood next to her, looking concerned.

'It was on Nick Nash's grounds. My name's in the file, apparently.'

'But what did they want with you?'

Patti sighed. 'I don't know. I don't think they did, either. They just wanted to tell me – God knows why!'

To hear Patti use the deity's name in this fashion was a measure of how disturbed she was.

'I don't get it.' Libby scowled at Ben, who backed away. 'They must have had a reason. Who was it?'

'They didn't say.'

'Do you want me to come over?'

'Well . . . I don't see what you could do . . .'

'Moral support. Shall I?'

'Would you mind?' Libby could hear obvious relief.

'Of course not. Just let me get out of my workman's clothes, and I'll be with you.' Libby rang off.

'What's happened?' asked Ben. Libby told him.

'They must have had a reason for telling her,' he said. 'Perhaps simply because she's the local vicar and it was a courtesy? Doesn't sound likely.'

'No,' said Libby, handing over her paintbrush. 'I'll see you later.'

After a quick wash and change of clothes, Libby called Fran, climbed into the silver bullet, and set off for St Aldeberge. When she arrived at the vicarage, once more she found Fran sitting in her car on the drive.

'I called Patti and asked if she wanted me to come too. She said yes.'

'Poor Patti.' Libby locked her car.

Patti let them in, casting a quick look round before she shut the door.

'So what do you think?' she said, as soon as they were in the kitchen.

'Ben said maybe it was simply a courtesy because you're the vicar and your name had appeared in the file on Nick Nash.'

'But why would it?'

'Ian would have put in about Nash's connection to the church,' said Fran, obviously thinking more clearly than the other two.

'Oh!' Patti's face sagged with relief. 'I never thought of that!'

'Tea? Coffee?' offered Libby.

'Wine!' said Patti. 'I don't care how degenerate it is.'

'Let's hope none of the old biddies call round,' said Libby. 'So come on – did they say anything else, these officers?'

'No – just that they were sorry to tell me that a body had been found on Mr Nash's land, and under the circumstances it was thought I should be – actually, they said "the Church" – should be informed.'

'There you are – it's what Ben said. A courtesy.'

'But they said they may want to speak to me again.' Patti was looking worried.

'They always say that as a precaution,' said Fran. 'Doesn't mean they actually will.'

'They didn't say if it was male or female?' asked Libby.

'No, nothing like that. I suppose I shall just have to wait and see.'

'Well, there's got to be a link,' said Fran, 'so we're bound to hear something one way or another.'

'You don't think it could be Nash's wife, do you?' said Libby, after a moment. 'Ian said they couldn't find her.'

They looked at one another uneasily.

'It would make sense,' said Fran.

'If not, who else?' asked Patti.

'Could be anyone. Probably the same person who killed Nash himself,' said Libby.

'Could we ask Ian?' ventured Patti nervously.

'No!' said Libby and Fran immediately.

'He'll tell us if he wants to,' said Fran. 'Otherwise we keep out of it.'

'He'll ask Colin,' said Fran.

'Oh, Lord, so he will,' said Libby. 'Should we warn him?'

'Better not,' said Fran. 'That would get us into trouble, too.'

'So we can't do anything?' said Patti.

'Nothing,' said Libby. 'Frustrating, I know. Just let's hope the news doesn't start any more scurrilous gossip.'

'It will,' said Patti with a sigh.

They stayed with Patti for another hour until Libby was sure she had regained her normal equilibrium, then took their leave.

'Come back for a cup of tea?' suggested Fran, as they went to their cars.

They arrived at Coastguard Cottage under a lowering sky and dived inside just in time to avoid the impending rain. Fran went to put the kettle on, and Libby laid the fire.

'So – the ex-wife or the murderer?' asked Libby, as they settled by the fire.

'As we said earlier, could be either,' said Fran. 'And it certainly leads the investigation away from missing girls and possibly wicked priests.'

'I'd still like to know the truth behind that, though,' said Libby.

'Nothing to do with us, now.' Fran stared into the fire. 'And I have to admit I'm intrigued. I can't help thinking something must have happened to those girls.'

'I know. Even if Sarah – the only one we've found who actually *was* there – dismisses it.'

'Was she telling the truth though? Did you like her?'

'I liked her Aunt Amy.'

'That's not what I asked,' said Fran.

'Yes, I suppose I liked her. Perhaps you should have spoken to her.'

'Why?'

'You might have sensed something – I don't know – off-kilter.'

Fran sent her a searching look. 'Does that mean you thought there *was* something off-kilter?'

'Not at the time.' Libby swallowed some tea. 'Bother. Now I'm going to question everything I've heard.'

'Particularly Connie and Elaine,' said Fran.

'And Dora. Although I think Dora has her feet more firmly on the ground than the others.'

'All right.' Fran put her mug down on the hearth. 'Pam. How can we find out about her?'

'Kerry's mum didn't seem to know where she was.'

'But Pam went to Dover. I don't suppose it's any use trying to trace a "Pam White, Dover", do you?' Fran tapped her long fingers on the arm of her chair. 'If we could find some of the other girls – do we know what school they went to?'

'No, but Pam and Kerry were older than the others. They wouldn't necessarily have been friends.' Libby put her own mug down and sighed. 'I'll try and think of something, but I think you're right. We're off the investigation.' She stood up. 'I'd better go home. I haven't even thought about dinner yet.'

When she arrived home, it was to discover that she didn't need to think about dinner.

'Colin called,' Ben told her. 'We've been invited to Steeple Farm. Gerry's cooking – it's a sort of thank you, apparently.'

'Just us?'

'He asked Pete and Harry, too, but as Harry couldn't go, Pete declined as well.'

Despite not having many of his own belongings, Gerry had managed to make Steeple Farm feel much more homely, and delicious smells wafted from the kitchen.

'Nice!' said Libby appreciatively.

'I love it here,' said Gerry, handing her a glass. 'I don't suppose Peter would sell?'

'Harry said you'd want to buy it,' grinned Libby. 'But no, it's not for sale.'

'Still belongs to the family,' said Ben. 'Sorry! Anyway, I thought you wanted to be near the sea.'

'I thought I did.' Gerry smiled round. 'I didn't know Steeple Martin then.'

It was just after the first course was finished that Libby's mobile rang.

'Ignore it,' said Ben. Libby looked doubtful, but did as he said. A few minutes later it rang again – and then again. Ben sighed.

'Go on then,' he said. 'It must be urgent.'

'One of the kids,' muttered Libby, leaving the table to retrieve her phone.

'Libby! Where the hell are you?'

'Ian? We're at Steeple Farm having dinner with Gerry and Colin. What is it?'

The three men were looking as startled as Libby felt.

'Damn! Look – could you just excuse yourself for a moment? I need to ask you some questions.'

Libby felt as if she'd suddenly been deprived of breath. She put her hand over the phone.

'He needs to speak to me.' She gestured outside. 'Do you mind?'

Out in the hall, she lifted the phone again. 'What is it?'

'I expect you know a body was found on Nick Nash's land this morning?'

'Yes, two constables told Patti.'

'Well . . .' he was silent for a moment. 'I don't want this getting around, but can you remind me of all you know about the girls who were supposed to have gone missing?'

Libby was going down in a lift. 'Oh, no!'

'I'm afraid so. Female, and at least fifteen years in the ground, if not longer.'

Libby swallowed hard. 'What do you want to know?'

'Names. Details.'

'I only know a couple. Kerry Palmer, the one who *really* went missing – we met her mum, Liz – and Pam White, who ran away to Dover. The only other one was the one who didn't go missing at all, Sarah Elliot. We met her and her mum. I did tell you all this.'

'I know, but we were following the other lines of enquiry, so this wasn't followed up. Now, it has to be. Forensic examination is telling us the remains are that of a girl between twelve and fifteen. Roughly. Could be a bit younger or a bit older. All to do with the bone development, particularly the pelvis. Have you got any addresses?'

'Only of Sarah Elliot's mother, Angela. Mavis at the Blue Anchor got hold of Liz Palmer for us. Or rather Liz got hold of us through Mavis.'

'OK, thanks.' Ian paused. 'Try not to say too much in front of Gerry Hall.'

'I shall have to tell them something,' said Libby. 'I've just left the table in the middle of dinner – which he cooked for us – which is fairly rude, you have to admit.'

Ian sighed. 'I'm sorry. OK, you'll have to tell them. But the bare bones—'

Libby gasped.

'Sorry. I meant – don't go into detail.'

'I know what you meant. All right.'

'Apologise for me.'

'OK.'

Libby ended the call and returned to the dining table.

'He said he's sorry for interrupting our dinner.'

'So what was so important?' asked Ben. All three men were look-ing curious.

Libby took a deep breath. 'They found a body on Nick Nash's land this morning.'

Colin went pale and Gerry's mouth fell open.

'And it's a young female. Ian wanted to know the names of any young girls I'd found out about.'

'My God,' Colin whispered.

'Shit,' said Ben.

'Yes.' Libby took another deep breath. 'But please don't say any-thing to anyone else. Ian said I could tell you, but that's all.'

Silence fell around the table. Then Gerry stood up.

'Does anyone want anything else? I didn't make a dessert, but there's cheese and biscuits . . .'

'Nothing for me, thanks, Gerry,' said Ben.

'Nor me, thank you,' said Libby.

Colin merely shook his head.

'No, it has rather taken away the appetite, hasn't it?' said Gerry. 'Coffee? Or shall we stick with alcohol?'

The general consensus was alcohol, and after helping Gerry with clearing the table, they adjourned to the sitting room.

'Well, I'm sorry to have spoilt the dinner party,' said Libby. 'And it was such a lovely dinner, too.'

'Not your fault,' said Gerry. 'I guess this is what it means to be part of Libby's Loonies.'

Chapter Sixteen

That broke the tension.

'Are we allowed to speculate?' asked Gerry. 'I'm new to all this.'

'Well, let's hope you don't have to get used to it,' said Ben.

'It depends,' said Libby. 'I speculate because I can't help it. But you're involved, even if only marginally, so you're bound to.'

'What does Ian think?' asked Colin, rousing himself. 'What about his Spanish crime theory?'

'He didn't say. But obviously, the gossip that I've relayed to him has made him take that theory more seriously. I expect he'll carry on with investigating the Spanish connection, or his team will. They can't afford to ignore anything. But now they've got two murders to cope with.'

'Honestly, I didn't realise so many murders could possibly take place in such a small area,' said Colin.

'Beginning to regret coming back?' asked Ben.

Colin gave a reluctant smile. 'No, not really. They don't happen all the time, do they?'

'No, we have a break now and then,' said Libby, with a grin. 'Talking of speculation, Fran and I wondered if the body could be Nick's wife before this.'

'You knew about the body earlier?' asked Gerry.

'Yes, Patti called us this morning. The police told her.'

'Patti – that's the vicar? Why did they tell her?'

'Because her name was in the file already. They don't think she's got anything to do with it, obviously.'

'I would have thought that was an obvious conclusion,' said Colin. 'They can't find her, can they?'

'Apparently not. She came back here, you said?'

'Yes, so I gathered, but I don't know when. She didn't seem to be around much in Spain, and then she didn't appear at all. Nick gave the impression that they had divorced, or at least separated.'

'And you didn't take to her?' said Ben.

'No. She was a sort of over-made-up type. Wore unsuitable clothes and very high heels – you know the sort?'

'Yes,' said Libby, with another grin, 'but they aren't always bitches.'

'No, I know. But she was.'

'Why would it have been her? The body?' asked Gerry.

'Nick's been murdered and they can't find her.' Libby shrugged.

'I would have thought she was more likely to be the murderer,' said Gerry. 'She'll inherit the property and whatever he had in Spain.'

'Apparently not,' said Libby. 'So we're given to understand.'

'Does he still suspect me?' asked Colin suddenly.

Libby looked surprised. 'I don't think he ever did. I told you.'

'Well, whatever he thought, he's going to have to think again, now,' said Ben.

Ben and Libby left after another hour.

'What do you really think Ian's going to do next?' Ben asked as they walked down the hill into the village.

'I don't know. He can't ignore the missing girls now, but he can't ignore anything he's turned up in Spain, either. You know, I've got to find out about those scouts and that Sergeant Peacock.'

'Will you be allowed to, now that it's turned into an official investigation? Anyway, the policeman might be dead by now.'

'I don't know.' Libby sighed. 'If the police don't look into it, I expect I can.'

Fran, appealed to on Friday morning, was of the same opinion.

'Even if there's no reason for us to look into it,' she said. 'After all, the reason we were allowed to talk to people was because the police weren't taking that angle seriously. They are now.'

'So no need for us to track down Pam White,' said Libby. 'They will.'

'Well, let's make sure whatever we do isn't out of bounds first,' said Fran. 'Why are we doing it, anyway?'

'What do you mean, why are we doing it?' Libby was affronted. 'Justice, of course.'

'Ah, yes.' Fran sounded amused. 'Not simply nosiness, then.'

'Stop it!' Libby thought for a moment. 'Should I tell Patti, do you think?'

'I think that might fall under the heading of gossip. She'll find out, anyway.'

'Hmm. OK.' Libby paused again. 'I can't help wondering, though . . .'

'I know. First thing I thought of. Kerry Palmer.'

'I do hope not. That poor woman.'

'At least she'd know,' said Fran. 'Let me know what you want to do, and when.'

There didn't seem to be anything to be done, however. During the rest of Friday, while shopping and doing a little desultory house-work, Libby wracked her brains, but nothing emerged. She eventually resorted to starting a new small picture for Guy to sell in his gallery, where he insisted there was a market for her output. But inspiration even here seemed to have deserted her, and in the end she gave up.

Colin appeared on the doorstep later in the afternoon.

'Sorry to disturb you,' he said. 'I wondered if you'd heard anything more today?'

'Nothing, I'm afraid,' said Libby. 'But come in – I was just about to have a cup of tea. I've just lit the fire.'

He followed her into the kitchen, where the big brown kettle was gently burbling away on the Rayburn.

114

'Only teabag tea, I'm afraid.' Libby fetched two mugs. 'I've got lazy, these days.'

'I never have anything else,' said Colin.

They settled by the fire with their tea, and Sidney glared at Colin. 'He doesn't like me.'

'Yes, he does. He looks like that at everyone,' said Libby. 'You see, he'll be trying to jump on your lap any minute.'

Sure enough, with a flick of his tail, Sidney jumped onto Colin's knee, very nearly causing a tea disaster.

'I was thinking, said Colin, putting his mug down carefully. 'I kept going over what we knew—'

'Or thought we knew,' put in Libby.

'Yes, thought we knew – and there's one person I hadn't thought of. I expect the police have, but I'd completely forgotten.'

'Who's that, then?'

'The gardener.'

'The – who?'

'The gardener, remember? You asked who had discovered Nick's body.'

'Oh, yes – you thought he might have hired her to tart up the garden – or the land.'

'Yes. Although there didn't seem to be much of a garden. It was just the land down to the cliff top. You haven't heard of her any more? Ian's not mentioned her?'

'Not a word. I'd forgotten all about her, too. What was she called?'

'I don't know. Do you think anyone would know? Patti?'

Libby frowned. 'Nobody I've talked to has mentioned a gardener. I could ask – but Patti didn't come into the equation until after the two ladies got in touch with her.'

'Worth asking?' Colin looked hopeful.

'I suppose so, but what could she offer? I doubt she knows anything.'

'I know. I'm clutching at straws, aren't I?'

Libby smiled at him. 'I do it all the time.'

115

Colin finished his tea and gently removed Sidney from his lap. 'I'd better go. I've interrupted you for long enough.'

'That's all right.' Libby stood up. 'Look, how about you and Gerry coming to dinner tomorrow. To make up for your spoilt party last night?'

'I'd like that. And you didn't spoil it – it wasn't your fault.'

'Is Gerry all right? He does seem to have been thrust right into the middle of all this.'

'He's fine. He realises Ian must still be investigating him, but he knows he hasn't got anything to worry about. And he loves the village – and the house.' Colin grinned. 'The trouble is, he says it's spoilt him for other houses.'

'He still wants to move to the area, then?'

'Oh, yes.' Colin went faintly pink. 'That was the long-term plan . . .'

'You two are all right, then?' Libby opened the door.

'Yes. It seems to have . . . oh, I don't know.'

'Brought you closer together?' Libby grinned. 'These things do. Ben and I bonded over a murder.'

She relayed the conversation to Ben when he came home a little later.

'I suppose,' he said, 'we could offer them Steeple Farm on a long-term lease.'

'Peter might not like that.'

'Well, he won't ever need it again,' said Ben. 'Shall I ask?'

'No – let him go on his house hunt. We might need Steeple Farm again.'

'More refugees?' Ben grinned. 'OK.'

Libby called Patti early on Saturday morning.

'Thought I'd get you before any weddings happened,' she said.

'You're all right,' said Patti. 'Not until two o'clock. What is it?'

'Colin reminded me that it was a gardener who found Nick Nash's body. You wouldn't happen to know who that was?'

'No idea,' said Patti. 'I do know about the body being found, though. Do you know anything about that?'

'Nothing, except that it's a young female. Ian wanted names from me.'

'Oh, no! The shop talked about nothing else yesterday. Honestly, Libby, they were positively excited!' Patti sounded angry and bewildered.

'I don't know why you're surprised,' said Libby. 'They'll be different if they find they know the person.'

'I wouldn't bet on it,' said Patti. 'Anyway, do you want me to ask around about this gardener?'

'If you think it won't start even more gossip.'

Gerry and Colin arrived that evening bearing wine and flowers.

'Very traditional,' said Ben, relieving them of both. 'And, being traditional, we're eating in the kitchen!'

Gerry, as guest not host, revealed himself to be very good company. Colin sat looking on like a proud parent.

'So where do you think you'll look for your new house?' asked Ben, as they helped themselves to Libby's special fruit salad.

'I think I might steer clear of St Aldeberge and Felling,' said Gerry. 'Colin was telling me about Nethergate.'

'If you want coast,' said Libby, 'there's plenty the other way. Towards Creekmarsh, where another friend of ours lives.'

'And I bet he knows about properties in that area,' said Ben. 'Ask Adam to talk to him.'

'Your son Adam?' said Colin.

'Yes. He works for the chap who owns Creekmarsh.'

'You've seen Adam,' Colin said to Gerry. 'He works in the Pink Geranium sometimes.'

'And lives in the flat upstairs,' said Libby. 'It's all a bit cliquey round here. That's the trouble with villages.'

'That's also possibly the best reason for not moving here,' said Ben. 'Gets a bit claustrophobic.'

Gerry laughed. 'I suppose it would.' He smiled at Colin. 'Seems to suit old Col here, though.'

'I asked Patti about the gardener, by the way,' said Libby. 'She didn't know a thing.'

'Worth a try,' said Colin. 'I suppose I shouldn't worry about it, really.'

'No.' Libby patted his hand. 'Best not.'

To Libby's surprise, Patti called on Sunday, just before she and Ben left to go to the Manor.

'Your gardener,' she said. 'Needless to say there was a lot of gossip after the eleven o'clock service today.'

'Coffee time?'

'Yes, indeed, and even Dora was there. They are a load of ghouls. Anyway, I just threw in a mention of the gardener, and someone immediately said they knew her.'

'Actually *knew* her?'

'Yes. A woman I don't know very well, and I didn't like to admit I didn't know what her name was, but she said, "Oh, yes, my friend Jemima. She's a landscape designer. She told me all about it." That was about all, and I didn't like to push any harder.'

'Well done, Patti! And don't worry – I know who will know her if she's a local landscape gardener. Two people, actually. Adam's boss Mog, and my cousin Cass's bloke, Mike.'

'He's the one with the nursery, isn't he?'

'Yes – and I don't know why I didn't think of those two before.'

'You are not phoning either of them now,' warned Ben, as Libby ended the call.

She grinned at him. 'I wasn't going to,' she said. 'I wouldn't dare be late for Hetty.

118

Chapter Seventeen

When Adam turned up at Peter and Harry's house later that afternoon, Libby sent Ben a triumphant look.

'Didn't even have to phone!' she said.

'What?' Adam looked from one to another.

Libby told him.

'Jemima . . .' Adam frowned. 'The name rings a bell.'

'Well, don't worry about it now,' said Ben. 'Ask Mog tomorrow.'

'No, it isn't through Mog.' Adam continued to frown. 'Oh, it'll come to me.'

'What's all this about then?' asked Harry, sprawled as usual, in a corner of the sofa. 'Come on – we're involved, too.'

Libby and Ben brought them up to date.

'And now,' said Ben, 'for goodness sake let's talk about something else.'

On Monday morning, Libby decided that she ought to think about buying some new floral decorations for Christmas.

'It's a bit early,' protested Ben. 'This is just an excuse to go and see Cass and Mike, isn't it?'

Cassandra, Libby's cousin, now lived permanently with Mike Farthing of Farthing's Plants, a nursery just past the village of Shott. Cass was a dab hand at creating decorations out of natural materials, and had increased the demand for these over the last few years.

'Well, it won't hurt,' said Libby, on the defensive. 'And we've got to go and choose trees from Cattlegreen as well.'

Cattlegreen Nursery was just outside Steeple Martin, run by Joe and Nella, who also had the farm shop in the village itself. They had a small tree plantation, from where Ben and Libby chose trees for themselves and the Manor.

'So you're planning to visit both of them and institute enquiries?' Ben asked innocently.

'No use having contacts if you don't use them,' said Libby.

When she arrived at Farthing's Plants, Cass was in the office and came out to greet her.

'To what do we owe the pleasure?' she asked, tucking her arm through Libby's and leading her towards the office. 'Do you need another protective hedge?'

'No, Christmas stuff.'

'Bit early,' said Cass, raising her eyebrows. 'And what else?'

'Am I that transparent?'

'When I know there's a local murder, I can guess that you're involved somehow. And that means you're on the hunt for something.'

Libby sat down near the heater in the office, while Cass went to plug in the kettle.

'Well, you're right, of course. I wanted to know if you or Mike knew a gardener called Jemima something.'

'Bit of a tall order,' said Cass. 'I mean, we know a lot of gardeners – or Mike does – but not sure I could call to mind all their names.'

Libby sighed. 'I suppose not, but I thought with it being an unusual name . . .'

'I'll call Mike.' Cass picked up a small radio transmitter. 'See? Persuaded him to get these, so that I don't have to trail through the greenhouses looking for him.'

'Wouldn't a mobile have done just as well?'

'He never carries his. He's happier with this, and he can leave it in the greenhouse at the end of the day.' She pressed a button.

Summoned, Mike said he'd be with them in a moment.

'Which means almost straight away, or within the next hour,' said Cass.

Mike arrived, however, in a few minutes and greeted Libby with a hug.

'She wants something,' said Cass, handing over mugs of coffee.

'What is it this time?'

'A gardener,' said Libby.

Mike's eyes widened. 'You've only got a pocket handkerchief! What do you want a gardener for?'

'Not for her – a particular gardener,' said Cass. 'Someone called Jemima.'

'Oh!' Mike nodded, enlightened. 'Jemima Routledge. She's a garden designer, landscaper, actually.'

'Really? Yes, I suppose that would be the one.' Libby frowned.

'So what's it all about?' asked Mike. 'Is this a murder?'

Libby told them.

'Does it seem likely that she would have been called in to do a tidy-up before selling?' she asked. 'I would have thought a designer and landscaper would be a bit too grand for that.'

'Near the Dunton Estate, you said.' Mike frowned. 'I know it. Actually, I can imagine the seller wanted to create a proper garden – at the moment, it's just open land right up to the cliff, isn't it?'

'Yes – everyone seems to treat it as common land.'

'But it isn't. That house owns it. It was sold off with the house by the original estate owners.'

'In that case I can see why she was called in. It also explains why she was rooting around on the cliff top.'

'Perhaps the owner wanted it fenced off,' suggested Cass.

'Instead, it killed him,' said Libby. 'How ironic.'

'Why did you want to find her?' asked Cass. 'The police will already have spoken to her if she found this body.'

'We wondered if she knew anything about the land. If the murdered man had told her anything about it.'

'Who's "we"?' said Mike. 'You and your mate Fran?'

'No, it was Colin Hardcastle. He brought the victim over here

121

from Spain, because he had a buyer for the house. He now feels responsible.'

'I suppose he would,' said Cass. 'I would.'

'Hold on.' Mike stood up from his perch on a packing case and went to the desk. Rifling through a small letter rack he soon found what he was looking for. 'There. That's Jemima's card. She uses us to source plants, and occasionally, extra labour. She's not far.' He peered at the card. 'No – Bishop's Bottom. Just up the road, really.'

Libby took the card. 'I'll give her a ring, thank you, Mike. And I really do want some new stuff for Christmas, Cass. Big bits, to decorate the theatre and the Manor.'

'Leave it to me. I shall create, just for you!'

Libby left the two tall, grey-haired figures standing, arms linked, on the forecourt.

'A real case of autumn romance, that,' she said to herself as she drove away. 'Bit like Ben and me.'

She debated with herself whether to drive past Jemima Routledge's address on the way home and decided against it, opting for Cattlegreen Nursery and Christmas trees instead.

The minute she pulled up on the forecourt, Joe and Nella's son Owen, appeared, beaming widely.

'Hello, Libby!' he said, opening her door for her. 'Shall I make chocolate?'

Owen's invariable habit was to make Libby a mug of hot chocolate, of which he was inordinately proud. Even with Cass's coffee still sloshing about inside, she was not about to refuse him.

'That would be lovely, Owen.' Libby climbed out. 'When I've chosen a couple of trees?'

'I'll fetch Dad, then.' Owen ran back inside, and a moment later Joe appeared wiping his hands on a rag.

'Potting up,' he explained. 'You after trees?'

'As usual, Joe, yes.'

'Right. I've got your ribbons here.' Joe waved some lengths of red ribbon at her. These were used to tie on to her selected trees to show that they were sold. They would be dug up a week or so before Christmas.

'You mustn't let Owen force you into having his chocolate,' Joe said, as they walked between rows of Norwegian Spruce.

'No – it's lovely chocolate. I feel very honoured.'

Joe looked at her sideways. 'Doesn't do it for everybody. Very fond of you, Owen is.'

'And I'm very fond of him,' said Libby. 'By the way, Joe, do you know of a garden designer called Jemima Routledge?'

'Jemima?' Joe looked surprised. 'Known her for years. Knew her dad.'

'Oh.'

'Why - what's she done?'

'Found a body,' said Libby.

'What?' Joe stopped dead. 'Don't tell me she's involved in one of your murders?'

'No, I shouldn't think so. She just found the body of a client. Hardly likely to be involved.'

Joe looked at her shrewdly. 'Why do you want to know about her, then?'

'Just to see if she knew anything about the client, or his land . . .' Libby trailed off. 'That was all.'

Joe shook his head. 'I dunno. You don't 'alf get mixed up in some things.' He resumed walking down the line of trees.

They chose a small, neat tree for number seventeen, and a more majestic version for the Manor, and walked back to the main building, where Owen had mugs of hot chocolate waiting.

'So – Jemima.' Libby sipped at her mug. 'She nice?'

'I like Jemima,' said Owen simply.

Joe smiled. 'She always played with Owen when she came here with her dad. He passed away a few years ago, now, and she took over the business. But he'd just been a gardener – good one, mind – young Jem went to horticultural college, got proper qualifications. Tell you who knows her – your cousin's bloke, Mike Farthing.'

'Yes, he gave me her card.'

'Aye. And tell you who else – that Lewis Osbourne-Walker.'

'Oh!' Libby put down her mug. 'I thought my Adam's boss might . . .'

'Mog!' Joe laughed. 'Well, he would. Doesn't Adam know her?'

'He said the name was familiar.'

'Kids, eh?' Joe smiled fondly at Owen sitting quietly by his side.

Later that afternoon Libby called Fran to update her, before calling Jemima Routledge's number.

'Routledge,' said a brisk, efficient sounding voice.

'Oh!' said Libby. 'Er – I'm sorry to bother you, but . . .' she searched for something to say next. 'My name's Libby Sarjeant,' she began again, 'and—'

'I know who you are.' Jemima Routledge laughed. 'I'm surprised I haven't heard from you before.'

'Really?' Libby was confused.

'Well, I discovered a body and you're in the business of discovering bodies, aren't you?'

'I wouldn't put it quite like that,' said Libby.

'Don't worry. Look I've heard all about you from Lewis, and his assistant, who's your son, isn't he?'

'Adam, yes.'

'I assume you're calling about that man Nash's death. Right?'

'Um – yes.'

'So – what do you want to know?'

'Would it be possible to come and see you? As I said, I don't want to bother you.'

'Of course.' There was a pause and Libby could hear pages rustling. 'I'm going over to Steeple Mount in the morning. I could come back via Steeple Martin – that's where you are, isn't it? – and maybe have a bite of lunch in the pub? I could meet you there.'

Libby sagged with relief. 'Perfect,' she said. 'What time? Or would you prefer to ring me when you're ready?'

'Good idea,' said Jemima. 'I'll be the one with mud on her boots. Look forward to meeting you.'

She rang Fran again.

'So I wondered if you wanted to come, too?'

'No, she's only expecting to see you. We don't want to overwhelm her.'

'She didn't sound the type to be overwhelmed,' laughed Libby, 'but I expect you're right. Talk to you tomorrow.'

Libby arrived at the pub on Tuesday morning to find their small bar inhabited by one person.

'Hello! Are you Libby?' Jemima Routledge stood up and held out her hand.

'Yes – and you're Jemima?' Libby saw a woman of about her own height – not tall – with a cheerful face and hair in a long mousy plait even more untidy than vicar Beth's usually was.

'Chap behind the bar told me this was where you usually sat.'

'Yes – Tim knows us all very well,' said Libby. 'Can I get you a drink?'

'No – got one.' Jemima indicated her glass. 'And I've ordered sandwiches.'

'Right,' said Libby, and went to the bar.

'New friend of yours?' asked Tim, as he poured Libby's half of lager.

'I don't know yet,' said Libby.

'You said "us all",' said Jemima, when Libby returned to the table.

'There's a group of us who meet here regularly,' said Libby.

'Ah. Nice to have a proper local.' Jemima sat back comfortably. 'Now – what did you want to ask me about?'

Libby regarded her carefully. 'It probably sounds a bit odd, but I was hoping you could tell me how much you knew about Nick Nash.'

'Very little, actually. He called me – oh, about four weeks ago, maybe – because someone had recommended me. He said he was

125

selling his house because he now lived permanently in Spain, and wanted to know if I could get his grounds in some sort of order because they'd been neglected for years.'

'And you said yes.'

'Well, not straight away. I said I'd have to have a look first, and could he meet me to show me round. He said he wasn't in the UK, but I could go and have a look myself, because the grounds weren't fenced off.' Jemima shrugged. 'Sounded a bit odd, but he told me how to get there, so I went.'

'And discovered it was more or less open cliff top.'

'Exactly. I poked around a bit, and when I called him back, I said there wasn't much I could do, I could create a proper garden near to the house, but the rest of it was best left as it was. You'd be destroying all sorts of habitat, and rare plants for all I knew, if you tried to do anything else, and I bet the environmentalists would be up in arms.'

'I would have thought that, too,' said Libby.

'And then he said that he really wanted to change it as much as possible.' She shook her head. 'So we compromised. I said if he could perhaps cut some of the grassy areas near the house, I'd do what I could, but he was in a hurry. Said his buyer was going to view quite soon. I couldn't go until the day he said this was happening, but I went over that morning.' She paused for a sip of her drink. 'And I was quite shocked to find that he'd obviously taken a motor mower to it and done quite a lot of damage. In my opinion, anyway. And that was when . . .'

Jemima stopped and swallowed. 'It wasn't pleasant.'

'I'm sure it wasn't.'

'But it puzzled me.' She frowned. 'It seemed as if he'd concentrated on a particular area quite a way away from the house. It almost looked as if he'd been moving boulders.'

Chapter Eighteen

Libby sat up straight. 'Boulders?'

'Yes. Does that mean something?'

Libby opened her mouth to speak just as Tim leant over the bar and called, 'Libby! Sandwiches.'

'I ordered enough for both of us,' said Jemima. 'I hope you don't mind.'

'Of course not,' said Libby, getting up to collect the tray.

'So,' she said, helping herself to a sandwich as she sat down, 'you thought he'd been moving boulders.'

'Yes. When I'd been before, there were outcrops of rock, the sort of thing you often find on cliff tops, and when I went back, it looked as though a couple of them had been moved.'

'Did you tell the police?'

Jemima frowned. 'No. I didn't think of it at the time, and I suppose I didn't think it was relevant. You obviously think it is.'

'Yes.' Libby nodded slowly. 'You see, another body has been found there. On Nick Nash's land.'

Jemima stopped chewing, her cheery face losing a little colour. 'Oh, no!'

'It's all right,' said Libby, 'it wasn't done then – the body, I mean. It had been in the ground a long time. Years.'

Jemima ate for a little while in silence. Libby followed suit.

'I suppose that's why you were asking what I knew about him,' she said eventually.

'Yes, and you were actually helpful,' said Libby. 'It sounds as if he wanted to hide – or obscure – something, doesn't it? Especially moving boulders.'

'It does.' Jemima stared at her empty plate. 'I've just remembered.'

'What?' Libby sat up, alert.

'Nothing to do with Nick Nash,' said Jemima with a small smile. 'I just remembered you've got some kind of connection with Mike Farthing, haven't you?'

'Yes, he's my cousin Cass's partner.' Libby grinned. 'And Joe up at Cattlegreen told me he knew your dad, and you used to play with Owen when he was young.'

Jemima laughed. 'Well! How the hell have we avoided one another for so long with all these connections?'

'I've no idea! I sometimes think everyone in this part of Kent must be linked by invisible wires.'

'I suppose you get connections within any business community. Mine's gardens and nurseries, but if you were a musician it might be the same.'

'It is. We ran a little beer festival here a couple of years ago,' said Libby, 'just behind the pub, and we were amazed at how many of the little bands and musicians knew one another.'

'Food producers are the same,' said Jemima. 'All the little independent ones.'

'And that's one of the problems.' Libby leaned back in her chair with a sigh. 'Nick Nash hadn't any connections. He left the area twenty years ago.'

'Oh? I had the impression he came back a lot.'

'He came back, yes, but his old connections had all gone. He used to be a churchwarden at St Aldeberge, down on the coast.'

'Really? And he was retiring to Spain? He didn't sound like an old man. And I couldn't really see from the cliff.' She shuddered. 'I didn't want to look any closer.'

'He wasn't.' Libby stared into the remains of her drink.

'There's more to this than meets the eye, isn't there?' said Jemima shrewdly, after a pause.

'Yes.' Libby sighed. 'The police didn't know any of this when you found his body, it's all emerged since.'

'Did you find it?' Jemima leant forward. 'Mog and Mike have both told me how you investigate this sort of thing.'

'Some of it,' said Libby. 'My friend and I do get involved somehow. It's partly because I'm nosy, and partly because we know so many people.'

'What was it this time? Sorry if I'm asking too many questions . . .'

'I don't mind. It's what I do! No, this time it was because we know people.' Libby finished her drink and Jemima waved at Tim, pointing at Libby's glass.

Libby gave an edited account of the discoveries about Nick Nash and how she and Fran had become involved.

'So, you see, it wasn't simply nosiness, I was actually asked in,' she concluded.

'You're helping the police, then?'

'In a peripheral sort of way, yes.'

'Will you tell them what I've said?'

'If you don't mind, unless you'd rather tell them yourself. I think they'll probably want to talk to you.'

Jemima nodded. 'They said I'd have to give evidence at the inquest, anyway, so yes. I'll do it myself. Can I say you asked me to?'

'Of course. Do you have a number to ring?'

'Yes – I've got a card.' Jemima smiled. 'I'm glad you asked me.'

Tim arrived with a refill for Libby.

'I hope you've given a good impression of us,' he said, smiling hopefully at Jemima.

'Oh, yes.' She smiled back. 'I'm hoping to be invited back.'

'Really?' said Libby, as Tim retreated to the bar. 'Welcome any time, obviously.'

'I get the feeling that you and the pub have a very interesting little community. And from what I've heard elsewhere, of course.'

'Yes, I think we do. Just a bunch of mates, of course. I expect you could find the same anywhere.' Libby sipped her new drink.

'Could you bear to keep me updated with the case? I'll do the same for you, obviously.'

'Course. You deserve to know.' Libby laughed. 'You see? This is what happens. Someone gets roped in and never gets away!'

Later that afternoon, Libby was surprised to receive a phone call from Detective Sergeant Rachel Trent.

'Hello, Rachel! You working on this St Aldeberge case, as well?'

'Yes, I'm playing sidekick on this one. They tried to tie DCI Connell to the desk, but you know what he's like. We've got local officers, too, but mostly it's Canterbury. We've even got a little incident room down here – in the church hall. Courtesy of your friend, the vicar, I believe?'

'Patti? Oh, I didn't know that.'

'Well, we're pretty sure the murders are linked – be odd if they weren't, wouldn't it? So we need one. Anyway, what I rang for was to check something.'

'Oh?' said Libby.

'We received a phone call from Ms Routledge, the lady who found Nash's body.'

'Yes?'

'She says you prompted her to call us with some information.'

'That's right.'

'You thought it was important?'

'Well, yes!' Libby was beginning to get exasperated. 'Don't you?'

'We don't know yet.'

'Why are you checking with me, then? Do you think she made it up?'

'No!' Rachel sighed. 'It's just having to check all the details. Dotting the i's and crossing the t's. You know.'

'For what it's worth, she just mentioned these boulders in passing. I thought it might be important.'

'What exactly did she say?'

'That he'd done quite a lot of damage in a particular area, and that he seemed to have moved some boulders. I thought it sounded important.'

Rachel sighed again. 'So do I. But the DCI isn't here, and no one's taking me seriously.'

'That's daft,' said Libby. 'Who do you need to convince?'

'The local team. Oh, don't worry. I'll run it by the DCI as soon as I get a chance.'

Libby decided not to tell Jemima about this development, but did call Fran.

'Would it be worth sending Ian a text?' she said.

'He might get cross,' said Fran. 'I expect you'd get told to butt out.'

'I wonder why the local police are being obstructive to Rachel, though?'

'Don't like having been taken over?' said Fran.

'I suppose so. It's odd, though, especially after finding out that Sergeant Peacock didn't take anything seriously twenty years ago. War between St Aldeberge and Canterbury?'

'I wonder if it is a hangover from that time,' said Fran.

'Maybe Ian will tell us tomorrow – if he can get away,' said Libby. 'Are you going to come up and have a drink with us?'

'Oh – Wednesday Club,' said Fran. 'I'll ask Guy.'

It was just after ten o'clock that evening when Libby heard Ben on the phone in the sitting room while she was in the kitchen. Curious, she hastily poured the drinks she had gone in to fetch, and returned to the sitting room.

'Here she is, now, bearing whisky,' he said, then laughed. 'Yes, I'm sure. Hang on, I'll pass you over.'

He handed Libby the phone. 'One of your other men.'

Libby scowled at him.

'Hello?'

'Good evening, Libby,' said Ian 'Getting restless?'

'Eh?'

'Well, you've got nothing to investigate, have you? Is that why you dragged in poor Ms Routledge?'

'Hey! She asked to meet me, I'll have you know!'

'After you'd been asking around about her.'

'We have a lot of friends in common. She even knows Adam.'

'I should have known. You've far too many contacts in the land-scaping world.'

'Good job I have. Otherwise you wouldn't have known about the moving boulders, would you?'

Ian laughed. 'The case of the moving boulders. I like it.'

'Rachel said the local force weren't happy about investigating.'

'There's a certain amount of resistance,' admitted Ian.

'Don't like you invading their territory?'

'Something like that.' Ian sounded uncharacteristically uncomfortable.

'By the way, did you look into Sergeant Peacock?' asked Libby.

Ian was silent for a minute. 'Are you implying some kind of residual local solidarity?'

'I just wondered.'

'As it happens, I did look into that aspect of what the gossip-mongers told you. He's actually still alive. Hardly surprising – it was only twenty years ago. He's in his seventies.'

Libby sat down abruptly. 'Have you spoken to him?'

'No – no reason to, at the moment. We need to know a lot more.'

'About what?'

'Come on, Libby! We need concrete evidence that there *was* actually something going on. We haven't got that, have we? Despite what your nose might tell us.'

'Right.' Libby was quiet while she thought about it. 'So are you going to check what Jemima's told you?'

'Of course.' Libby could hear the smile in his voice. 'I thought we'd ask her to come down and see if she can pinpoint the area she was talking about. Do you want to come with her?'

'What?' Libby was so surprised she spilt whisky.

'Well, it's due to you we heard about it.'

'But you don't like me interfering! And the local force certainly won't!'

'Let me worry about that. Now, will tomorrow suit you?'

'Yes.' Libby glanced at Ben, who was attempting to look uninterested. 'When?'

'I think I'll let Ms Routledge decide. Someone will ring you in the morning.'

Libby relayed this surprising conversation to Ben, who immediately vetoed a further phone call to Fran.

'Far too late,' he said. 'Besides, I wouldn't be at all surprised if Ian decided to ask Fran along anyway.'

'Oh! In case she can – er – see something.'

'Sense something,' corrected Ben. 'Now, I'd better top up that whisky you slopped all over the place.'

Sure enough, DS Rachel Trent called on Wednesday morning.

'Will twelve o'clock suit you?' she asked. 'Ms Routledge said she can be here by then. Oh, and Mrs Wolfe is coming, too.'

'Is that Ian's idea?' asked Libby.

'Yes, how did you guess?'

'He's always had a great respect for her – um – investigative powers.'

'Her funny psychic moments, you mean,' said Rachel. 'Well, I can't deny she's helped in the past. So we'll see you then?'

'Yes. Where?'

'The church hall. We'll take you all out to the site.'

Naturally, Libby had to consult Fran before they met in St Aldeberge.

'Quite a turn-up,' she said. 'Who knew he'd let us be involved?'

'Perhaps it's my "moments" he wants,' said Fran gloomily. 'I hardly ever get them these days – you know that. And I've told him.'

'Never mind. You often get flashes of inspiration apart from "moments".'

'I suppose so. So I'll see you at the church hall at twelve?'

'Yes. And I'll just give Patti a quick ring to warn her. Perhaps we can pop in to see her when we've finished.'

Chapter Nineteen

Patti was in the church hall car park when Libby arrived.

'I know I'm not needed,' she said, 'but I thought you might like to pop in when you've finished.'

'Fran's been invited, too,' said Libby, 'and we'd planned to do that anyway. You won't want Jemima Routledge, though, will you?'

'Play it by ear,' said Patti. 'But if she's not familiar with the whole scenario, perhaps not. Look, Fran's arriving.'

Inside they found Jemima sitting at one of the tables manned by Rachel Trent. Introductions made, Rachel stood up.

'Come on, then, DCI Connell's meeting us over there.'

'Is this your partner in crime?' asked Jemima, once they were seated in the back of the car, with Fran in front next to Rachel.

'Fran, yes.' Libby turned to look at her. 'You knew about her?'

'From Mike and Cassandra mainly. Sorry. They weren't gossiping.'

'That's all right. We get bracketed together all the time.'

'You both help the police, then?'

'Yes.'

Fran turned round. 'DCI Connell calls us special advisors.' She grinned. 'I think that's to appease his bosses.'

'Oh.' Jemima looked vaguely puzzled. 'I didn't realised it was quite so – so – *official*.'

Libby smiled, but kept quiet.

Rachel drove them onto the wild headland beyond Dunton

House, the woods, and the Willoughby Oak, much loved by the Wiccan community.

'We'll get out here,' she said, pulling in to the edge of the path. 'We go this way.'

They began to walk across the rough grass.

'Did you think Nash had used the mower here?' asked Rachel.

'Not this part,' said Jemima. 'I didn't come this far over. He told me specifically which area to concentrate on, and it wasn't near the house. It was more over that way.' She gestured towards the house seen in the distance. 'Is that the house?'

'Yes,' said Fran. Jemima looked startled and Rachel smiled.

'Have you been here before?' Jemima peered at Fran.

'No,' said Fran, and turned away. 'Look there's Ian.'

Ian came striding over the turf, wellingtons looking incongruous against his dark suit.

'Sir,' said Rachel. 'This is Ms Routledge.'

Ian held out his hand. 'It was very good of you to come, Ms Routledge.'

'Happy to help, and please call me Jemima.' She looked at Libby. 'Or even Jem.' She looked back at Ian. 'If I knew what I was looking for of course.'

'You told Libby you thought some boulders had been moved.' Jemima nodded.

'Could you remember where that was and show us, please?'

'I think so. It was between here and the cliff top.'

She began to lead the way across the turf. Libby, looking round, wondered how she had planned to turn this into anything like a garden. As they got slightly nearer to the house, Jemima began to veer away towards the cliff top, and a group of white suited SOCOs came into view. Jemima stopped.

'There,' she said. 'Where they are.'

Ian regarded her cautiously. 'Could you be a little more specific?' he asked.

She made a little moue of disgust. 'Must I?'

136

'There's nothing to see.' He tried to reassure her.

'Why are they there, then?' Jemima narrowed her eyes at him.

'Looking for clues,' said Libby briskly. 'Come on, then, Jem! Let's see if we can find some.'

So saying, she led the way towards the white suits, and stopped when she deemed it was a safe distance.

Jemima squinted. 'I can't quite see . . .' She turned to Ian. 'The rocks I thought had been moved. They aren't there.'

'Two big rocks, lying almost on their sides?' asked Ian.

'Yes! They were there, where those men are. And I'll show you where they were before.'

She turned and moved away to their right, to a small dip in the ground surrounded by ferns.

'I know what that is!' said Libby, stopping suddenly.

'So do I!' said Fran.

Ian and Jemima looked surprised. Then, 'Ah!' said Ian. 'I should have realised.'

'What?' said Jemima. 'What am I missing?'

'It's the entrance to an old tunnel to the shoreline,' said Libby. 'We've been here before.' She began to head for the entrance to the tunnel.

'No, Libby, wait.' Ian stopped her. 'I'll get the lads over here. DS Trent, go and fetch them, please.'

Rachel set off at a trot.'

'Do you know who the body is yet?' asked Fran.

'We're waiting for confirmation,' said Ian.

'Dental records?' suggested Libby.

Ian inclined his head.

'Not giving anything away,' said Libby. 'Ah, well.'

The SOCOs arrived with Rachel and Ian led them to the patch of ferns.

'What now?' asked Jemima.

'If we just wait for DCI Connell, he'll tell us.' She smiled at Jemima. 'You've been a big help.'

'I just wish I'd mentioned it before. It could have been an even bigger help, couldn't it?'

'We don't know that,' said Rachel, as evasive as Ian.

'Just one more thing, Jemima,' said Ian, coming back to them. 'Could you walk us over the area you were supposed to – what? – tidy up?'

'I suppose you could call it that. Yes,' Jemima began to walk back to the house. 'He didn't actually want it landscaped, and by the time I came that day, I was regretting taking it on. He wanted to start here.'

She stopped about a hundred yards from what appeared to be the front entrance of the house. 'And then stretch out right along here and here,' she gestured right and left, 'for about a hundred yards and then fan out in a sort of wedge shape towards the cliff top.'

'So quite an area, then,' said Ian, frowning. 'It certainly gives us parameters.'

'Have you finished with us, then?' asked Libby.

'Yes.' Ian looked at Fran. 'Unless?'

She shook her head.

'You knew that was Nash's house, though,' said Libby.

'Deduction,' said Fran.

Jemima was looking puzzled again.

'I'll take you back to the incident room, then,' said Rachel. 'All right, sir?'

'What was that about?' asked Jemima, on the way back to the car. 'What did he want with you, Fran?'

'She's very noticing,' said Libby airily. 'She picks things up, sometimes.'

Jemima didn't ask any more questions, but still looked puzzled.

'Can we leave our cars here while we pop in and see Patti?' Libby asked when they reached the church hall.

'Of course,' said Rachel. 'Thank you so much for coming, Jemima. It really was a huge help.'

'Don't you want a formal statement?' asked Libby.

'DCI Connell would have said if he wanted one. We'll be in touch if we want anything else.' She turned back to Jemima. 'I'm sure Libby will keep you posted – if you want her to.'

'Of course I do.' Jemima grinned at Libby. 'Now I've got involved I need to know!'

Rachel went in to the church hall, and Jemima went to her rather battered 4x4.

'Will you keep me up to date, Libby?'

'Of course.' Libby glanced at Fran. 'Tell you what – are you over this way again soon? Or near Nethergate?'

'Ah, yes.' Fran picked up the hint. 'If you are, perhaps you could come and meet us at my house for coffee, or lunch. By that time, we'll know more.'

'I'd like that!' Jemima brightened. 'I'm actually over this way on Friday. I won't be free until the afternoon, though.'

'That's all right,' said Fran. 'Lib can come over, and you ring when you're on your way. I live on Harbour Street, right opposite the beach in Nethergate.'

'I know it! Great. I shall only be about ten minutes away. I'll see you then.' She got in her car and rattled off into the village street.

'I was worried she'd want to hang around,' said Libby.

'I could see you were,' said Fran with a grin. 'But she's nice – I like her.'

'So do I. In other circumstances, I'd have asked her to the pub tonight, but we can't talk about all this in front of her. At least – not yet. Come on – Patti will be waiting.'

Patti was indeed, waiting, and to Libby's horror, so was Alice Gay.

'Alice!' Libby tried, and failed, to sound pleased. 'How nice to see you after all this time.'

Alice gave a somewhat vinegary smile. 'Well, now you're looking into something else for the village, and as I introduced you in the first place . . .'

'Always grateful for that, Alice,' said Patti. 'You remember Fran, don't you?'

'Of course,' said Alice, leaving 'how could I forget' carefully unspoken.

'Tea? Or coffee?' asked Patti. 'If you've got time, of course.'

From which Libby inferred that lunch wasn't on offer because Alice would have wheedled an invitation.

'Coffee, please,' said Fran. Libby nodded and Patti switched on the kettle.

'So is there any news about the body?' asked Alice, her nose almost twitching. Patti rolled her eyes.

'The body with the lawnmower?' asked Fran innocently. 'Nothing yet.'

'No! The new one. The one they found the other day. It was a girl, wasn't it?'

'No idea,' said Libby. 'They don't know anything about it yet.'

'Ah, but they do.' Alice sat back with a satisfied nod. 'Bob met one of those crime investigator people in the pub. He said it was a girl.'

'Do you mean a scenes of crime officer?' said Fran. 'He shouldn't have been talking about a current investigation in a pub!'

'You do!' said Alice.

'Only to people who are involved,' said Libby. 'That was well out of order, Alice. I hope Bob isn't spreading it about.'

Alice's face was now an unlovely red. 'Of course not,' she said. 'Well, I'd better get back.' She tried a smile, which didn't come off. 'On grandson-sitting duty, I'm afraid.'

'Your Tracey's boy? Do you still pick him up?'

'He's a bit old for that, now.' Alice stood up and pulled her brown coat around her more firmly. 'Don't bother to see me out, Patti. Nice to see you Libby – Fran.' And she whisked through the kitchen door.

'Phew!' said Patti, leaning back in her chair. 'OK, still coffee? Or wine?'

'Much as I'd like wine,' said Libby, 'we're both driving – and you will be later this afternoon.'

'All right.' With a reluctant grin, Patti stood up and went back to the kettle. 'So what happened with Jemima?'

Between them, they related the events of the last hour.

'I think Jemima was a bit fazed by it all,' said Fran. 'That's the trouble with someone coming in from outside.'

'Definitely wondered about you,' said Libby.

'Yes, that's why I said she could come over to see us. We'll have to explain.' Fran sighed. 'No point trying to hide it. It's too well known, now.'

'Sounds as though she might well turn up at Wednesday evening meetings,' said Patti, putting mugs on the table.

'After this is over, possibly,' said Libby. 'What did Alice really want?'

'Just being nosy. She saw you arrive at the church hall on her way to the shop. Thought she'd get something out of you. Playing the "old friends" card.'

'Huh,' said Libby.

Shortly after this, Fran and Libby left.

'See you tonight,' said Patti.

'What a social whirl,' said Fran, as they walked back to their cars. 'No wonder you get bored without an investigation.'

'Or panto,' said Libby.

'Yes.' Fran dug her in the ribs. 'Won't do that again, will you?'

'As long as they let me come back after two years off,' said Libby. 'I do miss panto.'

'We'll come up this evening,' said Fran. 'I want to see what Ian's got to say.'

'If he's able to get away,' said Libby. 'He didn't say he could.'

'He never knows,' said Fran. 'Go on, off you go. I'll see you later.'

Libby drove slowly home to Steeple Martin deep in thought. What was worrying her now was what Ian and his team might have discovered in the entrance to the tunnel. She couldn't help but suspect that it might be another body.

Chapter Twenty

Fran and Guy arrived at Allhallow's Lane that evening and walked to the pub with Libby and Ben.

'Is this going to be a post-mortem on the Nick Nash investigation?' asked Ben.

'And the discovery of the other body,' said Libby.

'And whether any more have been found,' said Fran.

'That was what I was worried about, too.' Libby turned to Ben. 'It was that tunnel, you see.'

'Like the one you found before,' said Ben. 'Yes, you told me.'

'The one you found where something – or someone – was landed on the beach and taken up to the cliff top?' asked Guy.

'That's the one. I'm not saying it's exactly the same one, but it's similar.'

'The original would have been blocked up,' said Fran.

'But surely they would have looked for others,' said Ben.

'Perhaps they did. If so, I can't think why they didn't check them before,' said Libby.

'Well, no doubt we'll find out – if Ian's allowed to tell you.' Guy tucked his arm into Fran's. 'Come on, there's a pint waiting with my name on it.'

Fran and Guy had decided to stay overnight with Libby and Ben, so no one had to drive home.

Anne and Patti were already at the pub with Peter, but as yet, there was no sign of Ian.

'No news, I suppose?' said Patti.

'No. How are you, Anne?' Libby settled herself next to the wheelchair.

'Same as usual,' said Anne, ever cheerful.

'Here's Colin and Gerry,' Fran turned and waved.

The drinks had just arrived at the table when Edward and Ian walked in.

'Full house tonight, then,' said Ian, leaning back in his chair and crossing his legs. 'Did you warn everyone, Lib?'

She grinned. 'No. We're just here for the company.'

'So not because you want to know what happened after you left today?'

There was an immediate chorus of protest.

'What were you doing today?' asked Colin. 'Has something been happening?'

'We – er – went to – to . . .' Libby looked at Ian.

'It's all right. Everyone knows about the body we found on Nash's land. Well, Libby found the gardener for us—'

'With Patti's help.'

'With Patti's help,' Ian smiled at her, 'and she came to show us where she was supposed to start on the landscaping.'

'Why did you want to know that?' asked Gerry.

'In order to make sure we were searching the right area.'

'And were you?'

'We were.' Ian glanced at Patti, who was looking pale. 'You don't need to know any more details.'

'Or who it was?' asked Fran.

'Not positively. DNA and other results don't come in as quickly as they do on television, I'm afraid.'

Libby recognised this as a sign that no more discussion of the case would take place and changed the subject. 'How's the flat coming along, Colin?'

Everyone else was quick to follow her lead, except Gerry, who still looked puzzled. When Ian excused himself to take a phone call,

Libby leant across. 'He only tells us what he's allowed to,' she said. 'We'll find out in time.'

'But—' began Gerry, just as Ian returned.

'Sorry, folks, I'm going to have to go. I've ordered a taxi, Edward, and checked that yours is still booked.'

He left in a flurry of goodbyes.

'Does he ever relax?' asked Gerry.

'Oh, yes!' Edward laughed. 'I live in the flat beneath his, don't forget. When he's relaxing, all you hear is very loud bursts of Mahler.'

'Classical music fan, is he? I never knew that,' said Ben.

'No, but it figures,' said Fran. 'Goes with the rather austere personality.'

'He's not always austere,' said Libby.

'And forbidding,' said Patti.

'Scary,' agreed Anne.

'I'd love to see him let his hair down,' said Gerry.

Libby carefully avoided looking at Fran, with whom Ian had had a very brief relationship before she and Guy got together. She was probably the only person in the group who actually had seen him let his hair down.

Over a nightcap back at Allhallow's Lane, Fran and Libby discussed plans.

'We can't do anything until we know what the police are doing,' said Fran.

'I suppose not.' Libby pulled at her lower lip. 'I still want to know about Sergeant Peacock, though.'

'Ian told you he was still alive.'

'I know, but that was all.'

'Because, if I remember rightly, he said there was no concrete evidence.'

'Perhaps we ought to find some.'

'How? If the police can't.'

'I don't know.' Libby shifted in her seat. 'I wonder what was so urgent in that phone call? Must have been something to do with the case.'

Ben looked over from his seat at the table. 'Are you two still picking it over?'

'She is,' said Fran. 'I'm trying not to!'

Fran and Guy left early the following morning, and Ben persuaded Libby to help him at the Hop Pocket. Redecoration was almost complete, and the bar furniture, sourced from a specialist supplier, was due to be delivered.

Once again, Libby found the process of helping out with something purely physical a rather soothing distraction. This time, there were no interruptions, and at lunchtime, the new furniture arrived, followed swiftly by Harry and Peter, bearing a picnic lunch.

'Have you closed the caff?' asked Libby, surprised.

'Donna's in charge. I'll go and prep for tonight later.' Harry began unpacking his basket. 'Pete tells me Ian wasn't forthcoming last night?'

'Too many people, probably,' said Ben. 'Gerry's still an unknown quantity, after all, and mixed up in the case.'

'Only on the periphery,' objected Libby.

'As far as you know,' said Peter, leaning against the bar and stretching out his legs. 'He seems nice enough, but . . .'

'Exactly,' said Harry. 'You ought to know that by now, young Lib.'

'All very well trusting Patti and Anne – he's known them a long time, now. But not Gerry – or even Colin, come to that,' said Ben.

'I thought Colin was a friend now!' said Libby.

'Yes, but we've not known him long. I like him, we all do, but we also know that we can often like the bad guys.'

Libby repeated this rather dispiriting conversation to Fran later that afternoon.

'I have to agree with them,' said Fran. 'That's why I think we have to be careful what we say to Jemima tomorrow.'

'Just fill her in on past activities, perhaps? After all, she can hardly be involved in this, can she?'

'Why not? She discovered Nash's body, and she was surveying the land.'

'Don't, Fran! I shall become paranoid!'

Libby's normally optimistic attitude had reasserted itself by Friday when she arrived at Coastguard Cottage.

'Jemima's on her way,' reported Fran. 'So let's just be upbeat and jolly, shall we?'

'I don't know about jolly,' said Libby, 'but definitely upbeat.'

Jemima arrived bearing a box of home-made biscuits. 'Gluten free,' she said. 'Just in case.'

Fran made coffee and brought it into the living room. 'Now,' she said. 'What can we tell you?'

'I looked you up,' said Jemima. 'Apparently you've worked with the police several times. And you,' she said to Fran, 'are apparently a psychic.'

Fran looked uncomfortable, so Libby answered for her.

'Only in a mild way. And DCI Connell takes her seriously. She's saved lives in the past.'

Jemima was round eyed. 'Really?'

Libby embarked on a brief history of Cases We Have Solved, with particular reference to Fran's 'moments'.

'They don't happen very often these days,' said Fran, 'but Ian's always hopeful. He hoped I'd pick up something on Wednesday, but I didn't.'

'What about your vicar friend – is she all right with it?'

'All modern diocese have Deliverance Ministers – the people who used to run so-called Exorcisms. She's fine with it, and tends to quote the *Hamlet* line at people.'

'The what?'

'You know: "There are more things in heaven and earth, Horatio, than are dreamt of in your philosophy." That one.'

'Oh.' Jemima looked slightly bemused.

'Anyway, now you've got the background.'

'How do you come to be involved this time?'

Fran took over. 'Libby was approached by some of Patti's parishioners because we'd helped in a previous case concerning St Aldeberge. They were concerned because Nick Nash had once been a churchwarden.'

Neatly sidestepping the issue of young girls, thought Libby.

'I see. So the police ask you in case people talk to you when they wouldn't tell them?'

'More or less,' said Libby. 'Mind you, I'm nosy, so I don't mind. It just gets rather uncomfortable, some times.'

There was a pause while they all drank coffee.

'Have you heard any more about that tunnel they found yesterday?'

'Nothing,' said Fran.

'But then, we aren't police, or even intimately involved with the investigation, so there's no reason why we would,' said Libby.

'Frustrating,' said Jemima.

'And the other thing is, we might let something slip to the wrong person,' said Fran. 'So best not to tell us in the first place.'

'Well,' said Jemima, helping herself to a biscuit, 'I can assure you I'm safe! I tend to work alone, and I don't socialise much. I've been to supper a couple of times with your cousin, Libby. They're a nice couple.'

'Libby virtually introduced them,' said Fran.

'No I didn't! They already knew one another because Cass was an online customer of Mike's. It just happened that she came to stay when Mike was involved in something we were doing at the theatre.'

'I can't imagine Mike doing anything theatrical!' laughed Jemima. 'Tell me about the theatre.'

The next hour passed pleasantly with Libby and Fran regaling her with theatrical tales.

'And Libby's missing panto this season, because someone else is doing it.' Fran grinned at her friend.

'I love panto,' said Libby. 'But you can't do it all the time.'

Jemima laughed. 'I'll come and see your next one.' She stood up. 'You will keep me posted, won't you?'

'As far as we can,' said Libby, 'of course.'

'I still like her,' she said, as Fran closed the door. 'And I don't think she's got anything to do with this case.'

'Doesn't seem like it, certainly. And she wasn't unduly curious about it, either.' Fran picked up the mugs. 'Do you want more coffee?'

'No thanks. I ought to get back and see how Ben's getting on at the Pocket.'

'Open in time for Christmas?' asked Fran.

'If he could get staff by then, perhaps,' said Libby, 'but there's a lot left to do.' She gathered up her basket and coat. 'Will I see you over the weekend?'

'Is something happening, then?'

'Not that I know about. Will let you know if there is.'

That was when her mobile rang.

Chapter Twenty-one

'Libby.'

Libby, surprised, mouthed 'Ian' at Fran.

'Hello, Ian.'

'You're not at home.'

'No. I'm at Fran's. We've been having coffee with Jemima Routledge.'

'You didn't tell her anything, did you?'

'Nothing to tell. She wanted to know about our previous adventures.'

'Hmm.' Ian paused. 'I've got two pieces of information for you. Please keep them to yourself – yourselves – but I have to tell you because you may be contacted by people concerned.'

'That sounds . . . ominous.'

'Yes. Well, the first is the body of the female.'

Libby sat down again abruptly.

'I'm afraid it is Kerry Palmer. Identified by dental records.'

Libby's stomach dipped. 'It's Kerry,' she said to Fran.

'And the second, if you've recovered?'

Libby made an inarticulate noise.

'I'm afraid we found more remains.

Fran was by her side, arm round her shoulders. Libby held out the phone.

'Ian? Libby seems rather shocked . . . OK . . . I see. Yes, I'll tell her. All right.' Fran ended the call and handed the phone back to Libby.

'More bodies?' whispered Libby.

'Yes. One male, one female, both young, they think.'

'Oh, God.' Libby hid her face in her hands.

'Ian wants to talk to us about our gossipy women. He may have to interview them. Including Amy and Angela. And Sarah, of course.'

Libby sat back. 'I can see that. I suppose he's already spoken to Kerry's mum?'

'He didn't say, but I expect so.'

'When does he want to talk to us? And where?'

'He said we could decide that. It's to be informal until he knows more. He said he's free, as far as he knows, this evening and hopefully, tomorrow evening.' Fran smiled. 'So it looks like another trip to Steeple Martin for me.'

'I could come here,' said Libby.

'Better for Ian at yours. I'll ring him and let him know.'

Ben wasn't entirely surprised when Libby announced they were to have visitors that evening.

'Tell her to bring Guy and we'll go to the pub. Always nice to have an excuse,' he said, dropping a kiss on top of her head.

Fran arrived just before Ian.

'What do you suppose he wants to talk about?' said Libby, after Guy and Ben had departed for the pub. 'We've told him everything already.'

'But that was more or less unofficial,' said Fran. 'This time he's got to take notice.'

'But he said this was informal.'

'But he's going to follow it up properly this time.'

When he arrived, Ian confirmed this.

'Frankly, I'm kicking myself for not taking it more seriously in the first place,' he said. 'By the way, Edward's gone to join Ben and Guy at the pub. We can join them later, if you like.'

'So what can we do?' asked Libby.

'Let's go over everything you were told by your various informants,' said Ian, taking out a tablet and swiping the screen. 'I've got notes I made at the time, so I can prompt you, if anything gets forgotten.'

'Patti was with me when I spoke to Amy and her family, not Fran, so you might need to check with her.'

'I shall speak to her anyway,' said Ian. 'Now, let's start with Patti's phone call to you about . . .' he referred to the screen, 'Connie and Elaine.'

Painstakingly, they went through every conversation they'd had and everything they'd learnt since Nick Nash's body was first found.

'Right,' said Ian, when they were up to date. 'Now tell me again what you were concerned about that we hadn't followed up.'

'Sergeant Peacock, for a start, although you said you'd discovered he was still alive,' said Fran. 'Libby was, anyway.'

'Tell me why, Libby.'

Libby thought for a moment. 'I suppose I was guilty of stereotyping. Peacock not only helped run the youth club and attended the meetings with Nash and the vicar, but he ran the Scout troop, and you know what they used to say about scoutmasters.'

'Is that all?'

'Well, no. He seemed to head off any enquiry into what was going on, when you would have thought he would at least have wanted to provide reassurance to the villagers.'

'Point taken. Right – what else?'

'The Pam girl. Everyone said she was really the only one apart from Kerry who really disappeared.'

'We've been trying to find out more about her,' said Ian, but we keep hitting a dead end.'

'Liz Palmer said she'd turned up in Dover,' said Fran.

'But we can't trace her there. We can't trace her mother, either.'

'Liz might tell you now you've found Kerry,' said Libby. 'She didn't want to give anything away before.'

'Pam White, wasn't it?' mused Fran. 'Not exactly an unusual name.'

'We checked with the school,' said Ian. 'They knew nothing other than her address when she still lived in St Aldeberge.'

'Well,' said Libby, 'if she was in Dover six months afterwards, it can't be her in the ground, can it? Not if the bodies are all the same age.' She thought for a moment. 'I suppose it still could be her, actually. Do you know yet when they were buried?'

Ian shook his head. 'Not exactly. We've been assuming it was at the same time that Kerry disappeared, at least for her. The other two, it's merely a guess. Someone knew about the tunnel, though.'

'And one was a boy.' Libby frowned.

'Gives weight to your scoutmaster theory,' said Ian.

'You don't take that seriously, though,' said Libby.

'There's as much abuse of boys as there is of girls,' said Ian.

'I just want to know how they were persuaded,' said Fran. 'I mean, twenty years ago children would have been aware of that sort of thing, surely.'

'Not as much as they are now,' said Ian. 'And there wasn't so much opportunity for online grooming there is now.'

'Do you think that was what it was?' said Libby. 'Grooming, of a sort?'

'Possibly. I think I have to talk to Sarah Elliot.'

'I'd do it without her mum, though,' said Libby. 'Nice though she is.'

'Hopefully Sarah's gone home. You said she was there on a visit?'

'Yes. I get the feeling Angela's still a very protective mum, though.'

'Well, I don't think there's anything more I need.' Ian put away his tablet. 'Do you fancy joining the others at the pub?'

They found Ben, Guy, and Edward at their table in the small bar.

'We've just been playing darts,' said Edward.

'And he beat us hollow,' said Guy.

'Did you do whatever it was you wanted to do?' asked Ben.

Ian nodded, before giving his order to Tim.

'But it wasn't much,' said Libby. 'We could have done it here.'

'It would have been too boring for everyone else,' said Ian.

'At least Colin and Gerry weren't here,' said Fran. 'They would have been curious.'

'Naturally enough,' said Edward. 'Not that I know much about it.'

Libby grinned. 'More than you should, probably.'

On Saturday morning, as she was preparing to go for her weekly shop to the supermarket in Canterbury, Libby was surprised to receive a phone call from Maria Stewart. Maria was married to former rock star Ron Stewart, who had helped out on previous investigations, including the most recent which had involved Colin Hardcastle and, interestingly, Felling.

'Libby, tell me if we're butting in, but we were talking to Mike Farthing yesterday, and he told us you were involved in this body that was found near St Aldeberge.'

'Yes? Nice to hear from you, by the way.'

'And you. Sorry we only seem to get in touch when there's something unpleasant going on.'

'Story of my life,' said Libby.

'Well, Ron remembered something that struck him as a bit odd at the time.'

'Oh?'

'You remember we told you about those girls and that party they all went to? Well, there was something about the policeman that was supposed to be involved.'

'I thought that it wasn't reported to the police at the time?'

'Officially, it wasn't. But Ron heard, through the grapevine, that this policeman ran some sort of boys' club.'

'That doesn't sound suspicious.'

'No, but it seemed it was being kept quiet. We don't know if it helps or not – it just seemed a bit odd. We heard that this business of the body on the Dunton Estate had some sort of link with a youth club or something—'

'And a scout troop run by a policeman!' said Libby. 'Yes, I see.'

'It does sound a bit tenuous, doesn't it?' said Maria. 'I think we could be putting two and two together and making five.'

'I do that all the time,' said Libby. 'But it could mean something. We did actually ask the police to look into this policeman – apparently he's still alive.'

'Well, he wouldn't be much more than sixty at the most,' said Maria.

'Police say he's in his seventies.'

'I do hope we haven't set you off on a false trail.'

'No, it's very helpful,' said Libby. 'I just wish we had the resources of the police.'

'But you're working with them, aren't you?'

'Yes, but as usual, we mustn't interfere. Only do what DCI Connell tells us.'

'Ah! Your nice policeman. How is he? And Fran?'

They fell to discussing mutual acquaintances before Libby rang off and called Fran.

'I'm in the shop,' she said. 'We're getting busy on Saturdays.'

'Sorry, but I just had a call from Maria Stewart.' Libby reported what Maria had said.

'It is a bit tenuous, as she said. But I wondered if Peacock still ran his boys' club.'

'If it is Peacock,' said Fran.

'Seems a bit of a coincidence too far,' said Libby. 'How could we find out?'

'No idea. Look I've got to go. I'll call you later.'

Libby drove to Canterbury musing on what she'd heard. It was indeed tenuous, and, as Maria had said, it probably was two and two making five. But how could she find out?

By the time she returned from Canterbury, she was thoroughly dispirited. There seemed to be nothing more she and Fran could do to help Ian's investigation, whichever way she looked at it. The more she thought about it, the less relevant the boys' club seemed to be.

The rest of Saturday was uneventful. On Sunday morning she and Ben went for a walk round the village before getting ready for the weekly lunch with Hetty. Ben wisely kept quiet about the investigation, but Libby was still brooding. However, when they reached home, there was another surprise. Once again, Patti called.

'Another Sunday morning call?' said Libby. 'What is it this time? More parishioner's gossip?'

'Sort of.' Patti sounded worried. 'Look, I didn't want to worry you, and I did think I ought to tell Ian, but . . .'

'What?'

'When I came out of church after seeing off the last of the congregation, there was a little group waiting for me.'

'Group? Who?'

'I don't know any of them. There were four women and a man. All around mid-thirties, I would say.'

'And? Come on, Patti, spit it out. Was it important?'

'I think it could be.' Patti took a deep breath. 'They wanted to talk about . . . you know.'

'No, I don't. What?'

'Nick Nash.'

Chapter Twenty-two

'What do I do now?' Libby asked Ben when she came off the phone.

'Tell Ian.'

'But they wanted to talk to me.'

'This is way beyond you, now,' said Ben. 'Ian needs to know. Have you got a contact number?'

'Patti has. I said I couldn't take it now, I'd ring her back later.'

'They won't be expecting an immediate response, will they? Leave it for now and think about it.'

'They might clam up if Ian barges in.'

'Ian never barges in.' Ben smiled at her. 'Come on, let's go to lunch.'

But when they arrived at the Manor, it was to find both Edward and Ian at the kitchen table.

'What are you doing here?' Libby blurted out.

There was another of the chorus of protests which so frequently greeted Libby's remarks.

'I was invited to lunch,' said Ian, smiling. 'What have you got to hide?'

Libby felt heat creeping into her cheeks. 'Nothing!'

'You are a terrible liar,' said Edward. 'Shall I go outside? Then I won't hear what you've got to say.'

'Don't be silly,' said Ian. 'Come on, Libby – what have you turned up now?'

Libby turned desperately to Ben.

'Some people approached Patti saying they wanted to talk about Nick Nash,' said Ben. 'I do wish everyone would be honest right from the start. If people know the police are looking into Nash's death, why don't they come out with it straight away?'

'Always the way,' said Ian. 'People are scared of saying the wrong thing. So, Libby, who are they?'

'Patti doesn't know. They were waiting for her after morning service. A group in their thirties. She's got a phone number.'

'Go on, you can phone,' said Hetty from the Aga. 'Time before dinner.'

'And they wanted to talk to Patti? Or the police?' asked Edward.

'Libby,' said Ben.

'Ah.' Ian nodded. 'This will be on the back of Connie and Elaine?'

'And Amy, I would imagine. And possibly Sarah,' said Libby. 'You said you were going to talk to her?'

'We are. And don't worry, Sergeant Peacock and Pam White are also on the list.'

'Sounds like Cluedo,' said Libby.

'So it does!' said Ben, much struck. 'I used to love Cluedo.'

'Anyway, Libby, don't worry about it,' said Ian. 'Get the number from Patti and tell her you're going to pass it on to me.'

'She'll think I've betrayed her and these people.'

'Then why doesn't she call them herself and explain?' suggested Ian. 'We can't let this slip.'

Flo and Lenny arrived and put a stop to all talk of the murders, and Libby tried to forget all about them.

But Flo wasn't having any of it.

'Come on, then, gal. What's going on?' She poured herself a generous glass of wine and peered at Libby over the top.

Libby glanced nervously at Ian.

'Nothing to report, Flo,' said Ian. 'It isn't always like the TV.'

'I know that.' Flo sniffed. 'Len and me want to know if you found any o' them Spanish tykes.'

'An' that woman,' added Lenny.

'Woman?' echoed Edward.

'Nick Nash's ex-wife.' Ian was amused. 'Not yet, Lenny. Why are you interested?'

Lenny shrugged. 'Just wondered.'

Libby eyed Edward, who was looking decidedly shifty. He shook his head at her.

They ate roast beef, Yorkshire pudding, roast potatoes, cabbage, and peas, followed by blackberry crumble, and all sat back replete.

'At least Ian eats properly when he comes here,' said Edward. 'I don't think he eats at all during the week sometimes.'

'Always welcome,' said Hetty gruffly. 'Go on, then, load up the dishwasher. I'll do the pots later.'

She, Flo, and Lenny retired to her sitting room while the others cleared the table.

'He wouldn't have talked while they were there, anyway,' said Edward quietly to Libby, nodding towards where Ian was decanting the remains of the crumble into a dish.

'Why, is there something to tell?' asked Libby.

'Might be,' said Edward.

Ian turned round.

'Strictly off the record,' he said, 'We've got a trace.'

'Where?' asked Libby.

'Don't pester,' said Ben.

'I can't tell you yet. But it's another line of enquiry. And we've now got rather a lot to look into, so don't hold your breath.' Ian put another dish in the dishwasher. 'Are you going to Peter and Harry's?'

'As usual,' said Ben.

'I won't come with you, if you don't mind,' said Ian. 'While I can, I ought to catch up with things at home.'

Ian left and Edward, Ben, and Libby walked down the drive to Peter and Harry's cottage.

'Are you keeping him in line?' asked Libby. 'You sound more like flatmates than neighbours.'

'He's there so little of the time,' said Edward. 'It's handy for me to take in post, put the bins out, and so on. And lend a sympathetic ear if necessary.'

'And is it? Necessary?' asked Ben.

'Sometimes.' Edward grinned sideways. 'Little helper, that's me. He knows I can keep my mouth shut and it does him good to off-load in the evenings if he's had a bad day. And it can help iron out problems.'

'Lucky Ian,' said Libby, subduing a twinge of jealousy.

'Ian needed a friend,' said Ben suddenly. 'I don't know what other friends he has, but in our group it's almost all couples, and just by virtue of his job he was a loner.'

'Exactly,' said Edward. 'And it's not as if he had a romantic partner. He says he couldn't commit anyway.'

'And you'd hate it if he did,' said Ben to Libby. 'Be honest.'

Peter let them into the cottage, where Harry, as usual, lounged on a sofa in his chef's whites.

'OK,' he said after one look at Libby's face. 'What's happened now?'

'Nothing,' said Ben. 'Just Libby being disgruntled.'

When they'd caught their hosts up on recent events, Harry was obviously all ready to dissect the news.

'I'm interested in this ex-wife,' he said. 'I always thought she was the obvious suspect.'

'She looked like it,' said Libby, 'but then Ian, and Colin, said she'd disappeared, and anyway, she was left nothing in the will.'

'If they were still married,' said Peter, 'even if she'd been cut out, she'd be entitled to make a claim on the estate, wouldn't she?'

'I think so,' said Ben, 'but wouldn't you think, if he really was mixed up with a gang of ne'er-do-wells on the Costas, most of his money would be hidden?'

'Even the houses?' said Harry.

'Maybe not them.'

'Well, Ian did sort of intimate that the police had a trace on her,' said Libby. She looked at Edward. 'Do they?'

He grinned. 'Maybe. He doesn't tell me everything!'

'Stop being so nosy!' said Ben.

'Can't be done,' said Peter. 'The old trout has "nosy" written right through her.'

On Monday morning, Libby did as she was bidden and called Patti.

'Ian says will you phone the number those people gave you and say that you must tell Ian. The police. I'm sorry, Patti, if it seems like a betrayal, but he says it's important. And I can see it is.'

'I know.' Patti sounded sad. 'And I'll do it. But before then, I want you to give Ian the number. I don't know which of the group it belongs to, but I suppose it doesn't matter.'

She gave Libby the number and rang off. Libby sent it in a text to Ian and sat staring out of the window at the rain which poured down outside, almost turning Allhallow's Lane into a stream.

What to do now? 'Think, Libby,' she told herself. 'What aspect of this case could you find out about?' Rarely did she find herself at such a loss, but then, rarely was she so little personally involved. She pulled the laptop towards her. There must be something.

After staring fruitlessly at the screen for some time, she gave up, collected her basket and coat, and left the house.

The high street was deserted. She hesitated outside the eight 'til late, decided against it, and walked on.

'Oi! Libby!'

She came to a halt. Harry was leaning against the door jamb of the café.

'You're in a brown study,' he said. 'What's up?'

'I'm stuck.' She wandered towards him.

'To what?'

'On the case.'

Harry tilted his head. 'On that there murder case the police are investigating, by any chance?'

'Stop it.' Libby sighed. 'I don't know what to do.'

'Look, petal, it's not your job. Leave it to Ian and his merry men and women. They know what they're doing.'

'And I don't?'

'You haven't got their resources,' said Harry tactfully.

'No.' Libby sighed again. 'I tell myself that every day.'

'What we've got to do,' continued Harry, pushing himself upright and holding open the door, 'is find you something else to do. Coffee? There's some on.'

'OK.' Libby followed him inside. 'Go on then, think of something.'

'Well, I did actually, last night. Only I doubt if anyone will approve.'

Libby brightened. 'Sounds like my sort of thing.'

'How about,' said Harry, filling two mugs, 'doing a bit of research?'

'Research? On what?'

'One,' Harry held up a finger, 'boys' clubs, and two, Nick Nash's wife.'

Libby stared. 'You think they're connected?'

'Of course not, you wassock! Separately. See if there's something dodgy about local boys' clubs – and see if you can find anything about Mrs Nash.'

'Where will that get me?'

'I've no idea, that's up to you.' He put the mugs down on the table. 'I just started thinking last night. First, what sort of woman was Mrs Nash, what links might she have to the area, that sort of thing and then, youth clubs – or boys' clubs. What might go on in them. Were they open to abuse? That's what you've been thinking, isn't it?'

'Well, yes, but I expect the police are going to look into that aspect now. Especially with one of these latest bodies being a boy.'

'I don't suppose you'd be able to look into this particular one, but you could find out what sort of things went on. It might give you somewhere to look.'

'I could . . .' said Libby.

'And Mrs Nash. If you could find out if she was known in the area – well, you could do some nosing around. And that's what you're missing.' He sat back and looked at her triumphantly.

Libby laughed. 'You were right, they wouldn't approve. How do you suggest I go about it?'

'You've got a computer, haven't you? Online.'

'The thing is,' said Libby, 'from all I've heard, Mrs N didn't come from here, and Nash wasn't married when he lived here. I rather gathered that he'd met her in Spain. She was part of the ex-pat community.'

'But she was English, wasn't she? I thought it was rather implied that Nash was going to live permanently in Spain to get away from her.'

'Yes, it was, wasn't it?' Libby frowned. 'Perhaps she had a home here before they married and kept it on, the same as he did. But not in Kent.'

'Well, it would be nice to find out,' said Harry.

'Mmm . . . And boys' clubs?'

'I'm pretty sure you could Google "abuse in boys' clubs". Bet you'd find something.'

'But not about Felling or St Aldeberge. Anyway, I've got a feeling we might be about to learn about Nash's activities very soon.'

'Oh?'

'I told you yesterday, Patti had some people asking to see me.'

'And you've passed it on to Ian?'

'Of course. I'd only have told him afterwards, anyway. I don't suppose they'll be too pleased, but they ought to have gone to the police in the first place.'

'Of course they should, dear heart, but you don't always, do you?' Harry grinned. 'Drink your coffee. I've got ordering to do.'

After leaving the Pink Geranium, Libby went into the eight 'til late after all and managed to find something for dinner, before turning for home. It was just as she reached Allhallow's Lane that a taxi

162

stopped on the corner opposite. After a moment a young woman got out, bundled up in a sheepskin coat. Anxious not to appear to stare, Libby hurried on, slightly puzzled, but did turn back a little way along the lane. The woman was staring at something in her hand and not moving. The temptation to ask if she could help was almost overwhelming, but somehow she restrained herself and continued into her cottage.

And five minutes later, Colin rang.

Chapter Twenty-three

'Are you alone?' Colin sounded breathless.

'Yes – why?'

'I've just seen Simone Nash.'

The woman in the taxi, Libby guessed immediately.

'Was she wearing a big sheepskin coat?'

'Yes – how did you know?'

Libby explained. 'Where did you see her?'

'Just going into the pub. She must be asking for me.'

'I suppose so,' said Libby. 'You ought to tell Ian.'

'Really?'

'Of course! Look, what are you doing now?'

'Unpacking. The furniture arrived this morning.'

'Is the van still there?'

'No, why?'

'Because she might see it. I take it you don't want to see her?'

'I certainly bloody don't!'

'Then phone Ian – or nice Sergeant Rachel. And don't answer the door!'

'She won't find me here!'

'She will if she asks in the pub. They know where you are.'

'Couldn't you phone Ian?'

'I can't keep phoning him! Go on – if I did it, it would simply be hearsay.'

All right.' Colin was grumpy. 'Can I phone you back?'

'Yes. Go on.'

'Well,' said Libby to Sidney, 'that was a coincidence! Do you think she heard us through the ether?'

Sidney turned his back and curled his tail round his nose.

The phone rang again.

'I spoke to someone who said they would pass the message on,' said Colin. 'What shall I do now?'

'Have you told Gerry?'

'No, he's gone to London to see his solicitor. He wants to get everything in place before he finds a house.'

'Do you want me to come round? Or pop into the pub and find out if she's there?'

'Could you come here and pop into the pub on the way?'

Libby sighed and grinned to herself ruefully. 'OK. I'm just going to make myself a sandwich first.'

'Oh – I suppose I ought to eat something,' said Colin. 'But I can't go out . . .'

'All right, I'll bring you a sandwich. Ham all right?'

Sandwiches made, Libby went out again, wondering what she would do if she came face to face with Simone Nash. In fact, once inside the pub, there was no sign of her. Tim spotted her and came out from behind the bar.

'Someone asking for Colin in the other bar,' he said quietly. 'I said I knew him but he wasn't staying here.'

'Well done,' said Libby. 'Keep to it – she's a person of interest, as they say.'

'In this murder?' Tim's eyes widened.

'More than one, but yes. I'll nip off, now. See you later.'

She darted across the road and round to the back of the Garden building. Colin waited at the top of the steps.

'It's all right, she's in there, but Tim hasn't said where you are.'

'I must buy him a very large drink,' said Colin. 'So what do you think will happen now?'

'No idea. I just hope your message gets passed on.'

'What do you think she wants?' Colin led the way into the large open plan space that was combined kitchen and living room. 'You can actually sit down, now!'

Libby perched on the edge of a plastic wrapped armchair. 'I would imagine she wants to know what happened. What I'd also like to know is how she found out. Ian said the police hadn't traced her, so who told her? Has it been in the papers?' 'She could have been in touch with someone who knew Nick.'

'Could have been. When did she leave Spain?'

'I'm not sure,' Colin told her. 'All I know is she'd gone by the time Nick told me he was selling the house. Could have been any time in the last year.'

'So she's likely to still have friends and contacts over there.' She stood up again. 'Which window did you see her from earlier? This one looks out at the back.'

'Bedroom,' said Colin. 'Look.'

Libby followed him into a smaller room which looked out at the high street and had a perfect view of the pub, the Pink Geranium, and the Manor drive.

'Well, there's no activity there now,' she said. 'No sign of police cars.'

'Should I ring again?' asked Colin.

'No, they'll only think you're fussing. Leave it for a bit.'

As they went back into the living room, Libby's phone rang.

'It's me,' said Ben. 'Are you with Colin?'

'Yes! How did you know?'

'I've got DS Trent here at the Hop Pocket. She was looking for you. They had a call from Colin, apparently?'

'Yes – can you send her up here? I suppose she didn't know where to find him.'

'That's about right. OK, she's on her way. Tell me all about it later.'

'Sergeant Trent's on her way,' Libby said. 'Can you let her in?'

Colin went and opened the door, looking slightly nervous. Rachel appeared, beaming at them both.

'Now, Mr Hardcastle,' she said. 'What's this about?'

Colin told her.

'And Libby thought I should tell you,' he concluded, 'as Ian – DCI Connell – had said the police hadn't traced her.'

'Quite right,' said Rachel. 'Where is she? Do you know?'

'Half an hour ago she was in the pub,' said Libby. 'I told Tim to keep an eye on her. As far as we know she hasn't come out.'

'I think,' said Rachel, 'I'll see if I can raise DCI Connell. I don't know if he'll want me to bring her in or not.'

'On your own?' said Libby. 'She might refuse to come – or make a run for it.'

'Shall we come over there with you?' said Colin bravely. 'Might it help?'

'Let me try the inspector first.' Rachel turned away, phone to her ear. Colin and Libby exchanged glances.

Rachel turned back. 'Yes, let's go over there. If you don't mind?'

'Course not,' said Libby. Colin shook his head.

Libby led the way down the steps, across the road and into the pub, where Tim met them as soon as they walked in.

'In there,' he said indicating the back bar. 'Just in time. She's finished her lunch.'

'You lead the way,' murmured Rachel to Colin. 'You know what she looks like.'

Colin put his shoulders back and made for the door.

Simone Nash was putting on her sheepskin coat. Her brown hair was stylishly cut and her face immaculately made up. Libby felt distinctly shabby.

'Colin!' Simone stopped pulling on her coat and fixed Colin with what could only be described as a basilisk stare. 'I want to speak to you.'

Colin stood aside. 'Sergeant Trent, this is Simone Nash. Simone, Detective Sergeant Trent.'

Smiling, Rachel stepped up to Simone, whose mouth had dropped open. Libby was aware of a smothered chuckle behind her, and the interested stare of the group of locals at the bar.

'I'm very pleased to meet you, Mrs Nash,' said Rachel. 'We've been looking for you. Shall we step outside?'

'Please don't!' Tim muttered in Libby's ear. She aimed an elbow in his direction.

Simone stayed seated. 'How did you know I was here?' She glared at Tim. 'You told him!'

'No, I didn't,' he said truthfully.

'I did,' said Libby. 'I saw you getting out of a taxi.'

'How did you know who I was?' Simone's voice was growing shrill.

'I saw you from my window,' said Colin.

'And I decided we ought to tell the police,' added Libby.

'Oh, village busybody, eh? Well you won't get anything out of him. Bats for the other team, dearie.' Simone stood up and grabbed her bag. 'I'm going.'

She tried to push past Rachel, Colin, and Libby, but came up against a solid and amused wall of locals.

'I think the nice police lady wants to talk to you – *dearie*!' said the largest of them.

'Thanks, lads,' said Rachel. 'Come on, Mrs Nash. My car's just outside.'

Still Simone resisted, but with the gentlest of persuasion, she was manoeuvred outside, and surrounded by her interested captors, while Rachel darted off to fetch her car.

'You can't do this!' screeched Simone. 'It's illegal!'

'We're helping the police,' said Tim.

'With their enquiries,' added a burly builder. 'Always helpful to the police.'

There was a murmur of assent. Colin, by now, along with Tim, was openly laughing, which was enraging Simone even more.

'You're making her worse,' said Libby. 'Leave off.'

Rachel drew up beside them.

'Shall we go, Mrs Nash? Much quieter, we can talk properly.'

'I don't want to talk to you,' growled Simone.

'No, I'm sure. Especially as you've just lost your husband – I'm very sorry for your loss.'

Tim and the locals looked somewhat abashed, and backed off.

Rachel managed to persuade Simone into her car and looked at Colin. 'I shouldn't ask,' she said, 'but it might help . . .'

'I'll come,' said Colin.

'Shall I follow, so I can bring him back?' asked Libby.

'We could send him home,' said Rachel, 'but I expect you'd prefer . . .?'

'Yes please,' said Colin. 'Thanks, Libby.'

'I'll go and get the car,' she said. 'Tim – give the lads a drink and put it on the slate.'

'Good job I know you,' said Tim, good-humouredly.

'Incident room?' Libby asked as Rachel got into her car.

'See you there.' Rachel waved.

Libby collected her car, called Ben to tell him where she was going, and set off for St Aldeberge.

It was odd, she thought, that just as Harry had advocated looking into Simone Nash, she had turned up, as it were, on the doorstep. It wouldn't, of course, mean that there was anything for Libby to investigate – that had already been turned over to the police – but it was, perhaps, a loose end that could now be tied up. And, who knew, it could be the answer to the mystery.

But, Libby argued with herself, would Simone have had the necessary knowledge and expertise to tamper with the lawnmower, if that was what had been done? Still less, to have the strength to push it, and Nash himself, off the cliff. Though she had to admit, she had assumed the machine, having been tampered with, just hadn't stopped when Nash tried to brake.

She arrived in front of the church hall, and put her head round the door. A police constable noticed and came to speak to her.

'I'm just here to wait for Mr Hardcastle,' she said, looking round, unable to see him.

'Yes,' Mrs Sarjeant, he's in with DCI Connell at the moment. Shall I tell them you're here?' He was watching her carefully.

What's all that about, she wondered. What have I done? 'No, just tell him when he's free I'll be at the vicarage.'

'As long as Patti's in,' she added to herself. Luckily Patti was, and saw her coming.

'What's happened?' she asked immediately. Libby told her.

'Does this mean Ian won't want to speak to those young people?'

'I expect he will. Did you tell them he'd be in touch?'

'It was the man who answered the phone. He didn't sound delighted, but he agreed it was sensible. I didn't ask any questions.'

'Can I wait here?' asked Libby. 'I won't get in your way.'

'Of course you can. I've got to go over to the church, anyway. If you're ready before I get back, just stick your head round the door and shout.'

After Patti had left, Libby wandered into the study. There was a shelf of books about local history, including several about witch-craft, which Libby loved to look at, and she made for these.

She was deep into a small pamphlet discussing the folk culture of Kent when she heard the front door of the vicarage open.

'Hello?' called Colin.

'In here.' Libby closed the pamphlet and stood up. 'How did it go?'

Colin came into the study looking tired.

'I don't know. They couldn't interview her formally with me there, but she wasn't exactly helpful at first. She kept accusing me of telling lies.'

'About her?'

'About her and Nick. I don't actually know what help Sergeant Trent thought I could be.' Colin sank down in a chair. 'She kept saying something about Nick's precious band of hope.'

'What?' Libby was startled. 'That's a religious movement, isn't it?'

'Is it? Whatever it is, she was being nasty about it.'

Libby turned back to the bookshelves. 'There's bound to be a book here,' she muttered.

'There are a lot of books there,' said Colin. 'Shelves of them.'

'No – about youth organisations.'

'Oh, you're on that again.' Colin leant back and shut his eyes. 'I'm exhausted.'

Libby eyed him irritably. 'All right, we'll go home. Come on.'

'Wait here for me,' she said outside the church. 'Just going to let Patti know we're going.'

She shouted 'Going!' round the church door, and Patti popped up from the narthex.

'I think,' she said, face alight, 'I've just found something out.'

Chapter Twenty-four

'What?' Libby looked over her shoulder to where Colin stood impatiently at the end of the path.

'Look, call me when you get home,' said Patti. 'He doesn't look happy.'

'He's not. But listen, to add to coincidences of the day, can I just tell you that Simone Nash mentioned in passing Nick Nash's band of hope. Wasn't that a youth movement?'

Patti laughed. 'It still is. And yes, it is a coincidence. Go on, go home. Call me.'

Once they were in the car, Colin seemed to relax.

'That was pretty horrible. She was just ranting about everything.'

'Where's she staying?'

'I don't know. I just hope she doesn't come after me again.'

'What do you suppose she wanted in the first place?'

'To find out what had happened, I suppose. They very politely chucked me out, saying thank you so much for my help. Do you think they'll tell me later?'

'They might. It depends how much help they still want.'

After dropping Colin in the high street, Libby drove home, and was still going through the front door when she rang Patti.

'Come on – what is it?'

Patti laughed. 'I was talking to an ex-parishioner of mine when you arrived. She dropped in to see me.'

'Why is she ex?'

'She moved. She now lives with her sister in Canterbury, but she used to live here, and – get this – used to be a member of the choir!'

'In Nick Nash's time?'

'Exactly. So of course, I was telling her all about the case. And she said, yes she remembered the girls going missing, but wasn't it to do with the Reverend Turner, not Nash? Because Turner ran the youth club "like a sort of secret society" were her words.'

'Blimey! Why haven't we heard this before?'

'Well, we have, in a way. When Connie and Elaine first came round?'

'But the emphasis has always been on Nash, and how he was blamed.'

'But was that perhaps because his body had been found? So of course that was who people were focusing on.'

By this time, Libby had shed her coat and managed to put the kettle on.

'Is this something else we ought to tell Ian?' she asked.

'I suppose so,' said Patti. 'Personally, I think I'd like to talk to Amy. Or you should. Or Sarah again. They seem more level-headed.'

'What a good idea.' Libby poured water into a mug. 'Do you think I could phone her?'

'I don't see why not. I'll dig out her number, hang on a moment.'

'I was wondering – should I ask her up here? Perhaps to the caff for a meal?'

'Excellent! Yes. Tomorrow lunchtime. Can I come?'

'Wait and see what she says,' said Libby. 'Got the number?' She wrote it down and ended the call. Now it all depended on Amy's availability.

She didn't call Amy's number until she was well into her cup of tea. It needed thinking about. Finally, she keyed it in. To her relief, it was answered.

'Amy?' she said. 'It's Libby Sarjeant here.'

'Hello, Libby.' Amy sounded surprised. 'Can I help you with something?'

'Well, yes, actually, you can.' Libby paused. 'This is a bit awkward, but we needed – oh, I don't know – verification.'

'About what Sarah told you?'

'Not exactly. It was another old parishioner of Patti's. She was a member of the choir when Reverend Turner ran it.'

'Oh? I told you, though, I wasn't even a member of the church.'

'No, I know. It was what this lady said. She told Patti he ran the youth club like a sort of secret society. Do you remember anything like that?'

Amy didn't speak for a moment. 'Well,' she said at last, 'there was talk. And, of course, he was so good-looking.'

'Good-looking?' yelped Libby.

'Yes!' Amy laughed. 'No one's mentioned that?'

'No! Not one!'

'I suppose I'm not surprised in a way. You know it's a cliché about church hens and vicars?'

'And very often true.'

'Indeed. Well, in this case, Reverend Turner caused more than a fluttering in the dovecots. I'm sure that was one reason there was all the gossip.'

'You mean all the old dears were put out because he didn't take any notice of them? They said he wasn't popular.'

'It's only a guess,' said Amy. 'Look, I'd rather talk about this in person.'

'I'm glad you said that! Patti and I wondered if you'd like to come up here to Steeple Martin and have lunch at the Pink Geranium tomorrow. Your sister and niece know it, apparently.'

'So do I – it's a lovely idea. Perhaps Patti and I could share a lift?'

'Of course – I'll leave that to you to sort out. Shall we say about one?'

'So what do you think now?' asked Ben, when Libby told him about this later. 'All the little girls had mad crushes on the vicar and Nick Nash was the front man who recruited them?'

'Something like that,' said Libby. 'It actually makes more sense than any other theory.'

'But why, in that case, have you got bodies turning up?'

'Oh, I don't know. And it's only three.'

'Only!'

'You know what I mean. Not a mass grave.'

'And one's a boy.'

'Look, I don't know, OK? Perhaps we'll find out now we know more about it all.'

'When are you going to tell Ian?'

'Tomorrow, after we've spoken to Amy.'

'And what about Fran? Are you going to leave her out?'

'Oh, hell. No, I'll tell her. I'd better warn Amy first, though.'

Fran, however, was dubious about muscling in, as she put it.

'Amy knows you already, that's different. You can tell me all about it afterwards. And I agree, it does make a weird sort of sense.'

Harry, having been warned that a high-level meeting was due to take place on his premises, promised to be on his very best behaviour.

'Luckily, your son won't be there to make trouble,' he said. 'And Donna's not on till tomorrow. See you at one.'

Promptly at one o'clock on Tuesday, Libby arrived at the Pink Geranium, to find Patti and Amy already installed at the table in the window.

'Thought I'd keep any other diners on the other side,' said Harry. 'Not entirely private, but better than nothing.'

'We'll all huddle round in front of the window,' said Libby. 'Then we can keep an eye on everybody else.'

'Bottle of red?' offered Harry, 'or are we being good and sticking to coffee?'

'I'm driving,' said Patti. 'Parish meeting later, so I'll stick to coffee.'

'Amy?' asked Libby.

'I'd quite like red wine, please.' Amy smiled up at Harry.

'Right,' said Libby, as Harry departed to attend to the drinks. 'So where do we begin?'

'Reverend Turner,' said Patti.

'The glamorous Mr Turner,' said Libby. 'Yes. Ben asked if we thought all the little girls lusted after him and Nick Nash recruited them into this club.'

'Well, I'm afraid it did seem a bit like that,' said Amy. 'Not that anyone put it into words, but for all his otherworldliness some people thought he encouraged the girls. I wasn't happy about it, I told you.'

'But Sarah never saw anything – well, untoward?'

'No. But I gathered if you didn't actually join up, you wouldn't get invited to participate.'

'Participate?' echoed Patti and Libby, wide eyed.

'I don't know exactly what *in*,' said Amy.

'Lord,' said Libby. 'How did you find that out?'

'Sarah.'

'She didn't say anything like that to us,' said Patti.

'No.' Amy looked up, as Harry reappeared with a tray.

'Sorry to interrupt,' he said. 'Are you ready to order food yet?'

All three shook their heads.

'Fine.' Harry grinned. 'Just shout when you're ready.'

'He's a friend, I gather,' said Amy.

'Family friend,' said Libby.

'I always say Harry's Libby's best friend,' said Patti. 'So does her partner, Ben.'

'Doesn't he mind?' asked Amy.

'Not in the least. Harry's civil partner is Peter, Ben's cousin,' said Libby. 'In fact, I knew them both before I knew Ben.' She took a sip of wine. 'Back to the Rev Turner.'

'What did Sarah say?' asked Patti, looking worried.

'I phoned to ask how it had gone with you.' Amy looked at Libby. 'And that was when she said . . . well, she said it had been a bit difficult with her mother there.'

'So she didn't tell us everything,' said Libby.

'No, I'm afraid not. I nearly asked her to come with me today as she's still at her mum's, but I thought I ought to talk to you first.'

'Did she mind?' asked Patti.

'No. She realised she should have said something before.'

'Go on, then. What did she say?' Libby sat forward, concentrating.

'Well, she said that a lot of the girls had crushes on Turner.'

'That's what Ben thought.'

'Yes, well, he was very good-looking. In that remote aesthetic sort of way. And he used to single them out. I never knew what for, but they always came away from "conversations" with him looking rather flushed. And he would ask for another girl to go in. And sometimes, the boys. Sergeant Peacock's scouts.'

'Sarah said there was an atmosphere.'

'She said the girls used to go into little huddles and giggled a lot.' Amy frowned. 'And she said that when Turner started having his meetings with the other men, he chose various girls to go and serve them refreshments.'

'We heard that from the old ladies,' said Patti.

'But it was then that some of the parents started to take the girls away.'

'Ah!' said Libby. 'Now, we didn't hear that. We just heard the girls disappeared.'

'But Sarah says the only girls who disappeared were Kerry and Pam.'

'We heard that, too.'

'So really, you knew all this anyway.' Amy looked disappointed.

'No. We didn't know about Turner's "conversations", or that the parents obviously knew all about it,' said Libby. 'But they didn't spread it around, or the old biddies would have known.'

'I wonder if that was when Nash and Turner both left the parish,' said Patti.

'I expect so.' Libby scowled at her menu. 'Ian really ought to know about this.'

'And you,' said Harry, coming up silently, 'really ought to order food before I stop serving.'

All three hastened to order lunch and Harry left.

'So what are you going to do?' asked Amy.

'I'm going to phone Sergeant Trent.' Libby stood up. 'Will you two be OK for a minute?'

Libby went to the kitchen and asked Harry if she could go through to the back yard.

'Police business, is it?' said Harry seriously. 'Go on then.'

Libby sat at one of the little iron tables and found Rachel's number. Luckily, she answered.

'Thanks for telling us,' she said when Libby had finished. 'I think we'd guessed most of it, but it's good to have it confirmed. I wish we'd been told earlier, though.'

'I know. We'd guessed, too. Why do people keep these things to themselves?'

'Scared of getting into trouble, or getting someone else into trouble,' said Rachel.

'And the parents! Why on earth didn't they report this at the time? They must have known about the gossip.'

'Same thing,' said Rachel. 'They'd be protecting their children.'

'You don't know who most of them are, though, do you?'

'No. And frankly the old ladies aren't liable to provide anything concrete.'

'Will you talk to Sarah?'

'Yes.' Rachel sounded grim. 'As soon as possible. Thanks, Libby.'

Libby returned to the table.

'She's reporting it,' she said.

'Good.' Amy sat back in her chair. 'I don't feel so grubby, now.'

'For reporting it?' said Libby. 'Did you feel guilty?'

'Yes. I'm just glad Sarah didn't get caught up in it.'

'I expect she knew slightly more than she told you, though,' said Patti. 'The same would apply to you as to her mother.'

'I can't help thinking of all those families who must have been devastated at the time,' said Libby. 'I mean, the one person you think you can trust with your kids is the vicar, surely?'

Chapter Twenty-five

Patti forgave Libby her somewhat tactless remark and they all parted on amicable terms. Libby detoured to the Hop Pocket to check on progress and found Colin sharing a companionable beer with Ben.

'I was just telling Ben, I shall be able to move into the flat this week.' He beamed. 'So all round to mine to christen it!'

'Excellent! And you look a lot more cheerful,' said Libby.

'I am. I realised that I was making this whole thing about me, when it wasn't,' said Colin. 'Gerry gave me quite a telling off.'

Libby grinned. 'Terribly tempting, though. Especially after the last time.'

Ben laughed. 'I know someone else who does that!'

'I don't!' said Libby indignantly.

'Anyway,' said Colin. 'Is there any more news?'

'There's a bit more confirmation of shenanigans at the church when Nash was there,' said Libby. 'I haven't heard any more about Simone, have you?'

'No. Not that I want to, unless it's to hear she's gone off again.'

'I'd love to find out a bit more about her, though,' said Libby. 'Why was she here? Where's she been living? That sort of thing.'

'You don't really think she could be involved, do you?' asked Colin.

'It does seem rather obvious,' said Ben. 'Spurned ex-wife, you know.'

'We don't know that she was spurned. I rather understood you to say it was she who left,' Libby said to Colin.

'I thought it was. Mainly because I couldn't see how Nick could have thrown her out over there. She wouldn't have anywhere to go.'

'You don't know that. You said you didn't know her very well – she could have had hordes of friends.'

'Yes!' Colin looked surprised. 'Of course she could. So could he.'

'Exactly. The police were looking into that, weren't they? In case it all linked up with the Costa del Crime.'

'Oh, hell! I do hope not!'

'Now don't start worrying again,' said Ben. 'It's nothing to do with you. Leave it to the police. And Libby.'

Libby sniffed.

'Time for a review,' she told Sidney when she reached home. 'I wish Fran was here.'

Her phone rang.

'Me,' said Fran. 'Are you in?'

'Blimey! You psychic? I was just wishing you were here.'

Fran laughed. 'Just leaving Canterbury. Thought I'd pop in on the way home.'

'Lovely!' said Libby. 'I'll have the kettle on.'

Fran arrived twenty minutes later.

'So fill me in on what's been going on. I gather something has?' She followed Libby into the kitchen.

'Well,' began Libby. 'You know Amy came to lunch?' While she made tea – in a proper pot – she told Fran what Amy had reported.

'So,' she concluded, 'I think we need a review. We've got a lot of new people in the mix now.'

'There are always new people in a murder case,' said Fran. 'You ought to be used to that by now.'

'What do you think Ian and his team are following up, then? Simone?'

'And the young people who talked to Patti.'

'I wish we'd been able to talk to them after all.'

'That's just nosiness. You'll find out.'

Libby poured two mugs of tea and pushed one across the table.

'Where do you suppose Simone's gone to?'

'No idea. I doubt if she'll come back here, though. She'll know the police will be on the watch for her. Same applies to St Aldeberge.'

'I feel sorry for Patti, though,' said Libby after a pause. 'She's got thoroughly mixed up in this again, hasn't she?'

'She could stay out of it if she wanted,' said Fran. 'She can always say no when people come bothering her.'

'Not in her nature,' said Libby. 'And I think she feels she's got to redeem the church somehow. The Reverend Turner hasn't done her many favours, has he?'

'No.' Fran stared thoughtfully at her mug. 'I was thinking, his little club, or whatever it was, sounds suspiciously like a cult.'

'A what?'

'A cult. You know, like those terrible ones in America.'

'Ah, yes. But not as bad as that, surely? Not those mass suicides and murders?'

'Maybe not, but think about those young people. How were they persuaded to join up? And stay there?'

'Well, at first I guess they were flattered. The girls fancied Turner, and if he showed them attention . . .'

'But there were other men,' said Fran. 'What were they doing?'

Libby felt a cold trickle down her spine. She looked at Fran in horror.

'Surely you must have thought about that?' Fran raised an eyebrow. 'It struck me when we first heard about it.'

'So – what? Turner was supplying young girls to middle-aged men? That's a bit of a leap, isn't it?'

'I would think it's more like Nash was doing the supplying,' said Fran.

'For what, though? He wasn't the type to do something like that for nothing.'

'For money. Perhaps ostensibly for the Church?'

'Good grief! Do you think the kids knew?'

'They might have twigged. Don't you think? Not known for sure . . .'

'And tried to get away.' Libby stood up and ran her fingers through her hair. 'This is awful! I can't bear it! Surely, it can't be true.'

'Maybe not, but it makes sense of the evidence so far.'

Libby sat down again.

'I can't believe you hadn't thought of it,' said Fran. 'Right at the start you were told about young girls attending some sort of club where men met at the church. No women, just men. And rumours of disappearances – and then actual disappearances. And finally, bodies. And think about what Kelly's mother told us. This is what she was worried about, wasn't it?'

'Oh, God.' Libby put her head in her hands. 'Yes, of course it is. I was being deliberately blind, wasn't I?'

'Just avoiding something unpleasant,' said Fran.

'*Unpleasant*? God!'

'Anyway – how did they persuade them? Some kind of coercion?'

Libby cleared her throat and sat up straight. 'Right. Are we over-thinking this?'

Fran regarded her with amusement. 'Don't you usually over-think things? We're just going through what we know. Until we have more evidence, there isn't much we can do. And the police will be doing it already.'

'OK.' Libby sighed. 'You're right. I should just wait and see, shouldn't I?'

'Hard though it may be, yes, probably.' Fran stood up. 'Now I'd better get home. Phone if you want.'

Libby saw her friend off, stood staring down the lane after her for a long moment, then went back to the kitchen. Time to get on with real life.

It was almost six o'clock when her phone rang again.

'Patti. Listen, I've got a couple of the people who spoke to me after church the other day with me.'

'What?' Libby's heart missed a beat.

'They want to talk to you.'

'What about the police?'

'The police have already been in contact with them.'

'Then why do they want to talk to me?'

'I asked them that. Listen – I'm going to hand you over to Steve.'

'Wait!' yelled Libby.

'Er, Libby?' said a strange male voice. 'I'm really sorry to bother you. My name's Steve Plowright.'

'Hello, Steve.'

'I know you told the police what we said, and a policeman has already been in touch with me. We're all going in to the – er – incident room to give statements.'

'That's good,' said Libby.

'Yes – but we just wondered – could you tell us what you think they want? We're all a bit worried.'

The truth, obviously, thought Libby. Aloud, she said, 'I don't see how I can help, but I'm happy to talk to you if you think it will help, um, clarify matters.'

'I don't suppose we could see you this evening?' said Steve hesitantly.

'I'll just check,' said Libby, and covered the mouthpiece. Ben was sitting staring at her over his pre-prandial beer, a foreboding expression on his face.

'Can I go out this evening?' she asked.

'Where?'

'I guess St Aldeberge.'

'Then I'm coming with you.'

Libby uncovered the mouthpiece. 'Where did you want to meet?'

Patti answered. 'I've told them they can meet here. Sorry about this.'

Libby sighed. 'Don't worry, Patti. Are you sure you don't mind everyone invading you? Oh, and Ben says he's coming with me.'

'I should imagine he's thoroughly fed up,' said Patti with a short laugh. 'No, of course I don't mind. It's what vicars are for. I suggested eight thirty. Is that all right with you?'

'Fine,' said Libby. 'We'll see you then.' She ended the call.

'What is it this time?' asked Ben.

She told him.

'And Fran thinks it could be a cult?' Ben frowned.

'Yes, although now I've thought it over, I'm not sure. The girls weren't taken away from home to live in a commune or anything like that. It's more likely they were simply coerced somehow into having – what? Illegal relations? With Turner and possibly other men. That's about the size of it, isn't it?'

'I would have said so. Equally as awful.' Ben stood up. 'We'd better get on with dinner then, so we can go and find out from the horse's mouth.'

Before they left, Libby called Fran to tell her what was happening, and what her conclusions were.

'I think you're right,' said Fran. 'I was overstating the case when I said cult. But some sort of force must have been used.'

'Not simply the thrill of the unknown?'

'Maybe. Go and find out.'

Libby and Ben arrived at the vicarage by a quarter past eight.

'Sorry we're early,' said Libby.

'I'm glad you are,' said Patti. 'I wanted to talk to you first, anyway.'

'Do you know what they're going to tell us?' asked Ben. 'And shall I stay out of the way?'

'I don't know what they're going to say, and we'll wait and see, Ben. If the girls aren't happy, we'll go and wait in the kitchen.' Patti led them into the study, where she had already placed a tray of mugs with a plate of biscuits. 'Standard vicar fare,' she said.

At one minute past the half hour, there was a knock on the door. Patti gave them a rueful grin and went to answer it.

Voices were heard, then Patti came back.

'Libby, Ben, this is Steve Plowright, whom you've already spoken to. And these are?'

'Debbie Jones,' said a statuesque blonde.

'Nickie Taylor,' said a slim, plain brunette.

184

'Immi Bancroft,' said a diminutive person with an almost white crop.

Ben stood up. 'Pleased to meet you,' he said. 'Now, if you'd prefer to talk to Libby alone, I'll leave you.'

Steve Plowright looked at the others who all smiled. 'No, sir, it's fine. I presume, as you're here, you've been part of the investigation so far?'

Ben, secretly delighted with the "sir", nodded.

'Then we'd be happy for you to stay.'

Ben sat down again.

'Can I offer anyone coffee? Or tea?' said Patti.

Everyone declined.

'Right then,' said Libby, taking a deep breath. 'What did you want to talk about?'

Chapter Twenty-six

The three girls looked at Steve, who had obviously been voted the leader.

'We heard about Mr Nash's body being found,' he said, 'but we didn't think it was anything to do with us.'

'He hasn't been around since we were at school,' said Debbie.

'But then we heard that the body of a girl had been found.'

'We didn't know it was Kerry Palmer at first,' said Immi.

'Neither did the police,' said Libby. 'You hadn't heard about the gossip that's been going round about Nash and Reverend Turner?'

'No,' said Immi. Nickie had turned sickly pale.

'Go on,' said Libby.

'Well,' said Steve, 'when we heard that we did phone each other and talk about it. You see, none of us live here any more, and neither do our families. It was pure chance that we heard anything.'

'And how was that?' asked Ben.

'My mother lives just outside Nethergate, and when we take the children to visit her, we always go and have an ice cream on Harbour Street, and take Mum for a cup of tea with Mavis. She has a café called the Blue Anchor. I don't know if you know Nethergate.'

Libby gave a faint smile. 'We do. And we know Mavis very well indeed.'

'Oh.' Steve looked surprised. 'Well, she started telling Mum a bit about what had been going on, and about Liz Palmer trying to find out about Kerry.'

Libby nodded.

'So we had another phone conversation – well, on Skype actually – and wondered what to do.'

'How did our names come up?' asked Libby.

'That was me,' said Nickie. 'I came across Sarah Elliot at work some while ago, and we stayed vaguely in touch. I called her to see if she knew about—' she waved an expressive hand, 'all this, and she told me about you and the vicar.'

'So we came to see the vicar,' said Steve. 'We didn't know what else to do.'

'I can see that,' said Ben. 'You wouldn't want to waste police time, so you wanted to find out if what you knew was relevant.'

'Yes!' said four relieved voices.

'And now we know more bodies have been found, and that the first one *was* Kerry Palmer,' said Debbie. 'So we thought before we saw the police formally tomorrow, we'd like to talk to you.'

'We're not being wimps, honestly,' said Immi, gazing limpidly at them out of large round brown eyes.

'No, I can see you're not,' said Libby. 'Patti, if it's not too much trouble, I'd love a cup of tea.'

'I'll help you,' said Ben. 'I bet you've only got coffee ready.'

This, as Libby had intended, had relaxed the atmosphere slightly, and the other four all placed their orders for coffee.

'Where do you live now, then?' asked Libby.

'Bishop's Bottom,' said Immi. 'I expect you know it.'

'Cherry Ashton,' said Debbie.

'Canterbury,' said Steve and Nickie.

'And of course, once Sarah had told us about you, we all realised we'd heard about you,' said Nickie.

'Sorry about that,' said Steve.

Libby grinned. 'Not to worry. I'm beginning to get used to it.'

Patti came back with a cafetiere, followed by Ben bearing a steaming mug, which he gave to Libby.

'Right,' she said, when they were all supplied with coffee. 'Now we know how you came to consult us, start with why. Tell us what you know about the situation back in the day when Nash and Turner seemed to be ruling the roost.'

Steve looked at the girls. 'You'd better tell it,' he said.

The three of them looked at each other, nodded and turned to face Libby.

'We were all junior members of the choir,' Immi began. 'And then Mr Nash told us Reverend Turner was starting a little youth club. Just a few select members, he said.'

'And he began interviewing us. One at a time,' said Nickie.

'And we were all a bit flattered,' said Debbie. 'I was, anyway. I was always big for my age and I was never picked for anything at school.'

'Neither was I,' said Nickie. 'I was as plain as a pikestaff.'

'Anyway, he asked us all sorts of questions. Sometimes they struck us as odd, but we'd come out and talk about it with the others, and giggle a bit, you know . . .'

'I know,' said Libby. 'Sarah told us about the interviews. Although she didn't go into detail. Could you tell us a bit more?'

They fell silent for a moment.

'Well,' began Debbie, 'it was questions. About boys. And had we got boyfriends. And . . .' She stopped.

'How we felt about them,' said Nickie in a small voice.

'And about our own bodies. It made us – uncomfortable.' Immi cleared her throat.

'Then,' she continued, 'the club actually started.'

'And it was just ordinary,' said Debbie. 'We had table tennis, and tea and coffee and lemonade, and that was about it. Then the scouts joined in.'

'I wondered about that,' said Libby.

'Well, Sergeant Peacock was supposed to be running a scout troop,' said Steve, 'and our parents were keen for us to join, but there were none of the normal scout activities. No badges, or anything like that. We kept getting told there was time for all that. Some of us were all for leaving, but then we were told we'd been merged with the youth club. Of course, that meant girls, so we all hung on.'

'Well,' said Ben, 'you would.'

'Then,' said Immi, breaking an uncomfortable little silence, 'the "interviews" started again.'

The girls looked at one another again, and Libby noted Nickie's shortening of breath and Debbie's heightened colour. She glanced at Ben. He stood up.

'Shall I pop out to the kitchen?' he suggested gently.

Nickie looked doubtful, but the others shook their heads. He sat down again.

'Let me guess,' said Libby. 'This time the "interviews" were more personal?'

Immi nodded, her pointed little face becoming vicious.

'He touched us. And told us this was the will of God. We were there to serve. He stroked us and made much of us – you know what I mean?'

By this time Patti looked as though she was either going to throw up or pass out.

'How long did this go on?' asked Libby.

'Not long.' Debbie said. 'None of us mentioned it to the others at first. I don't know about them, but I was too ashamed.'

'But eventually we began talking to each other,' said Immi. 'Except some of them didn't seem to mind. They were still giggling, and they began to act as if they were superior to the rest of us.'

'And it sounds daft, but we were too ashamed to tell our parents,' said Nickie. 'I just kept saying I wanted to leave the church, but they wouldn't hear of it.'

'And by this time had the gossips started?' asked Libby.

'I don't think so,' said Debbie doubtfully.

'That wasn't until the meetings started,' said Steve.

They all went quiet again.

'Who were the men who came to the meetings?' asked Patti, softly.

189

Immi sat up straight again. 'I don't really know. We didn't see many of them. It was the older girls who were asked to help serve refreshments, and we were never there when they came out.'

'Some of the younger ones were asked to go in,' said Nickie.

'But you don't know what happened?' said Libby.

'No. By that time we were actually quite frightened, so we just stopped going to the choir and the youth club,' said Debbie.

'And that was what gave rise to some of the gossip,' Libby said to Patti, who nodded.

'And then Kerry and Pam ran away.' Immi looked down. 'And we didn't say anything.'

Libby let the silence go on for a minute. 'Your parents wouldn't have believed you,' she said. 'They would have said it was your imagination.'

'Exactly,' said Immi, and the others all nodded, relieved.

'What about you, Steve?' asked Ben, again, gently.

'Some of us were asked in,' said Steve slowly. 'With us, it was mainly the younger ones.'

Patti was looking sick again.

'I only went a couple of times, but we were told to be "on parade" and to serve the gentlemen.' He looked at Ben. 'It was odd. They all seemed to be – I don't know – excited. They all laughed.'

The girls all shifted uncomfortably.

'And the older ones were sent home. And I found one or two of the younger ones crying outside the church a couple of times.'

'And they wouldn't say why?' asked Libby.

Steve shook his head. 'I saw them home, if I found them. Of course, now I realise what was going on, but I didn't at the time. I wish we'd said something.'

'Do you think you've suffered permanent damage?' asked Libby. 'I'm pretty sure I would have.'

'A bit,' said Nickie. 'I was very wary of men for years after that.'

'So was I,' said Debbie.

'And me,' said Immi.

'I didn't actually suffer anything,' said Steve. 'It was just what I pieced together afterwards, and eventually what the girls told me. I did get a bit aggressive during my teens, which I think was a way of warding off any sort of approach.'

'I think you've been remarkably frank,' said Libby. 'And I think you should tell the police everything. I'm going to try and do something I expect I'll get into trouble for, but I'm going to try and talk to the police before they see you. Bear in mind, they won't talk to you together—'

'Collusion,' said Steve.

'Exactly. But I might be able to make them a bit more—'

'Approachable?' suggested Ben.

'Quite,' said Libby. 'Now, one more thing. Do you know what happened to the Reverend Turner?'

'Not that I'd call him Reverend,' said Patti, through gritted teeth.

'We all refused to go to church after that,' said Immi.

'Which wasn't popular with our parents,' said Debbie.

'But we did hear that he'd left,' said Immi. 'I asked my mum what had happened, but she was very vague.'

Debbie and Nickie nodded.

'We moved away,' said Steve, 'although I wasn't sure why. Dad and Mum didn't change jobs, or anything like that, and I didn't have to change schools, and you just accept what your parents do, don't you?

'And you never heard any more about Kerry or Pam White after that?' said Libby.

They all shook their heads.

'More coffee?' offered Patti, after a pause. They all declined.

'Well, we should let you get back to your homes,' said Libby. 'Have you all told your families?'

They all nodded.

'Then thank you again for being so frank. It's a horrible business, but I'm quite sure you'll have helped to clear it up.'

'I just wish we'd said something earlier,' said Nickie. 'Even back then. Even if we weren't believed.'

'It would have fuelled the gossip mill,' said Libby, 'which wasn't taken seriously, but now, your evidence will provide confirmation. If I need to speak to any of you again, shall I call Steve?'

'Yes, please.' Steve stood up and held out his hand. 'Thank you so much – may I call you Libby? I think you've made us all feel a lot easier.'

'And I'll feel better talking to the police tomorrow,' said Immi.

There was a chorus of agreement, a round of hand shaking, and Patti ushered them all out.

'Glass of something?' she said when she came back. 'I feel we need it.'

'Just a very tiny one,' said Ben. 'I'm driving.'

'You shall have an extra large one when we get home,' said Libby smiling at him.

'I intend to,' said Ben. 'That wasn't the pleasantest interview, was it?'

'Bloody harrowing,' said Libby, accepting a large glass of red wine from Patti. 'Those poor kids.'

'And that *bloody* man!' Patti sounded positively vicious.

'Now I've got to decide who to tell,' said Libby.

'Text Ian, as usual, on his private number,' said Ben. 'Tell him you've got something important to tell him.'

'He's going to get fed up with me,' muttered Libby, dragging out her mobile, 'but I really feel I must do it.'

Chapter Twenty-seven

The phone rang on the drive home.

'What is it now?' barked DCI Connell.

Libby froze. 'This was the reason I sent the text to Rachel rather than you.'

'Well, she forwarded it to me. So?'

'I have some information.'

'What about? Don't play games!'

Ben was making faces indicative of a desire to grab the phone. Libby turned away from him.

'I'm not. But knowing how you react when I get involved in something without meaning to, I chose to inform the police via Sergeant Trent. If you want me to tell you, you will please be polite about it.'

Silence.

'Right,' said Libby. 'How many did you count up to? I'm ringing off now.'

Suddenly Ian burst out laughing.

'All right, all right – I'm sorry! And it was going to be a hundred, but I only got up to twenty-five. If you must know, it frustrates the hell out of me when you manage to get important information out of people I'd never get in a million years.'

'Well,' said Libby, suppressing a small glow of satisfaction, 'you'll get this tomorrow, as long as you go gently.'

'Don't tell me,' groaned Ian. 'You've been coaching my witnesses.'

'I suppose you could call it that,' said Libby. 'But it wasn't my idea. Now do you want me to tell you what it is, or will you wait until you see them tomorrow?'

'If you tell me, at least I'll have an idea of what it's about,' said Ian. 'Where are you?'

'In Ben's car on the way home.'

'I'm on my way home, too. Could you bear for me to come and see you on the way?'

Libby turned to Ben. 'Could you bear for Ian to pop in and give me the third degree?' She heard a spluttering noise from the phone. Ben grinned and nodded. 'All right. We'll be about another ten minutes.'

'And I'll be about twenty.'

When Libby rang off, she and Ben both laughed.

'I do love it when you put him in his place!' said Ben.

True to his word, Ian arrived at Allhallow's Lane twenty minutes later. Ben let him in.

'Now,' he said. 'What have you got to tell me?'

'First,' said Libby, 'would you like coffee?'

'I'd love one,' said Ian.

'I'll get it, to show there are no hard feelings about you interrogating my beloved,' said Ben.

Ian made a face.

Libby embarked on the story which had unfolded that evening. By the time she'd finished, all traces of laughter had been banished.

'We thought it would be something like that,' said Ian. 'And it's all right – we'll go gently. You didn't sense any of them holding something back?'

'No.' Libby shook her head. 'They'd obviously thrashed the whole thing out between them over the last week or so, and now feel guilty that they hadn't spoken up about it before. I said if they'd told their parents at the time, they probably wouldn't have been believed.'

'Sadly, only too true,' said Ian. 'There are innumerable cases of that happening.' He leant back in his chair. 'This case is getting to everybody. Bad enough that these are all bodies of children, before we even try to figure out how they actually died.'

'Let alone Nick Nash,' said Ben.

Ian nodded. 'In a way we should be grateful to him – or his murderer – or we'd never have known about the others.'

'They are connected, though, aren't they?' asked Libby.

'I don't see how they *can't* be. We're tentatively working on the theory that someone from that time, a parent, maybe, is Nash's killer. And I didn't tell you that, by the way.'

'Contrary to what you might think,' said Ben, 'none of us gossips for the sake of it. We've seen what damage it can do.'

'I know.' Ian sighed. 'And I'm sorry I snapped.'

Libby smiled. 'I can be irritating.'

Ian and Ben exchanged eye-rolling glances.

'I'd better go.' Ian stood up. 'Enjoy your nightcaps.'

'That's what I like to see,' said Libby, after he'd gone. 'A mellow Ian. I felt almost sorry for him.'

'It's a pig of a case,' said Ben. 'I suppose all cases involving children are.'

'Let's just hope it doesn't get any worse,' said Libby.

The following morning, Jemima called.

'I don't suppose there's any more news, is there?'

'No, I'm afraid not,' said Libby. 'The police, as they say, are baffled.'

'Poor them. Can't say I envy them, do you? Anyway, the reason I called was I wondered if I was going to get my lawnmower back. Not that I'd actually want to keep it, but it might be able to be repaired and sold. The cliff isn't that high, or it would have been smashed to bits.'

'It was your lawnmower?' Libby was surprised.

'Yes. It wasn't exactly new, it was my dad's originally, and I rarely use it, which was why I lent it to Nash when he gave me the job. He said he'd get the wider landscape in trim before I started the actual garden.'

'So he'd had it for some time?' Libby's brain was whirling.

'Yes. Ever since he gave me the contract. The people who do the repairs took it over there for me. They had to check that it was in working order.'

'So,' said Libby slowly, 'if they checked it over, it would have been safe.'

'Of course!' Now Jemima sounded surprised.

'Do the police know this?'

'Course they do!' Jemima laughed. 'Right from the first day!'

'Yes, I suppose they would.' Now Libby felt a little foolish. 'Of course the police would know.'

'Your son would know the firm,' Jemima went on. 'He and Mog use them. So does Lewis Osbourne-Walker.'

'Right. Yes, Creekmarsh does have rather extensive grounds.'

'Yes.' Jemima sighed. 'I envy them. I love the ha-ha.'

'Mmm.' Libby had not terribly nice memories of the ha-ha.

'Anyway, they're no nearer solving the case, so I won't get my mower back?' said Jemima.

'Doesn't look like it,' said Libby. 'I might see Ian tonight, so I could ask, if you like?'

'If it won't seem intrusive, thank you.'

After she had ended the call, Libby sat in thought for a long time. Eventually, she dialled a number.

'Mum? What do you want? I'm working!'

'I know, Ad, and I'm sorry. I just wanted to ask you about a firm of repairers you use, you and Mog.'

'What on earth for? Oh, this latest case, is it? Something to do with a ride-on mower?'

'That's it, darling.'

'We use a couple. I think we might have put you on to one a few years ago . . . Anyway, the latest is a bloke from over near Creekmarsh. Lewis uses him as a contractor to do the heavy work over there. We usually get his young trainee. Surly kid.'

'You don't remember his name?'

'Who, the kid?'

'No! The bloke! Or his firm.'

'Marsh, I think. Coincidence, eh? Yes, Nobby Marsh. The boy's called Ryan, I think.'

'OK, Ad, thank you. So is the firm called Nobby Marsh?'

'I don't know. I suppose so. Why?'

'Just in case I need to get in touch. Go on, you get back to work. Thanks again.'

'OK, Mum. You in the pub this evening?'

'I expect so. Will you be there?'

'I'm helping in the caff tonight, so probably.'

'See you then,' said Libby, and rang off. She wasn't sure why she'd wanted the details of the repair man, or what she'd do with them now she'd got them, just that what Jemima had told her presented all sorts of new avenues. Except that she couldn't see where they would lead. As usual, when stumped, she called Fran.

'I'm in the shop, so I can't talk for long.'

'No, all right. Just wanted to bring you up to date.'

Libby reported briefly on the previous night's conversations, and Jemima's phone call that morning.

'And so I asked Adam if he knew the repair man.'

'Why? What can you do about a knackered lawnmower.'

'No idea. But it opens up possibilities, doesn't it?'

'Does it? Look, I've got to go. I'll talk to you later.'

Frustrated, Libby wondered what to do next. The post falling on the mat brought her to the realisation that Christmas wasn't far away and she'd done nothing about it except choose trees. Perhaps a little desultory shopping might be in order. At least she could do it from her laptop without having to venture into crowded streets and shops.

Eventually, she got so engrossed in browsing online shopping outlets, mostly on the basis of one for you and one for me, and one for them and one for me, she forgot all about lawnmowers, cliffs and Nick Nash. Until at just about lunchtime, Rachel Trent knocked on the door.

'Rachel!' Libby held the door open and peered into Rachel's face. 'You look a bit . . . er . . .'

'Tense?' suggested Rachel, coming in and collapsing in the armchair. 'I've just spent a harrowing morning.'

'Ah.' Libby sat on the sofa. 'Debbie, Nickie, Immi, and Steve?'

'Yes. You had them all together. We had them one at a time. The DCI actually asked me at one point if I was all right.' She gave a short laugh. 'I wouldn't be much good as a copper if I wasn't, would I?'

'I don't think you'd be a very good copper if you didn't feel anything,' said Libby.

'What did you make of them?' asked Rachel. 'Did you believe them?'

'Yes. Didn't you?'

'Of course.'

'Rachel – would you like something to eat or drink? Tea, coffee? A sandwich?'

'I'd love a cup of tea,' said Rachel. 'I don't think I could eat anything.'

'Right.' Libby got up and went into the kitchen. Rachel followed.

'What did you want with me, anyway?' said Libby, filling the kettle.

The DCI wanted me to talk to you. He said he spoke to you last night. Was that after I passed on your message?'

'Yes.' Libby grinned over her shoulder. 'Do you think it did any good?'

'He was certainly less intimidating than he can be,' said Rachel. 'Almost human, in fact.'

'Come on, that's not fair!'

'Oh, yes it is! You know what he can be like! You should see him with some of the people he interviews. Like God and the headmaster all rolled into one.'

Libby laughed.

'And don't tell him I said that!' Rachel grinned reluctantly.

'As if I would.'

'No, I know. You don't gossip.'

'I told him that last night.'

'Right. So what we wanted to ask you was, is there anything in what they told you that should be followed up?' Rachel sat on one of the kitchen chairs and leant her elbows on the table.

'I thought you would have found things yourself.' Libby was surprised.

'Yes, but Connell – we – have quite respect for your nose, if I can put it like that.'

'Well . . .' Libby poured water into mugs, 'Pam White again.'

'Yes, we're still trying with her.'

'And some of the other boys. Does Steve not know any names?'

'We thought of that, too. He's going to try and remember.'

'And I did wonder if any of them had been to Nash's house, or knew the headland.'

'Yes!' Rachel was suddenly alert. 'I didn't think of that.'

'And going on from that, although not to do with the interviews, what about the lawnmower?'

'Eh?' Rachel was startled. 'The lawnmower?'

'Jemima Routledge was asking after it. Apparently, it's hers.'

'Oh – yes. We looked into that right at the beginning of the investigation,' said Rachel. 'It was an obvious place to start to see if anyone could have tampered with it.'

'It was tampered with, then?'

'Yes. Don't ask me about the technical part, I didn't understand it at the time, but the company who brought it over had checked it out at the time, they said.'

'Yes, Jemima said. I must admit, when she asked, I immediately got suspicious.'

'I can imagine. Poor Jemima!'

'But when she explained – especially when she told me my Adam and his boss Mog used the company – I realised she wasn't involved.'

'But,' said Rachel, 'Nobby Marsh could be, couldn't he?'

Chapter Twenty-eight

'Yes,' said Libby, 'but how? Has he got any connection to the case?'

'That was the first thing we thought of,' said Rachel. 'Perhaps he was a parent.'

'But how would you know?' asked Libby. 'He's hardly going to admit it, is he? Has he got kids?'

'I think so.' Rachel looked vague.

'I suppose the boy who works with him would be too young?'

'Much,' said Rachel. 'I don't suppose he was even born at the time. Not a very nice specimen, actually.'

'Poor lad,' said Libby.

'So, nothing else, then?' Rachel sipped her tea.

'Nothing that wouldn't have been obvious to you at the time,' said Libby. 'If I think of anything I'll let you know. You, not Ian.'

Rachel smiled. 'Understood. Is he coming over to you this evening?'

'Oh, you know about our regular Wednesday club, then?'

'Of course,' said Rachel. 'We all do! I'm afraid the lads have given you a very rude name!'

'Go on, tell me!' Libby bounced in her chair.

Colour seeped up Rachel's neck. 'Er – Connell's Snouts.'

Libby burst out laughing. ' I love it!'

Rachel looked surprised and relieved. 'Don't tell him I told you that, either!'

'Does he know?'

'Of course he does! Bloody man knows everything.'

'OK, well, as a snout, what else can I do? Go ferreting in a trough somewhere?'

Rachel thought for a moment. 'What you said about the lawnmower.'

'Don't ask me to look into lawnmowers – I know nothing about machinery.'

'No, I was thinking about Nobby Marsh.'

'What about him?'

'Is there any way you could maybe look into his background?'

'But you're better placed to do that,' objected Libby.

'But not the way you do it. Ask questions. Find out about the man. If he works for your son . . .'

'Adam didn't really know anything about him or the firm. Just said the boy – Brian, was it? No – Ryan – was surly.'

'I'd agree with that. What about Adam's boss, though?'

'I doubt it. Hasn't got an inquisitive bone in his body. Lewis, though . . .'

'Lewis?'

'You know. Lewis Osbourne-Walker. Owner of Creekmarsh.'

'Oh, the TV guy. Yes you've had something to do with him in the past, haven't you?'

'Yes. Adam and his boss Mog work for him. They've even featured in his TV programme once or twice. He's helped us and the police before. And he loves finding things out.'

'Would he help?'

'I don't know. He might feel he was intruding. Especially if he doesn't know the bloke well.'

Rachel sighed. 'We'll just carry on digging.' She looked stricken. 'Oh, hell. I didn't mean that.'

Libby laughed. 'An everyday hazard, surely!'

'Like "I'll kill you!" said by practically everyone on the planet!'

'Exactly. Well, I haven't helped much, have I?'

'You have, you know you have. And I promise we won't mind if you ring up with odd bits of information.'

'Ben would say don't encourage me.'

Rachel laughed and stood up. 'And tell Fran the same thing. She's had no spectacular insights, I suppose?'

'No, nothing. She says she's too content these days for her sub-conscious to work.'

After Rachel had left, Libby sat in thought until hunger drove her to start raiding the fridge.

Parents. The obvious place to look for someone who wished to take revenge. Except that surely it would have been better to take revenge on Turner, who was the real villain, in Libby's opinion. But then, no one knew where Turner was. Both he and Nash had disappeared twenty years ago, and Nash had only been killed when he turned up recently. Although, Libby reflected, he must have been back on the odd occasion before now.

But Turner. Where was he? Why hadn't the police dug him up. Libby stopped in her tracks. Dug him up. Was that what had happened? Libby sat back down again. Had someone killed Turner? Was that why he had disappeared? Then she shook her head. No, if that was the case, the police would have looked into it. After all, he had lived here. Not that she liked to think of him living in Patti's vicarage, but all his things would still have been there, and at least the diocese would have looked into it, even if the police hadn't. No, he must have left voluntarily.

For the rest of the afternoon, Libby tried to busy herself with other things. Plans for the theatre, half an hour gazing at the latest half-finished painting for Guy's shop, a little more online Christmas shopping, and, finally, a book. None of these things held her attention, however, and she was relieved when Ben arrived, back from today's stint at the Hop Pocket.

'Coming along nicely,' he said. 'Pity we won't be open for Christmas, but there's too much planning to be done for that. Had a good day?'

'No,' said Libby. 'Is it too early for a drink?'

Ben raised his eyebrows. 'Steady! What's brought this on? As if I didn't know.'

Libby told him.

'Right. Let me have a quick wash, and we'll talk it through. Meanwhile, call Harry and see if he can fit us in tonight with Anne and Patti.' He disappeared upstairs and Libby picked up her phone.

When Ben appeared, having obviously had a shower rather than a wash, she reported.

'Yes, he can, but he says half past seven rather than eight, as he has a crowd coming in for a pre-Christmas meal.'

'OK. Now you can have a drink.' Ben went into the kitchen and returned with two glasses of wine. 'Go on, then. Tell me.'

'Well, what do you think about Rachel's suggestion that I should try and look into Nobby Marsh's background?'

'This is all a bit sudden, isn't it? You hadn't even heard about the whole lawnmower scenario this morning.'

'It does open up new possibilities, though. Rachel says the police have been looking into it.'

'And the possibility that a parent is responsible for Nash's death. Which seems the most likely place to look for a murderer.'

'I agree. But how do we find parents of possibly abused children? Steve, Immi, Nickie, and Debbie don't look like possible candidates.'

'What about Kerry's mum? You met her.'

'No.' Libby shook her head.

'And the other one? Pam?'

'Pam White. I still think they should be trying to find her, and Rachel says they are, but they don't appear to have even located her mum. Kerry's mum wasn't very forthcoming about her, either.'

'You don't think she could be one of these latest bodies they've found?'

'No.' Libby frowned. 'I think Pam was older, like Kerry – and Sarah, come to that. The boy and girl they've just found were younger, I think. I don't know why I think that, though.'

'How would you go about finding out about this Marsh's life? I would have thought the police could do that better than you could. Official documents and so on. You know, like the sort of thing you see on TV, where researchers look into old town records and censuses and so on.'

'I know – that's what I said. Although old town records and censuses wouldn't be much use in his case – too recent. But she said I could find out about the man. I think she meant what he was actually like.'

'Well, all right.' Ben surveyed her over his glass. 'How would you go about that? Without getting into trouble?'

Libby made a face at him. 'I could ask Ad. And I thought Lewis, too.'

'And Mike,' said Ben.

'Oh yes! I hadn't thought of him!' said Libby.

'You were quick enough to ask him about what's her name.'

'Jemima, yes. I'll do that tomorrow. Thanks, Ben.'

He grinned at her. 'Just please be careful.'

When they arrived at the Pink Geranium, they found Anne and Patti ensconced at a much smaller table than usual, and the rest of the café almost full. Adam and the latest of the "casual" waitresses darted among the tables, and even Donna was on duty behind the counter.

'How did he fit us in?' said Libby, sliding into a chair.

'With difficulty,' said Adam coming up behind her, and slapping menus down. 'What would you like to drink?'

A bottle of Libby's favourite Shiraz and Anne's favourite Sancerre ordered, Adam hurried off.

'Progress report?' suggested Patti. 'Anne knows all the background.'

Libby duly reported.

'I don't see how we can do any more to track down parents,' said Patti. 'We've had all the gossip from the old ladies, and from Amy, and Sarah and her mother.'

'And Liz Palmer,' said Anne. 'I feel so sorry for her.'

'And Steve, Immi, and the other two,' said Patti. 'I don't see how any of us can find out any more.'

'No,' said Libby, 'and I don't see how they're going to find out who those other two children are, either. Unless they were reported missing at the time.'

'Which it doesn't appear they were,' said Ben. 'Which is very odd.'

Adam returned with their wine, and they ordered food.

'Good job you all know the menu,' he said, as he scurried off leaving them to pour their own drinks. They all grinned at each other.

'The benefits of privilege,' said Ben, raising his glass.

'So where are we then?' asked Patti. 'You're going to investigate lawnmowers—'

'Lawnmower menders, actually,' said Libby, 'and Ben suggested I ask Mike Farthing about him.'

'That's the one with the garden centre? Farthing's Plants?' said Anne.

'Yes, my cousin's partner,' said Libby.

'And who knew how useful he was going to come in when we first met!' said Ben.

By the time Adam arrived with their main courses, they had thrashed out the whole case between them and got no further.

'I honestly don't know what we can do now, as I said before,' said Patti. 'I propose a moratorium while we eat.'

The pace of service had calmed down by the time they had finished their meal, and Harry strolled out from the kitchen looking slightly dishevelled, attracting a few admiring glances from the various ladies in the clientele.

'Hello, chicks,' he said, 'more wine? Or a sneaky brandy on the house?'

They all opted for a brandy, and Harry signalled Adam to fetch them.

'So, solved the case, have you?' He dragged a stool over from the waiting area and perched beside Ben.

'No,' said Libby. 'Suggestions?'

'I told you. That sexy Simone.'

'Yes, well, as you well know, she turned up the minute you mentioned her,' said Libby. 'And as far as I know, the police have dispatched her back to where she came from.'

'What's her background?' asked Anne. 'Where did she come from?'

'I don't know. What we do know is she apparently knew Nash's background, because she mentioned the "band of hope". Which we gather was the Rev Turner's club.' Libby sighed.

'Did he meet her here? Or in Spain?' asked Harry.

'No idea. Colin doesn't know.'

'Presumably the police know now,' said Ben. 'Perhaps Ian will tell you, if he comes in later.'

'Colin hasn't been in for a few days,' said Harry.

'He's tied up with the flat,' said Libby. 'He says he'll be in by the weekend.'

'And what about Gerry? I thought he'd be moving in with him.'

'He said at the start that wasn't the idea,' said Ben. 'It was a sort of trial for them.'

'We'll see when Gerry finds his house,' said Libby. 'Shall we adjourn to the pub? Then Harry and Ad can start clearing up.'

Harry stood. 'Go on, then. Shove off. We'll join you in a bit.'

They paid Donna, asked after her little girl, and said goodbye.

'I'm still slightly surprised that she comes to work here,' said Anne. 'She lives locally, now, doesn't she?'

'Yes, and needs the stimulation, apparently,' said Libby, holding the door for the wheelchair.

To their surprise, they found Ian already in possession of the small bar in the pub, along with Colin and Gerry, all looking serious.

'What's happened?' asked Libby, coming to a halt by the table. 'Can you tell us?'

Ian nodded. 'Get your drinks.'

Ben went to the bar, and Libby, Patti, and Anne arranged themselves round the table. No one smiled. Ben came back and sat down.

'So – what?' he said.

'Kerry Palmer was pregnant,' said Ian.

Chapter Twenty-nine

There was a minute's horrified silence. Then Patti put her head in her hands. Anne put her arm awkwardly round Patti's shoulders.

'Jesus,' whispered Ben. Then cleared his throat. 'Sorry, Patti.'

'No way of knowing who . . .?' Libby croaked.

'After twenty years, unlikely. I gather DNA can be retrieved sometimes, but it's open to question.' Ian stared into his pint glass. 'Bloody case gets worse and worse.'

Unwilling to pursue the topic any further, Libby took a healthy swallow of her drink and nearly choked. Gerry patted her on the back.

Ian looked up with a half smile. 'So. Is there anything else you want to know?'

They all looked at each other.

Then Colin sat up straight. 'Simone.' He looked at Ian warily. 'Did you find out anything else about her?'

'Very little.' Ian relaxed back into his chair. 'She has apparently been staying in a private hotel – for which read boarding house – for the last three months.'

'Where?' asked Ben.

'Ashford. We've checked, and she has.'

'So where does she actually live?' asked Gerry.

'She says she hasn't had a permanent address since she left Nash in Spain. And we certainly can't find any record of her over here. No results on any census.'

'I thought you couldn't check recent censuses?'

Ian grinned. 'The police can.'

'Alibi for Nash's death?' asked Libby.

'Firmly in her bedroom in Ashford.' Ian smiled. 'Almost as though she knew she would *need* an alibi.'

'No suspicious comings and goings? Or is it a rather free and easy establishment?' asked Anne.

'No, quite respectable. The landlady did say that Mrs Nash – yes, registered under her own name – often spent a few days away.'

'I wonder where?' mused Libby.

'We haven't yet had the chance to ask her,' said Ian. 'But she's in the clear for the murder.'

'But you don't know that she wasn't around St Aldeberge at the time of the Reverend Turner,' said Ben.

'I think we would have noticed an exotic name like Simone if it cropped up,' said Ian.

'But perhaps,' said Libby suddenly, 'she wasn't Simone! Suppose she changed her name?'

They all looked at her.

'No one said anything about Nash having a wife or even a girl-friend,' said Patti.

'No, but he could have kept her hidden,' said Libby, unwilling to give up her theory.

'We'll look into it,' said Ian. 'It's certainly an idea, Libby.'

Libby sat back, triumphant, just as Harry and Peter walked in.

'Oh, dear,' said Peter, 'what's the old trout been up to now?'

This eased the tension.

'No Edward tonight?' asked Harry.

'No. I got someone to drop me here – I'll get a cab home. He knows where we all are if he wants to join us.' Ian stood. 'Another drink, anyone?'

'I've never seen him so despondent,' said Ben, while Ian and Peter were at the bar. 'Really getting to him, isn't it?'

'I'm not surprised,' said Patti. 'It's getting to me, too.'

'Do you know,' said Libby, a faraway look in her eye, 'in books, village mysteries are always labelled "cosy". I think that's a stupid term, don't you? What's "cosy" about this?'

'Or any of the other murders you've been involved with,' said Harry. 'These people should live through one, then they'd soon see. And when Agatha Christie was writing hers, they didn't call them cosy, did they?'

'No,' agreed Anne. 'As a librarian, I can verify that. Mystery or detective stories. Didn't matter if the detective was professional or amateur, then.'

'That sounds an interesting conversation,' said Ian, returning with a tray.

'We were talking about books and TV shows,' said Libby, going faintly pink.

'Not about real-life detectives, then,' said Ian with a smile.

'Would we?' said Harry.

'It's all got a bit more serious, Hal,' said Peter. 'Ian's just told me. The girl whose body they found? She was pregnant.'

'Fu . . . bloody hell,' said Harry. 'Now what? At least *that* couldn't have been down to Simone.'

'Harry's got a thing about Simone,' explained Libby.

'And Libby thinks she might have been around when Nash lived in St Aldeberge and has changed her name,' said Gerry.

'Well done, petal. That sounds quite likely, don't you think?' He cocked his head in Ian's direction.

'We're going to look into it,' said Ian.

'That wouldn't make her a murderer, though, would it?' said Anne.

'Not of the girls, I wouldn't have thought,' said Harry, 'but definitely of Nash. Revenge, or something.'

'Could it not be just because he'd cut her out of his will?' said Patti. 'That's what I thought.'

'It's the obvious motive,' said Libby. 'Isn't it, Ian?'

Ian was regarding them all with amusement. 'Carry on,' he said. 'You might just hit on something relevant.'

'Don't be patronising,' said Ben.

'Me?' Ian said in mock surprise. 'What a thought!'

The door opened and Edward's smiling face appeared.

'Evening! Can anybody join in?'

Amid the exclamations of welcome, Ben noticed Libby about to ask a question.

'You're looking smart, Edward,' he said quickly. 'Not that you don't always look smart of course.'

On his way to the bar, Edward turned and winked over his shoulder. 'Thank you, Ben. I'll satisfy Libby's curiosity in a minute.'

Libby went even pinker than she had been before and everyone laughed.

'Yes, Libby.' Edward squeezed in beside her. 'I had a date.'

'Don't encourage her,' said Ian. Libby looked indignant.

'Well, everyone was wondering, weren't they?' said Edward. 'I dared to step outside the charmed circle.'

Libby groaned. Edward laughed and patted her hand.

'It's all right, Lib. We had a visiting lecturer who came from my old uni, so we went out for a meal for old times' sake. Officially broken up now, of course.'

'Where did you go?' asked Anne. 'I'm always keen to add to my list of good places to eat.'

'Oi!' said Harry. 'I am here, you know!'

'And you're top of the list, of course,' said Anne. 'Where was it, then?'

'Really good Turkish restaurant,' said Edward. 'You all ought to try it. You went to Turkey on holiday a few years ago, didn't you?'

Peter, Harry, and Ben nodded.

'Yes, Guy took us to a place he used to visit,' said Libby. 'Perhaps we should?' She looked round the table.

Luckily, this had the result of diverting the group away from speculation about Simone Nash and the murders, but Libby couldn't help returning to it as she and Ben walked home.

'So who do you suppose the father was?'

'Of Kerry's baby?' said Ben. 'Obvious answer's Nash, isn't it?'

'Hmm. Do you suppose he left Simone pregnant, too?'

'Hold on – she was his wife! Wouldn't matter if she was pregnant, would it?'

'No.' Libby frowned. 'Where have we gone wrong?'

'We? We haven't! We're only exploring possibilities.'

'What about Ian? Where has he gone wrong?'

'Libby! He hasn't! We don't know what the police are doing. They could have all sorts of lines of enquiry we don't know about.'

'He did look despondent, though. You said so.'

'Yes, but that's because it's turning out to be a complicated case, and a distressing one. He'll get there.'

But I need to, as well, Libby thought as she followed Ben into the house. Somehow.

Thursday morning she was somewhat surprised to receive a phone call from her cousin.

'Morning, Lib,' she said. 'Got a minute?'

'Of course! In fact, I was going to call you.'

Cass laughed. 'I bet I know what about, too!'

'Go on, then – surprise me!'

'Mike had a call from Jemima Routledge this morning.'

'About Nobby Marsh?'

'How did you guess? Yes, of course. She asked if we knew anything about him, as you seemed quite interested in her lawnmower.'

'I didn't know it was hers until yesterday,' said Libby. 'It was the fact that Marsh had been repairing it and would have known how to tamper with the brakes – or whatever was damaged. The police did look into him, right at the beginning of the case, though.'

'But surely, there would be the question of motive. *Why* would he tamper with it?'

'Yes, Cass, exactly. So?'

'Well, Mike's known him for years, so he started thinking about it. And he couldn't think of anything.'

'OK.' Libby frowned. 'So – what?'

'But he did remember something else.'

Libby bit down a scream. 'Shall I come over?' she asked, with barely a wobble in her voice.

'Yes, that would be good. About an hour?'

'A bit sooner,' said Libby.

'OK.' Cass sounded surprised. 'I've got a decoration for you, as well.'

'Lovely! Thank you,' said Libby.

She was out of the door in ten minutes, and then realised she would be at Farthing's Plants far too early, so she took the scenic route via Maria and Ron's house, and was surprised to see them both walking out of the gates. She pulled up.

'Are you out for essential exercise, or can I give you a lift?' she asked. 'Not that there's much room in here.'

'On our way to Mike's actually,' said Ron, looking at her curiously. 'Didn't seem worth getting the motor out.'

'That's where I'm going, too! Sure you don't want to squash in?'

'No, we're fine,' said Maria. 'We try and get out for a walk at least once a day.'

'OK – I'll see you there.'

OK, so was this a coincidence, she asked herself, or had Mike asked them to come and see her?

She pulled in to Farthing's Plants courtyard, and wasn't surprised to see both Mike and Cassandra waiting for her.

'Maria and Ron are on their way,' she said, as she climbed out of the car.

'We know,' said Cass. 'They just rang.'

Not a coincidence, then.

'Come into the office,' said Mike. 'Kettle's on, and the boys are off in the greenhouses.'

The boys ran the mail order side of the business, and all the more technical aspects with which Mike found it hard to deal.

They had barely got inside when Ron and Maria turned into the yard.

While Cass busied herself with tea and coffee, Mike took up a position on a stool and looked at Libby.

'I was thinking about Nobby Marsh,' he said. 'And I remembered you told Cass Maria had mentioned that policeman.'

'Did I tell you that?' Libby raised her eyebrows at Cass.

'No, I did,' said Maria.

'And I just wondered . . .'

'About whether I'd come across any more of the players in the drama,' said Ron. 'There's bound to be some sort of crossover between Felling and St Aldeberge, isn't there?'

'Well, yes, I thought so,' said Libby. 'We all wondered at first if the bloke who was killed by the lawnmower had been involved in all that business with Sir Nigel and his parties years ago. Even the police.'

'Yeah, well, I didn't know him, but, as I think I told you before, I never got involved, although they tried to make me.' He made a deprecating face, 'I never got into anything really dodgy.'

Cass began handing out mugs.

'So what did you remember?' asked Libby, blowing inelegantly into her mug.

'I remembered Nobby Marsh.'

Chapter Thirty

'You said you didn't know him!'

'I didn't. But I remembered him after I'd thought a bit. He was a mate of that copper's.'

'So he *was* involved at St Aldeberge!'

'I'm not saying that! Don't get excited,' said Ron. 'I just said he was a mate of the copper's. I only remembered because I called him Nobby Clarke – that's usually what a Nobby is, after all – and someone got irritated about it.'

'Who did?'

'I don't remember! It was twenty years ago!'

'Sorry.' Libby subsided onto her stool. 'Well, thank you, Ron. That's certainly a help.'

'Why?' asked Cass. 'How does it help?'

'I'm not sure I ought to say, really.'

'Libby!' Cass made an exasperated sound. 'Come on! We all help you! It's the least you can do.'

'Well—' Libby looked round the circle of expectant faces. 'Nobby Marsh mended Jemima's ride-on lawnmower – or gave it a service, anyway – before it was given to Nash. So he would have known how to tamper with it. And we wondered why he would do that. But if he was around St Aldeberge and Nash's little gang he might very well have a motive.'

'What were they doing?' Ron narrowed his eyes at her.

'That I really *can't* tell you,' said Libby, exceptionally uncomfortable.

'It really is classified. Take it from me, it appears to have been pretty nasty.'

Maria leant forward and patted her arm. 'Don't worry. We'll find out sooner or later.'

'It's really kind of you to help.' Libby smiled at her. 'I do appreciate it. And the police will, too.'

'Rather tell you than them!' said Ron. 'And now we'll go on with our walk. Thanks for the coffee, Cass.'

'Was it really a help?' asked Mike after they'd gone.

'Yes, actually. At least, I think so. It will help with elimination, anyway.'

'I've got something for you,' said Cass. 'Hang on – it's out the back.'

A few minutes later she came back and held up a beautiful twisted piece of wood, decorated with sprayed leaves and pine cones.

'Christmas!' she said.

'It's gorgeous, Cass!' Libby beamed. 'How much do I owe you?'

'Don't be daft,' said Cass. 'Present. Now, anything else we can help with?'

Ten minutes later, Libby left Farthing's Plants and found herself driving down the Nethergate Road. She debated going to see Fran and won the argument.

Fran was discovered sitting with her feet up behind the counter of Guy's gallery-come-shop.

'Not much business this morning?' asked Libby.

'No. It calms down on Thursdays. I think people are saving up for the weekend.'

'Good, then I can ask your advice.'

'What about?'

Libby told her about the discovery of Kerry's pregnancy and of Marsh's tenuous connection to Sergeant Peacock and St Aldeberge.

'So what advice do you need? To leave well alone?'

'No. I was wondering if I should go and see Marsh.'

'Libby! Don't be daft!' Fran put her feet down and stood up. 'That really would be stupid.'

'He might not be involved.'

'And he might be! That's why you'd go, isn't it? To find out? That's just idiotic. That's the heroine going down into the unlit cellar at night after hearing a strange noise in a strange house. Well, there might *not* be a mad axeman down there!'

Libby gave an unwilling chuckle. 'So how can we find out?'

'I know!' Fran held up a forefinger. 'Let's tell the police!'

'Oh, *you*!' Libby sat heavily on the stool provided for customers. 'All right. I'll tell Rachel. She said I could. I think the police are trusting us now.'

'The police have always trusted us,' said Fran. 'Well, Ian has. Remember he asked us in over that business with Laurence Cooper.'

'Who? Oh, the Anderson Place case. He didn't ask us, he asked you. And that was partly because he fancied you.' Libby gave her a wicked grin.

'Yes, well. Maybe, maybe not.' Fran sat back down. 'In any case, that's what has to be done. After all, it's only a snippet of news, isn't it? It might mean nothing.'

'No.' Libby sighed. 'You're right. What shall I do, then?'

'I told you! Tell the police. If they think it's worth investigating, they will.'

'Mmm, yes. I could go and chat to the old ladies again, I suppose.'

'What for?'

'Well, now we know more about what went on from the horse's mouth, it might be worth trying to find out if all the parents were involved in the gossip-mongering.'

'Unlikely, I would have thought,' said Fran. 'They'd be more likely to be in denial. And Liz Palmer would have known, too.'

'Mmm, yes.' Libby stared in silence at a rotating rack of Christmas cards. 'Isn't it annoying that we can't get hold of Pam White or her mum? I feel sure they hold the key.'

'They will. Eventually.' Fran leant her elbows on the counter. 'But go and talk to the old ladies again, if you can bear it. If it'll put your mind at rest.'

'Right. I will. Or at least ask Patti what she thinks.'

Libby drove the familiar route to St Aldeberge mulling over what she wanted to say when she got there. Another thing occurred to her: she could pop into the incident room to leave the information passed to her by Ron Stewart.

Which, after parking at the vicarage, was what she did. There were no familiar figures around, but a constable came forward and smiled at her.

'Mrs Sarjeant,' he said. 'What can we do for you?'

Libby told him and watched him note it down.

'I'll pass it on as soon as I can,' he said. 'Hope it's useful.'

'So do I,' said Libby, smiling back.

Patti was standing at the vicarage door looking puzzled when she got back.

'Wondered where you were,' she said. 'Coming in?'

'Just for a minute,' said Libby, following her inside. 'I wanted to ask your advice.'

She told Patti her idea.

'I suppose it might help, but I'm not sure it wouldn't just be going over old ground. And I don't want to end up with a flood of elderly ladies inundating the vicarage.'

'I hadn't thought of that,' said Libby. 'Nothing I can usefully do, then, is there?'

'No.' Patti grinned.

'That's more or less what Fran said.' Libby pulled a rueful face. 'Oh, well, I shall have to suppress my nosy gene, I suppose.'

'Difficult,' said Patti seriously. 'Have you had lunch?'

'No, I'm going to have it with Ben at home. I shall try and be a good little woman for a few days.'

Libby went home.

'I feel sure there's something I could do,' she said to Ben, when she joined him at the Hop Pocket. 'Fran and Patti both said that's enough, in effect. And they're right. Looking into Nobby Marsh would be foolhardy, after what Ron told me.'

'What, that he's been mixed up in the past with the bad guys? I agree with them.'

'I knew you would.' She looked round. 'This is virtually finished, isn't it?'

'Yes.' Ben smiled round with satisfaction. 'I've got stock lists drawn up, but I won't be able to start interviewing until after Christmas, so it looks like opening around Easter.'

'You could start advertising now, though,' said Libby. 'I mean, it'll be a whole lifestyle change for someone. It'll take some planning.'

'Yes, I will. You'll help me, won't you?'

Libby smiled. 'Of course. Never doubted it, did you?'

Ben gave her a hug.

With an effort, Libby allowed the whole St Aldeberge subject to drop over the weekend. Colin and Gerry had gone up to London to visit old friends, so they weren't there to remind her.

'I thought Colin said he was moving into the flat this weekend,' Libby said to Ben on Saturday afternoon.

'He moved in on Friday. He popped in to tell me about an hour before you got back from Patti's. He wants us to go round for a drink on Monday with Harry and Pete.'

'When does Harry start Christmas opening on Mondays?'

'Not this Monday, obviously.'

Sunday was the usual lunch at Hetty's, and as a special treat, Libby was allowed to take Jeff-dog for a walk on Sunday morning. Flo and Lenny joined them, but this week neither Edward nor Ian were there.

'Got plans, Edward said,' Hetty told them.

'Ooh, I wonder if it's that visiting lecturer again?' said Libby.

'We don't know, and we won't ask,' Ben warned her.

However, when they arrived at Colin's new flat on Monday evening, it was to find Edward already there. Gerry was bustling around in a tea-towel apron assembling a selection of party food.

'Thanks,' said Colin, accepting the bottle of fizz Libby presented him with. 'You shouldn't have.'

'You have to christen the new home,' said Libby. 'Looks lovely.'

Colin and Gerry exchanged looks.

'Actually,' said Colin, 'we wanted to talk to you about that.' He gave them both glasses and indicated a sofa. They sat. 'We've reconsidered a bit since Gerry's been here in Steeple Martin.'

'Yes,' Gerry said. 'I love Steeple Farm, and I love what I've seen of the village. But it does seem a bit silly for me to keep staying up there now Col's moved in here.'

'We did wonder,' said Ben. 'So you'll be moving in here?'

'If you don't mind,' said Gerry.

'Why should we mind?' asked Libby. 'I assumed you would move in here when we first heard you were – um – well . . .'

'I know,' said Colin. 'We were trying to – er – play it cool. Oh, dear, that's terribly dated, isn't it?'

'Well, we're very pleased for you. Take your time moving out,' said Ben. 'Not that you've got much to move, as I remember.'

'No. I'll have to go back to Spain to arrange for everything to be transported over here, but I'll do that after Christmas.' He looked at Colin. 'We saw my parents over the weekend, that's why we weren't around. They'd never met Col.'

'Ah,' said Libby nodding wisely and managing to refrain from asking all the questions she wanted to.

Peter and Harry arrived bearing a Welcome to Your New Home hamper, full of Harry's special delights, which Harry refused to allow to be eaten tonight.

'For when you're on your own, ducks,' he said, appropriating the second sofa. 'And where were you yesterday, you scallywag?' he asked Edward.

Edward laughed. 'I wondered how long it would take before someone asked.' He looked at Libby. 'I bet you were dying to!'

'Me? No!' protested Libby.

'I expect you'll meet her in the next week or so,' said Edward mischievously.

Six expectant faces stared at him.

'All right, all right,' he said after a minute. 'The visiting lecturer I told you about—'

'Told you so!' said Libby.

'Well, we had actually been a bit more than friends before, although nothing serious. But she's been down here for the whole Michaelmas term, and is likely to get tenure. So we've been seeing a bit of one another.'

'Where does she live?' asked Libby.

'The same digs I lived in before I moved to Grove House.' Edward grinned at her. 'And yes, she's been to the flat. And yes, she's met Ian.'

'He didn't say anything!' said Libby indignantly.

Everyone laughed.

'Has anything happened with the Nick Nash case?' asked Colin, when they had all settled down.

Between them, they told Colin and Gerry everything they had learnt over the last few days.

'Nobby Marsh.' Edward looked thoughtful. 'I know him.'

Gasps of amazement.

'You remember Ted Sachs, that builder who did some work for us on Grove House?'

'And turned out to be a bad lot? Yes,' said Ben.

'Well, we had some work done on the garden as well, and he recommended Nobby Marsh to come in and do the heavy work. You know, moving earth and breaking up old paving. He had all the machinery.'

'Why didn't Ian know about that?' asked Libby. 'He actually interviewed Marsh right at the beginning of the case.'

'Had him interviewed,' corrected Ben. 'I doubt if he did it himself.'

'Whatever, he knew about him,' said Libby.

'But he didn't really know anything about the garden,' said Edward. 'That's my domain.'

'But you must know where he's based?' said Gerry.

'Yes, you would have got in touch yourself, not through Ted the Red,' said Harry.

'Ted the Red?' spluttered Libby. 'Where'd you get that from?'

Harry grinned. 'Rhymes.'

Edward was thinking. 'Over near Steeple Mount, I think. Or – no, nearer to the next village along – Ashton something?'

'Cherry Ashton,' said Libby. 'I know it.'

'Does that matter?' asked Peter. 'You aren't intending to go and visit him, are you?'

'No!' chorused all the men in the room.

'No,' agreed Libby doubtfully.

'Look, petal,' said Harry, in his best avuncular manner, 'If this Nob bloke turns out to be involved with Nick Nash's Nasties you'd be in trouble. And if he isn't, well, nothing wasted and no point in going. And Ian looked into it. So if anything had been flagged up, it would have been dealt with.'

'Harry's right,' said Ben. 'Stop worrying at it.'

'But the police didn't know about his connection with Sergeant Peacock,' protested Libby.

'Solution.' Harry wriggled forward in his seat. 'Your Adam told you about him, didn't he?'

'And others.'

'But it was Adam who told you about the boy helper, wasn't it?'

'Yes . . .'

'Well, perhaps you could track him down and talk to him. Unless he's the Nob's son, of course.'

'I still don't like it,' said Ben.

'I can't help remembering Ted Sachs,' said Edward.

'Oh, all right.' Harry sat back again. 'Only trying to help.'

Peter smiled at him and patted his leg.

'Well, as everyone's told me to leave it alone, even Patti and Fran, I suppose that's what I'd better do, unless it pops up and bites me again,' Libby said. 'Ian will be pleased.'

'Nothing more about Simone, then?' asked Colin.

'No, nothing. I think the police might have hit a brick wall, let alone me,' said Libby.

'They'll keep plodding away in the background,' said Ben. 'You see if they don't.'

It wasn't entirely a wish to see an old friend that sent Libby over to Creekmarsh on Tuesday morning. She knew Adam and his boss Mog were working on a new section of the garden they were restoring for Lewis Osbourne-Walker, and had a desire to see how they were progressing. And she hadn't seen Lewis's mother Edie for a long time, and told herself she owed it to Hetty to check up on her.

As work on the garden had progressed, Adam and Mog had moved further away from the house, and were now in the mini-parkland designed, apparently, in the Georgian era. And, as Libby had supposed, this required a fair amount of re-landscaping, although on a grander scale than that at Grove House. She was gratified, therefore, to see two sturdy-looking mechanical diggers standing idly on the edge of the small lake.

'Hello!' Mog, faintly dishevelled as usual, appeared from behind a hedge. 'Did we know you were coming?'

'No, I dropped in to see Edie and thought I'd come and see how you were doing.' She looked around. 'Isn't it difficult to do this sort of thing in the winter?'

'Not ideal,' said Mog. 'But with most things dormant it could be worse. We'll have to stop in the spring, though.'

'Why? Oh! Birds!'

Mog grinned. 'Exactly. Once they start nesting, that's it. When I think how many birds were made homeless in the old days . . .' He shuddered.

'I suppose so,' said Libby. 'People weren't always so aware, were they?'

'They didn't care,' said Mog. 'Shall I tell Ad you're here?'

'Only if he's handy,' said Libby.

'He's only down there.' Mog waved an arm. 'Telling the bloke with the digger what to do next.'

Libby felt a surge of adrenalin which left her arms tingling.

'Oh, I don't want to disturb him,' she said.

'No bother,' said Mog. 'Hi, Ad! Your mum's here!'

Adam appeared from behind one of the diggers, accompanied by someone who definitely wasn't Nobby Marsh.

'Golly!' said Libby.

Mog laughed. 'Doesn't quite fit the surroundings, does he?'

'No.' Libby regarded the blue quiff adorning the otherwise shaven head thoughtfully. Ryan? 'Doesn't his employer mind him looking like that?'

'Doesn't appear to. And it doesn't really matter, does it? He's not meeting members of the public. And Lewis is the last person to worry about it.'

'True.' Libby grinned and realised Adam was beckoning her down the slope. 'Is it all right if I go down?'

'Yes – you can't damage much at the moment.' Mog gave her a mock salute and returned to his hedge.

'Mum,' said Adam, giving her a knowing look. 'Come and see what we're doing.'

The blue-quiffed one moved sulkily out of the way.

'This is Ryan. This is my mum, Libby Sarjeant, Ryan.'

Was it imagination, or had Ryan's blue eyes just sharpened?

'Hello, Ryan. Nice to meet you,' said Libby. 'So, what are you doing, Ad?'

Adam began to explain, drawing her right down to the edge of the lake. Ryan climbed back up into his digger and set it moving.

'It's all right,' said Libby. 'I wasn't going to start questioning him. I'm here to see Edie.'

'Is that right?' Adam looked unconvinced.

'I've been warned off.' Libby looked round. 'So what's going on?'

Adam explained what they were doing. 'The original design of the garden has got a bit lost over the years – well, you know that. And one thing we need to do is leave it less manicured than it was. Not quite re-wilding, but getting on that way.'

Libby nodded approval. 'And does Ryan agree with that?'

'I don't think he cares one way or another. His heart isn't really in the job. I gather he's only doing it because his mum said he had to get a job.'

'And did you sympathise?' asked Libby, with a grin.

'Of course! Makes a bond, you know.' Adam gave her an answering grin.

Libby bade them goodbye and began to make her way towards the house. Edie, unsurprisingly, was in the kitchen and saw her approaching.

'Libby, love! Come in, come in!' Edie gave her a hug. 'Haven't seen you for an age. How's Hetty?'

Over the inevitable tea and biscuits, they caught up on their mutual news.

'And you got another murder on your hands, Lewis tells me?' said Edie.

'How does he know?'

'Your Adam always tells us what you're up to.' Edie gave her a satisfied smile. 'Bit of excitement, you know?'

'I wouldn't call it that,' said Libby with a sigh. 'Not this time, particularly.'

'Oh, lovey.' Edie patted her hand. 'Nasty, is it?'

'It is. Oh, it didn't start off as badly as it carried on, if you know what I mean. Actually it started with someone doing a bit of landscaping, although nothing like Lewis's project here.'

'That lawnmower or something, wasn't it? Sounded like an accident to me.'

'Yes, a ride-on mower.'

'The chap who does the work for the boys has one of them,' said Edie.

'Is that Ryan? I met him just now.'

'No, his boss, love. Nobby something.'

Libby stared. 'Oh, yes . . . I think I heard something about him.'

Edie leaned forward. 'I've met some villains in my time – well, you know that – and I would have said he's definitely not kosher.'

'Really? Is it safe to have him round here?'

224

'He can't do much here.' Edie sat back. 'Never comes into the house. Don't think much of that Ryan, either.'

'Is that because of the way he looks?' Libby smiled.

'Nah! I'm a Londoner! Seen worse than that. No, he's just such a sulky specimen. Comes from a good home, though.'

'Oh?' said Libby, surprised. 'How do you know?'

'Lewis drove him home one time. Really classy little block of flats on the outskirts of Nethergate, he said. Must be his family home. He could never afford it on his own.'

'Right, the boys said he was only doing this job because his mum told him to!'

Edie laughed heartily. 'Much good that usually does!'

'So he's nothing to do with his boss, then?'

'Dunno, love.' Edie shrugged. 'But I wouldn't, would I?'

After another half an hour, Libby excused herself to go home.

'Now don't you leave it so long next time,' said Edie, giving her a parting hug. 'And bring Hetty, too. She can bring that dog of hers.'

Libby drove thoughtfully home. Interesting though all this information was, she couldn't see that any of it would be of use to the police investigation. She drove through Heronsbourne, briefly considered popping in to see George at the Red Lion, who might know Nobby Marsh, then decided against it and drove home past Steeple Mount.

As she drove past her own pub, she was surprised to see Rachel Trent emerging. She slowed to a halt and opened the window.

'Hello! What are you doing here?'

Rachel leant in. 'Tracking down Colin Hardcastle. Didn't realise he'd moved from the pub.'

'Only this weekend,' said Libby.

'I'm going to go up and see if he's in. Are you going home?'

'Yes. Want to come in?'

'Yes, please. Pop the kettle on!'

Libby drove home, lit the fire and, as per instructions, popped the kettle on. Rachel arrived ten minutes later.

'I expect you want to know what we wanted with Colin?' she said, as they settled in front of the fire.

'Only if you want to tell me.'

'Well, you need to know, too. We're closing the incident room in St Aldeberge.'

'Oh? Scaling down the enquiry?"

'Not exactly. It's just that DI Connell doesn't think we need a presence there any more. I agree with him. For the last week everyone's been sitting round doing very little. Waste of resources.'

'I can see that. But you're still looking into everything?'

'Including your bête noire Pam White particularly.'

Libby smiled. 'Actually, I picked up a little bit of information today. Not really to do with the case, but interesting.'

'Go on then, what?'

'I went over to see Edie at Creekmarsh this morning. You know – Lewis Osbourne-Walker's mum?'

'No, I don't know her.'

'No, I don't think you were around for any of those cases. Well, that's who she is – friend of Ben's mum Hetty. And while I was there Adam – you know he works over there on the gardens? – he introduced me to Ryan who works for Nobby Marsh.'

'Oh? You didn't ask him any questions, I hope?'

'Of course not! But when I saw Edie, she started talking about Nobby Marsh and Ryan. And it was nothing to do with me, either!'

'So what did she say?'

'She reckons Nobby Marsh is – or was – a villain, and she doesn't like young Ryan. But she told me something odd. She said he comes from a good home.'

Rachel frowned. 'How does she know?'

'Not so much a good home as a nice flat, actually. Lewis drove him home once. And Edie said Ryan couldn't have afforded it himself. But Adam told me the boy's only doing the job because his mum said he had to.'

'So presumably he's living with his mum.' Rachel quirked an eyebrow. 'I don't see that's anything to interest us.'

'No neither do I. But it looks as if Ryan has no connection other than work with his boss, so couldn't be connected with damage to the lawnmower.'

'As far as we could see, neither did his boss,' said Rachel. 'Why did this Edie think Marsh was a villain?'

'Instinct, I think. She had a bit to do with London lowlifes when she was younger.'

'Prejudice,' said Rachel, with a smile.

'Probably,' said Libby. 'I accused her of that with Ryan because of the way he looks.'

'Mind you,' said Rachel, 'there is some intel that Marsh was connected to Sir Nigel all those years ago.'

'Yes. Apparently he knew Ted Sachs – they worked together sometimes. And Ian might already know that.' Libby explained the connection.

'If that's the case, I expect it will have been looked into. I didn't do it, but I expect it's all written down somewhere. I really ought to catch up,' sighed Rachel.

'You have briefings, don't you?'

'Yes, of course, but not everything's included every day.'

'If there was anything important you'd know, though.'

'Yes, so it couldn't have been, could it?'

Chapter Thirty-one

Lewis rang in the evening.

'Mum said you were asking about young Ryan.'

'Not particularly,' said Libby. 'She mentioned him, and I said I'd just met him with Adam.'

'Yeah, well. Actually I thought it was a bit – you know – peculiar.'

'What – us talking about him?'

'Don't be stupid! No, where he lived. It just wasn't like him.'

'And that worried you?' Libby got up from the sofa and went into the kitchen.

'You know what he looks like,' said Lewis.

'And you shouldn't judge by appearances,' replied Libby.

'All right – but where he lives doesn't suit him at all.'

'From what Ad said, he lived with his mum, so it must be her flat.'

'Suppose so.'

'Where exactly is it?' Libby perched on the edge of the kitchen table.

'Right on the edge of Nethergate. Above the town, at the top of the hill. All newish bungalows and little blocks of flats.'

'Not Canongate Drive?'

'Yeah, that's it! Do you know it then?'

'I'll say! We even know the bloke who built it,' Libby laughed. 'And we have a friend who lives in one of the little blocks of flats.'

'At the end of the drive?' asked Lewis. 'That's where Ryan lives.'

'Well, well, well,' said Libby. 'Does seem an anomaly.'

'A what?'

'Seems a bit out of place,' elaborated Libby. 'Our friend who lives there is a retired Professor of History.'

'Might I have met him?' asked Lewis. 'Little bloke with a goatee?'

'That's him! Very dapper. Yes, you might have met him at a party or something. Anyway, not Ryan's sort at all.'

'Yeah, well. Worried me a bit.'

'Why?'

'I dunno. He's been coming here for ages now, but he's got grumpier and grumpier. I don't see so much of his boss, now. Which is no loss. Villain if ever I saw one.'

'That's what your mum said.'

'My mum knows everything!' Lewis laughed. 'Anyway, thought you needed to know. Especially if it's got anything to do with this lawnmower case.'

'What was that about?' asked Ben, when she went back into the sitting room.

Libby told him.

'He didn't seem to know exactly why he was worried,' she concluded, 'but I agree that it is an odd place for him to live, but if he's with his mum, it isn't odd, is it?'

'Convoluted, but I think I understand,' said Ben. 'And Lewis thinks this Nobby Marsh is a villain, too?'

'Yes. But I'm getting sick of reporting gossip and hearsay to the police, so I shan't say anything.' Libby sat down. 'Is it time for a nightcap, yet?'

'I'll tell you what you could do,' said Ben, getting up and going kitchenwards, 'pop over and see Andrew Wylie in the morning. He might know Ryan's mum, or something about the family, if you're really worried.'

'That's a good idea. And frankly, I don't know why it's ringing warning bells.'

'Because of the lawnmower of course,' called Ben from the kitchen. 'Although I think I'd be more worried about Nobby Marsh.'

'But nobody wants me to go anywhere near him,' objected Libby.

'Too right,' said Ben, returning with two large scotches. 'That's why I'd be more worried about him.'

Libby gave up.

On Wednesday morning Ben, having done all he could do at the Hop Pocket, returned to the estate office, and Libby, after opening one of the first batches of Christmas cards, set off for Canongate Drive. She gave Andrew a quick ring, saying she was on her way to see Fran (which she would) and could she call in to say compliments of the season.

Canongate Drive, built above Nethergate Bay by an old friend of Ben's, comprised three small blocks of flats, a few townhouses, and a clutch of spectacular bungalows. The upper floors of the flats and the bungalows all had wonderful views over the bay, and the prices would have made it unfeasible for anyone young and in a menial job to have afforded.

'This is a nice surprise,' said Andrew, standing aside and waving her into the flat, where Talbot, his large black and white cat, greeted her from the dining table.

'Still quite happy being a house cat?' Libby asked him, making a fuss of his big head.

Talbot had once belonged to a former partner of Andrew's, and lived a mainly outdoor life.

'Seems to be,' said Andrew. 'Getting fatter though. Are you having coffee? There's cake.'

'Go on, then!' said Libby.

'And then you can ask me whatever it is you've come for.'

Libby gasped. 'I haven't . . .'

Andrew threw his head back and laughed. 'Go on with you! I don't mind.'

'Well,' he said, when he returned with a laden tray. 'What is it?'

Libby thought. 'About a neighbour of yours. At least, I think it's a neighbour.'

'It? Man or woman?'

'Woman and boy. Youth.'

Andrew nodded. 'I think I might know who you mean. Would the woman be – not sure – one with a very *stylish* haircut, and fond of a sheepskin coat?'

'Yes, that sounds about right.'

'Rather over-smart, shall we say?'

'I don't know. I've never seen her.'

'And the youth, then. A little dated in style. Blue quiff? At least, it's blue at the moment.'

'That's them!' Libby was excited. 'You know them?'

'Not know, exactly. They live in the next block. Moved in a few years ago – three? I thought at first she had a toyboy, but apparently, the boy is her son. He didn't seem to do anything at first, and lived there a lot of time on his own, but now he seems to go out to work and she's there a lot of the time, too.' Andrew cocked his head on one side. 'Are you going to tell me why?'

'As much as I can.' Libby took a sip of excellent coffee. 'He's come up in an investigation, and we're curious.'

'Who's we? You and Fran, or the police?'

'Both,' said Libby. 'Not sure he's actually anything to do with it, but it's a – an anomaly.'

'Because they're an unlikely couple?'

'More that it didn't seem the right – um – *milieu* for the boy.'

Andrew laughed. 'Among all the middle-class retirees, you mean?'

'Sort of. Am I being a snob?'

'Not you. Have some cake.'

Libby helped herself. 'It's me being incurably nosy as usual. I don't know whether you've heard about the murder over at St Aldeberge?'

'The ex-churchwarden and the lawnmower? Yes – local TV news. Your friend Campbell McLean reporting. We don't seem to get local papers any more.'

'They are still produced, but it's mainly online now. Do you remember our friend Jane? She's online editor, now.'

'I remember.' Andrew nodded. 'Lives somewhere down near Fran?'

'That's right. Anyway, you've heard about the murder.'

'Yes. And hasn't there been another body discovered now?'

'Yes.' Libby sighed. 'And our Ryan – the blue-haired boy – doesn't seem to have anything to do with that. It's just that he works with lawnmowers and diggers and that sort of thing.'

'I see! Poor lad. Guilty by association.' Andrew pulled a face.

'Indeed,' said Libby. 'No, I won't have any more cake. I don't know how you stay so trim.'

Just before she left, Libby said, 'You don't know anything about the Dunton Estate, do you? Not the main house, but another one. The one that belonged to the ex-churchwarden.'

'Yes, I know the one. Used, like the main house was, in the last war. I *think*, although I'm not completely sure, that it was used as a base for one of the Special Duties bases.'

'Oh!' said Libby. 'Yes – I think I know about that. They had tunnels, didn't they?'

'They did. Not my area of expertise, but if it's useful I could look into it for you.'

'I don't think it's necessary, thank you, Andrew, but I'll come back to you if it is.'

Before driving off, Libby stood looking at the next block along from Andrew's. So this was where Ryan had lived for the last few years. And where had he been before that?

'It doesn't matter!' she told herself impatiently, and got into the car.

She drove down the hill into the town and along Harbour Street. She could see Fran, again behind the counter in Guy's shop, so drove along and parked behind the Blue Anchor.

Mavis appeared at the door as she went past.

'See you've found that Pam White, then,' she said.

Libby stopped dead. 'What?'

232

'Liz seen her, thought you would have.' Mavis folded her arms and frowned.

'Where?'

'I dunno. About. Didn't recognise her at first.'

'Has she told the police?' Libby stepped forward urgently.

'How would I know?' Mavis shrugged.

'Thanks, Mavis!' Libby turned and ran down Harbour Street until she reached the shop, breathless.

'Good heavens! What's up with you?' said Fran. 'Sit down, for goodness' sake.'

Libby was scrabbling for her phone. 'Just listen!' she gasped. 'Rachel? Libby! Have you heard from Liz Palmer? Well, Mavis – you know from the Blue Anchor? – she's just told me that Liz has seen Pam White! – I know, I couldn't believe it either. No, she didn't say where. No, go on, you pass it on. Will you let me know?'

Fran was sitting open mouthed. 'Did I hear right? So she isn't dead?'

'If Liz is right, no.' Libby relaxed against the counter. 'Although, how did she recognise her after all this time? She'd look a lot different from a fifteen-year-old, or whatever she was. I wouldn't recognise me at that age.'

Fran stood up. 'I think you need a restorative coffee.'

'I've just had one with Andrew. Oh, and that's something else I have to tell you.'

'Well, I need one,' said Fran. 'Let me call Guy from the studio.'

Guy emerged looking slightly dazed and also requested coffee. Fran and Libby retreated to the miniscule kitchen and Libby began her story.

'Well,' said Fran when she'd finished. 'There is an obvious answer to all this.'

'There is?'

'Let me take Guy his coffee.' Fran slid out of the room leaving Libby frowning over her statement.

'OK, tell me,' she said when Fran came back. 'I can't see anything obvious.'

'Pam White is Ryan's mother.'

To Libby, the silence that followed this announcement positively rang.

'Ticks all the boxes,' said Fran. 'Pam disappeared at the same time as Kerry, right? Suppose she was pregnant, too. So she vanishes to Dover, or wherever, and manages to bring him up. And makes enough money, somehow, to eventually buy this flat on Canongate Drive. But whatever it is she's doing, it takes her away from home sometimes. I could make a guess, but it would be uncharitable.'

'Prostitution?' hazarded Libby. 'High-class escort? Drugs?'

Fran inclined her head.

'Well, you're right, it does tick all the boxes, but it's pure speculation.'

'Isn't most of what we ferret out pure speculation?'

'I suppose so. How do we find out?'

'I imagine the police will be doing that. And if Ian goes to the pub tonight, he might tell you.'

'I can't believe it's a week since the last Wednesday club,' said Libby. 'But if Ian's deep into another line of enquiry, as he might well be, I doubt if he'll turn up.'

Chapter Thirty-two

Libby was wrong, however. She, Ben, Patti and Anne were joined by Colin and Gerry at about nine thirty, and to Libby's surprise, at just before half past ten, Ian arrived with Edward.

'Have you told them about today's startling revelations?' he asked Libby, while Edward fetched them drinks.

'Were they startling?' asked Libby. 'I told them Mavis said Pam White had been seen.'

'And did you and Fran not speculate about what that could mean?'

Libby glanced sideways at Ben. 'Well, yes.'

'What's all this about?' asked Anne. 'Or is it classified?'

'You all know most of the background,' said Ian, 'so go ahead, Libby. Tell them.'

Libby haltingly described the morning's meetings with Andrew, Mavis and Fran. 'And Fran thought Pam White might be young Ryan's mother.'

Gerry shook his head. 'I'm lost.'

Ian was amused. 'As it happens, we came to the same conclusion. We managed to get hold of Liz Palmer and asked where she thought she'd seen Pam, and as it happened it was in the big supermarket in Canterbury.'

'Could have come from anywhere,' said Ben.

'What about the flat?' asked Colin.

'We sent officers round there, and we found out which flat it was – the boy Ryan is hard to miss, apparently – but according to both the land registry and the freeholders, that's Butler Holdings, Ben, it's in his name.'

'Gosh! Is he old enough?' said Libby.

'He had a guarantor – Nobby Marsh.'

'Oh!' Libby was puzzled. 'Did he know Pam, then?'

'Well, according to your theory that he could have been mixed up with Nash and his cohorts twenty years ago, it might make sense. Perhaps he *is* Ryan's father.'

'What's Ryan's surname?' asked Ben.

'Unimaginatively, Black.'

'And what about Peacock?' asked Libby.

Ian laughed. 'Would you believe – he's in Spain?'

Libby didn't know whether to laugh or cry.

'Priceless!' said Colin. 'So I might have met him?'

'You certainly might,' said Ian.

'So where do you go from here?' asked Patti. 'No ideas about those poor children?'

'We're making enquiries,' said Ian, straight-faced.

Before they left, Patti took Libby aside.

'Steve Plowright called in to see me just before I left today.'

'Yes?'

'Apparently, he and the girls are worried.'

'Worried? What about? Have they spoken to the police?'

'Yes, and that's why they're worried.'

'Why?'

Patti was obviously finding it hard to formulate the right words.

'He thinks they've had warnings.'

'What do you mean, warnings?' Libby was horrified. 'Was this after they'd spoken to the police?'

'Yes. They all had phone calls.'

'Tell Ian! Quick, before he goes!'

'Should I? That was what the phone calls said . . .'

'Don't talk to the police?' Libby caught at Patti's arm. 'Come on, you must!'

236

Ian had noticed, and was coming towards them.

'Patti?' he said.

Patti went pink.

'It's Steve Plowright and those three girls,' said Libby. 'Apparently they've been warned off.'

Ian drew them both off to the small table by the fireplace.

'Now, sit down and tell me what they said.'

'Well . . .' Patti looked at Libby. 'I feel this is breaking a confidence.'

'No. This is aiding a murder investigation,' said Ian. 'If you tell me, the four of them haven't told the police. You have.'

'Well,' said Patti again, glancing over at Anne, who was studiously ignoring the table in the corner. 'Steve said they'd all had phone calls which just said "No more talking to the police." Just that. No return number. They didn't know what to do.'

'I can imagine,' said Libby. 'But how did they get all the numbers?'

Ian frowned formidably. 'I think I might be able to guess.'

'What?' both Patti and Libby gasped.

Ian stood up. 'Patti, you've done the right thing, thank you very much. No need to tell Steve or the girls yet, we'll attend to all that, but this means we're getting very close.'

He returned to the main group and spoke to Edward, who stood up and began his goodbyes.

'Come on, Patti, time to go,' said Libby. 'And don't worry, you really have done the right thing.'

'What do you think he meant? About being able to guess?'

'I don't know,' said Libby, who actually had a shrewd idea.

'What was all that about?' asked Ben, as they walked home.

Libby told him.

'I seem to spend my life telling people what other people said,' she complained.

'And you think he knew how whoever it was got the telephone numbers?'

'Well, yes. Think about it. Those four have all moved away,

more than once, and changed their names – well, the girls have – so the only people who would know about them, apart from Patti and me—'

'Are the police!' Ben stopped dead. 'Bloody hell! That means . . .'

'Yes. There's a mole.'

'Back to Sergeant Peacock, then?'

'And they've traced him, too,' said Ben, starting to walk again. 'What now?'

Libby shook her head.

'I don't know. As Gerry said earlier, I'm lost!'

Libby couldn't wait to update Fran in the morning, and called her just before eight thirty.

'Something's up?' said Fran immediately.

Libby explained.

'And now we really are on the back burner,' she finished up. 'Absolutely nothing we can do.'

'Good to hear you admit that for a change,' said Fran.

'I suppose so,' said Libby, with an unwilling laugh. 'I'm just worried about those four – Steve and the girls.'

'I would imagine Ian's going through his team with a fiery sword even as we speak,' said Fran. 'How galling for him.'

'But at least it will get him a lot closer, as he said last night.'

'Is someone panicking?' suggested Fran.

'But who? The murderer of the girls from twenty years ago, or the murderer of Nick Nash?'

'Same person?'

'I doubt it,' said Libby. 'Oh, well. I suppose we'll find out soon enough.'

Unsurprisingly, Libby heard nothing about the investigation for the rest of the day, and occupied herself with wrapping Christmas presents which had arrived after her bout of online shopping. It still felt odd having nothing to do at the theatre.

'I'll have to find something else to do with my time,' she told Ben over dinner. 'Preferably something that earns me money.'

'Shelf stacking?' Ben said, with a grin.

'Be serious. I feel such a parasite.'

'You do work,' said Ben. 'You work up at the Manor – you do most of the work on the holiday lets – and you work at the theatre. You do most of the admin, don't you?'

'That feels like volunteering,' said Libby.

'No pleasing some people,' said Ben.

Friday morning and time to organise collection of the Christmas trees. It was already early December. The one in the Manor would go up this weekend, but the one for Allhallow's Lane would stand in the garden until the week before Christmas. The Manor Tree would be delivered by Owen on Joe's flat bed truck, but Ben collected the smaller tree in his four by four. Libby went with him to Cattlegreen Nursery, where they were greeted, as usual, by Owen with hot chocolate.

It was while they were drinking this that Libby's phone rang.

'Does that thing never stop?' said Ben.

'It's Adam,' said Libby, glancing at the screen. 'Have to take it.'

Ben and Joe shook their heads at each other.

'Ad? What can I do for you?'

'I don't know, Mum, but Mog and I didn't know what to do. Ryan hasn't turned up for the second day running.'

Libby felt the familiar cold trickle down her spine.

'Doesn't his boss know?'

'No. And he's been round to his flat.'

'And he's not there?'

'No. Not answering his phone, either.'

'Do you think it's worth telling the police?'

Ben sat up at this.

'They'd say it was too early to worry,' said Adam.

'Oh, I don't know,' said Libby, thinking about what she'd told the police, and what they already knew.

'Well, could you do it, then? I'd feel such a fool.'

'I could try,' said Libby doubtfully. 'Leave it with me.' She rang off and looked at Ben and Joe. 'Sorry about that. Adam's got a problem, Ben.'

'We'd better get off, then,' he said.

'Look, Owen can deliver both trees,' said Joe. 'He'll leave them both at the Manor.'

They thanked Joe profusely and got back in the car.

'So what is it now?' asked Ben.

'That young chap Ryan. He seems to have disappeared, now.'

'Well, that could be serious, couldn't it? What do you want to do?'

'Apparently his boss Nobby Marsh has been round to his flat, but got no answer. Not sure I trust him, though.'

'How about,' said Ben after a moment, 'we go and see if Andrew's seen him?'

'Good idea!' said Libby. 'Now?'

Ben gave her a sideways grin. 'Yes, now. Ring Andrew.'

When they arrived, Andrew met them at the door before they even rang the bell.

'They're both there,' he said, having been warned to keep an eye out. 'He went out to buy something, I think, and I saw her at the window. Is there a problem?'

'There might be,' said Ben. 'Call the police now, Libby.'

They stood at the window while Libby called Rachel Trent, who, unluckily was attending to something else.

'I'll tell control,' she said. 'Keep your eyes open.'

Just then, Ben turned for the door. 'They're on the move!' he called and ran. Libby threw her phone at Andrew.

'Tell them!' she said, and followed Ben.

She found him standing by an open garage door at the side of the block.

'In there,' he murmured.

And Ryan appeared.

'Adam's mum. Nosy witch,' he said.

'Adam and Mog were worried about you.' Libby strove to keep her voice steady. 'They couldn't get hold of you.'

'Oh, worried, were they?' Ryan swore. 'So was bloody Marsh, was he?'

'Er, yes,' said Libby. 'Are you going to work, now?'

'No.' He grinned. 'My mum's keeping me off today.'

'And that's Pam White, is it?' said Ben, moving forward.

'What do you know about it, old man?' Ryan moved forward, too.

Suddenly, a noise behind them made them both jump. The garage door had been shut.

'Oh, dear, shame,' said Ryan. 'Now your friends the police won't know where you are.'

Don't bet on it, thought Libby, and avoided looking at Ben.

Another noise, and a personal door at the back of the garage opened. Libby gasped.

Simone Nash walked slowly in.

'What are you doing here?' stuttered Libby. 'Where's Pam?'

'God, you're thick, aren't you?' Simone sounded amused. 'You're looking at her.'

Libby and Ben gasped with amazement, and then the pieces began to fall into place.

'And don't think you're going to do anything about it.' Simone took a step towards them. Ryan moved up on the other side.

Ben moved closer to Libby.

'What do you plan to do now?' he said, his voice remarkably steady.

'Well.' Simone tapped a finger against her mouth. 'What do you think, son?'

Ryan growled.

'Not a great talker, my boy.' Simone laughed mirthlessly. She put her head on one side. 'No handy cliffs here, are there?'

Libby's stomach lurched.

'You can't . . .?' she began.

'Oh, can't we?' Simone moved closer. 'Two of you might be a bit more difficult, but . . .'

Ben made a sudden grab for her, and immediately Ryan was on him. Libby screamed.

'Very silly,' said Simone, shaking her head. 'Now—'

She got no further. To everyone's surprise, the personal door opened quietly once again and DCI Ian Connell cast a cool eye over the assembled company, before the garage door burst open to reveal a squad of armed police.

Chapter Thirty-three

'That could have been incredibly foolish,' said Ian, half an hour later in Andrew Wylie's sitting room.

'Yes,' said Libby, sitting in the circle of Ben's arms. 'But we didn't know . . .'

'We just wanted to see what they were doing in case they left before you got here,' said Ben.

'Well, it's a good job Andrew kept control on the line and talked them through what was happening.' Ian looked at Libby. 'A bit like when you kept Rachel on the line when you were in trouble.'

'But we didn't deliberately put ourselves in danger either time,' said Libby. 'We weren't even going to call on Ryan.'

Ian sighed. 'All right. But you'll have to come into the station to give a statement.'

'Now?' said Ben.

'Yes, please.' Ian stood. 'Thank you, Andrew, very much.'

Libby went and gave him a hug. 'Yes, thank you, Andrew. You'll have to come to the de-brief.' She turned to Ian. 'There will be one, won't there?'

'If you give me some time off from murders, I suppose so,' said Ian.

Ben and Libby arrived home late that afternoon and refused to give anyone details of what had been happening. Ian had promised to come to the village the following night, and they issued invitations to everybody to join them in the pub. Tim even gave them use of the upstairs function room, which, luckily had an unusually free Saturday night.

By the time all interested parties had arrived, and Ian had confirmed he would be there by eight thirty, the room quivered with expectation.

'Look, we don't know very much more than you do,' said Libby, at the centre of a circle of badgering friends. 'We'll find out soon enough. Despite what he says, he loves doing his Poirot bit at the end.'

Indeed, a little later, when Ian was ensconced in prime position on a leather sofa, he did seem to be enjoying himself.

'I'll have to go backwards on this one,' he said, accepting a large Scotch from Edward. 'And tell you what kicked it all off.'

'The band of hope?' said Libby.

'It was hardly that, but yes. The little club the Reverend Turner formed with Nick Nash's help. And, of course, Sergeant Peacock, who, it turns out, has a devoted nephew in my own team.'

There were shocked exclamations. 'I'm sure you'd figured that out, Libby.' He smiled at her.

'Not that it was a nephew, but yes, Ben and I did.'

'It was a kind of gentlemen's club. For those of – er – original tastes.'

'Horrible,' muttered Patti.

'Yes, it was. It started with Turner himself abusing the girls, but then extended to other – interested parties. Including Nash, Peacock, and a few other local businessmen. All very hush-hush, of course. And then Kerry Palmer got pregnant.' He looked round the room. 'I can only think she was going to tell someone – the police, her mother – I don't know. But Turner killed her.'

'*Turner*?' There was a horrified chorus.

'How did you find that out?' asked Colin.

'Simone. Who, of course, was really Pam White, who was also pregnant, but by Nick Nash. How they kept her quiet she won't say, but she was shipped off somewhere to have the child, who was then illegally fostered. After Nash had left the country, he arranged for

Pam to join him. He kept her quiet until he considered she was old enough for marriage. She insisted on that, she says. Didn't want him walking out and leaving her without anything.'

'Tough cookie,' said Guy.

'She was. Apparently the other two children we found were accidental deaths which had to be hushed up. It was Peacock who killed them.'

'Because of the abuse?' asked Guy.

'Reading between the lines, yes. They put up more of a fight. It fits with what Steve Plowright told you about finding those younger boys crying.'

'That's awful,' said Libby, horrified.

'Keeping them quiet, apparently.' Ian shook his head.

'And he went to Spain, too,' said Ben.

'So what about Nash?' asked Colin.

'The obvious is often the answer,' said Ian. 'What did everyone think?'

'The estranged wife,' said Fran.

'Yes, Simone,' said Colin.

'Exactly. And who was the obvious person to tamper with the lawnmower?'

'The people who serviced it!'

'And that was it. Simone, or Pam, had come back to the UK, "rescued" Ryan, as he rather sneeringly put it, bought the flat, and installed them both there. Meanwhile she fed him tales of his ghastly father. And then – well, it just fell into his lap. He and his boss, who had nothing to do with any of it - except that he had an affair with Simone, who blackmailed him to keep quiet and act as Ryan's guarantor - they delivered the mower to Nick's address, and all Ryan had to do was nip over under cover of darkness and work his magic. He says he didn't intend to kill him, but I don't think he cared if he did.'

'So did Simone put him up to it?' asked Fran.

'He says yes, she says no. The family feeling doesn't run too deep.'

'On his part, I'm not surprised,' said Libby. 'He's a lost soul.'

'What about Peacock?' asked Gerry.

'And Turner?' asked Patti, looking strained.

'One loose end we haven't been able to tie up. He just vanished. We'll keep looking though, and maybe something will come out under further questioning. Peacock will be repatriated.'

'Do you think Turner's dead?' asked Fran. 'A lot of people had reason to hate him.'

Ian shook his head. 'Neither Pam White nor Ryan have any idea, apparently. Well, Ryan wouldn't, but I would have thought Pam might have.'

'Can people really just disappear off the face of the earth?' asked Gerry.

'Yes – especially if they have contacts in questionable places,' said Ian. 'And don't forget all the – er – *businessmen* Turner knew, and what he knew about them.'

'False passports? That sort of thing?' said Colin.

'I know it sounds melodramatic, but yes. That sort of thing.' Ian frowned. 'We're going to keep looking.'

'At least he wouldn't come back here,' said Guy.

There was a murmur of agreement, but Ian looked doubtful.

'You think he might?' said Fran.

'He probably still has contacts in the area,' said Ian. 'It will make sense to trace them – if possible.'

'After twenty years?' asked Gerry.

'You'd be surprised,' said Ian.

'And Steve and the girls?' said Patti.

'Peacock's nephew. He kept his uncle abreast of the investigation, and when he found out that these four had passed on information, called each of them and warned them off. All quite simple when you know the basics.'

'Do you know who he is? The nephew?' asked Libby.

'Oh, yes.' Ian smiled. 'You met him.'

'I did?'

'I bet I know,' said Colin. 'I met him, too.'

Ian nodded. 'When you came to pick up Colin from the interview room.'

Libby gasped. 'The constable who took the message?'

'He was very interested when I came in with Sergeant Trent and Simone,' said Colin. 'I didn't think about it at the time.'

'I wouldn't like to be in his shoes,' said Ben.

'It's all quite, quite horrible,' said Patti.

Ian smiled and held up his glass. 'Murder usually is,' he said. 'No more before Christmas – please!'

Acknowledgements

First, I would like to acknowledge the contribution of my son Miles, who, once again, supplied the original idea for this story. Second, the help of my agent Kate Nash, my editor at Headline, Toby Jones and my editor Greg Rees. And, of course, my apologies to all police forces everywhere for playing fast and loose with their investigative procedures. And lastly, my whole family, Louise, Miles, Phillipa and Leo, for help and support during the trying times of 2020.